About the Author

Simon Northouse writes books that entertain. His stories include hefty doses of self-deprecating humour, ironic farce, and droll bathos delivered in a deadpan voice. His characters leap from the page, the plots twist and turn and he delves into the dark alcoves of modern life. However, as many of his fans have pointed out, there is much, much more to his books than laughter and a bit of social commentary.

He touches on issues that have plagued humans since the first man pointed at a woman on the back of a woolly mammoth and shouted, "Oi, love, come down from there. That's a man's job!" Racism, misogyny, sexism, elitism, classism, anxiety, self-doubt, and entitlement are a sprinkling of topics that intersperse his works.

Also By Simon Northouse

The Shooting Star Series

The Soul Love Series

The Discombobulated Newsletter Series

The School Days Series

I Will Survive

The Shooting Star Series

Simon Northouse

Flabbergasted Publishing

Cartography of Crusoe Island by Carol, the Cat's Mother, reproduced with kind permission.

Published by Flabbergasted Publishing

First Edition

Kindle e-book ISBN-13: 978-0-6487619-6-9

Paperback ISBN-13: 978-0-6489684-2-9

Hardback ISBN-13: 978-0-6489684-6-7

Contents

Chapter 1

Stranded

I pull the penknife from its sheath on my belt, slump onto a sun-bleached log and whittle. Flaky is frolicking in the sea twenty metres away.

'Daft bastard,' I murmur to myself. Geordie is spreadeagled on the white sand in front of me sunbathing. His Scottish alabaster skin is already turning a pink hue under the blazing sun. The canopy from a palm tree protects me from the celestial fireball but not the humidity, which is strength-sapping. A rustle of leaves and snap of twigs from behind has me peering over my shoulder. Robbo stumbles from the thick jungle, pulling at the zipper on his shorts.

'Hey Will, I'm not sure how much more of this I can take,' he whines bitterly. 'No weed, no pixie dust, no alcohol, not even any smokes. I can't last much longer.'

I glance at my watch. 'We've barely been here two hours,' I reply wearily.

'Exactly! What am I going to be like after four weeks!' he exclaims.

'Fit, detoxed, your body a temple of purity. I think they were your words when this hare-brained scheme was first raised. Be careful what you wish for. Anyway, I'm sure the next twenty-seven days and twenty-two hours will fly by.' Flaky skips from the sea and runs back to us like an eager child. He grabs a towel off the sand and vigorously rubs himself down.

'Oh, wow! Isn't this just magnificent? Isn't it wonderful? Isn't it simply divine and perfect?'

'No. It's a nightmare,' I grunt.

'The calm, the serenity. Man and nature living in harmony.' Geordie rolls onto his front and lets out a rasping fart.

'There goes the serenity,' Robbo comments.

'And the harmony,' I add. Flaky throws Geordie a prudish glance but says nothing. He stops drying himself and stares at me.

'What are you doing?' he asks.

'What does it look like I'm doing... I'm whittling.'

'I can see that, but what are you whittling?'

'A stick.'

'I can see it's a bloody stick! But what is the ultimate purpose?' he shouts, getting annoyed.

'A spear to kill things with,' I answer glumly.

'Hmm, well, I won't be killing any of God's creatures. There's an abundance of vegetation, fruit, nuts and fresh water on this island to make the eating of meat totally unnecessary.' I scrape a few more pieces of wood from the tip of the spear and touch the point with my finger.

'Yep, that should do it,' I say. I get to my feet, do a quick run-up, and release the missile with a half-hearted throw. The stick wobbles through the air before landing horizontally about fifteen metres down the beach. 'Hmm, it needs more weight on the tip. It could also do with some fletching to give it more stability,' I add thoughtfully.

'Fletching?' Robbo queries. 'Isn't that a perverse sexual practice?'

'That's felching, you moron,' I reply. 'Fletching is the craft of attaching feathers to the end, like an arrow.' I turn and glare at Flaky. 'So, you reckon you're going to last four weeks on this island by scrimmaging around in the jungle trying to find a turnip or two?' Flaky laughs in a pompous way; an annoying trait of his.

'I've done my research, Will. God's larder is bursting at the seams. There's breadfruit, ruka, seaweed, chillies, yams, sweet potatoes, bananas, oranges, coconuts, custard apples, mangoes—the list goes on and on.'

'A bit like you,' Geordie mumbles.

'It may have escaped your attention, but we are in the southern hemisphere,' I state.

'So what?' Flaky replies.

'It's the second month of spring. Most of the fruits you mentioned won't be ripe for another three months at the earliest. I'll bet you within a week you'll be ripping flesh from a bone with your bare teeth,' I barter. Flaky hangs his towel over a branch of a tree and sniggers.

'William, my good friend, I have been a vegetarian for over twenty years; a pescatarian for three. Why do you think I would suddenly turn into a raging carnivore in the space of a week?' I sit back down on the log and let out a deep sigh.

'Because you lot don't know what you've got us into,' I reply.

'I think I do,' Robbo curses.

'It may be easy to be a vegetarian at home, where you can nip down to the supermarket and get your broccolini and a bunch of asparagus tips—not so here. In a week's time, you will be ravenous and fatigued from hunger. Your gut will ache with emptiness and you, my good friend, will eat anything—even meat.'

Flaky smiles benevolently at me. 'My resolve is tempered in the cauldron of righteousness. I will survive.'

'Thank you, Billy Graham,' Geordie moans as he sits upright, squinting at us. The distant sound of engines distracts me as I peer down the beach. Heading towards us is a red quad bike followed by a yellow, two-man all-terrain vehicle with roll bars and cargo netting.

'Looks like our glorious leader is heading our way.' The others turn and stare at the rapidly approaching vehicles.

'I've never been able to take to Jerry,' Robbo drawls.

'No, me neither,' Geordie agrees. 'He's a pompous prig. Never trust a man who wears a cravat.'

'You two are so judgemental,' Flaky bristles. 'Just because he's got a posh accent, is well-educated and successful, you have it in for him. You're both inverted snobs.'

'It's nowt to do with that,' Robbo replies. 'I don't care what background or upbringing anyone's had. I take each man and woman on their own merits, and Jerry is a twat of the highest calibre.' The vehicles stop about ten feet away and the occupants alight.

'Christ, what *is* he wearing?' Geordie murmurs, as he slowly shakes his head. Jerry is dressed in a pale grey safari suit with a pink cravat adorning his neck. In his left hand he holds a black cane decorated with an ornate ferrule on the top. He walks towards us in a flamboyant, over-energetic manner, swinging his cane, as if trying to prove he's younger than his sixty years.

'He's forgotten his monocle and elephant gun,' Robbo chuckles.

'Ah, chaps!' Jerry calls out. 'Sorry for the delay. I've just had word the last of the contestants will arrive by chopper within the next thirty minutes. I'm sorry you've had to hang around for a few hours. We really couldn't begin until everyone was safely on the island, otherwise, it could be deemed you had an unfair advantage.' The other two guys, who for some bizarre reason are dressed like Australian Lifeguards, in red shorts and yellow shirts, grab a large trunk from the back of the ATV and follow Jerry.

'What's in the box?' Flaky asks with a welcoming smile.

'Basic survival supplies,' Jerry says. 'By the way, let me introduce you to Travis and Brent.' We nod our introductions. Travis and Brent drop the box in front of us as Jerry squats, releases a clasp on the lid, and throws it back in dramatic fashion. He lists the contents. 'Sixty feet of climbing rope, a ball of string, a small shovel, a metal bucket and a first-aid kit. Plus, four of the following: mess kits containing a mess tin, cup, knife, fork, spoon, kettle, canteens, dynamo torches, hunting knives with steels, machetes and one large pan.'

'Very handy, Jerry,' I say, 'because if we really were stranded on an island in the middle of the South Pacific, I'm not sure we'd have stumbled across a metal trunk containing all this clobber.' Jerry eyes me suspiciously as he rises and stretches his back.

'Aye, very fortuitous,' Geordie scoffs as he bends down and picks up a machete, then runs his thumb along the edge of the blade.

'Let me make it clear,' Jerry begins. 'First and foremost, this is a TV show. It's entertainment for the masses. If we didn't provide you with some basic equipment, I'm not sure any of you would survive more than a couple of days, let alone four weeks. You must still forage for your own food and water and make your own shelter. Talking of which, Travis,' he says as he fixes his attention on the young muscular guy with a shock of blonde hair.

'Yes, Jerry?' Travis replies in a slightly effeminate tone.

'Could you show the Shooting Tsars to their camp and explain the set-up to them?'

'Of course, Jerry. Delighted to,' he says, fluttering his eyelashes. Geordie's eyes furtively swivel towards me and Robbo.

'There'll be no filming for two days, so it will give you time to settle in to your new home on Crusoe Island and set up camp,' Jerry explains as he turns to leave. 'Oh, and your personal backpacks will be delivered to you once they've been cleared by security.' As quick as a flash, Geordie throws his forearm around Jerry's neck and holds the machete to his throat.

'One false move and you're a dead man,' Geordie whispers in his ear. Jerry's body stiffens as his two helpers stand frozen to the spot with horror etched on their faces. Geordie winks at me.

'What are you, you, do... do... doing?' Jerry stammers in a high-pitched squeal.

'I'm hungry, and there's plenty of meat on you. Remember the show's motto? Survival at any cost. There's nothing in the rules about cannibalism.' Geordie swiftly pulls the machete across Jerry's neck. He lets out a deafening scream as he clutches his throat. Geordie laughs like a drain as Jerry inspects his hands, expecting to see blood.

'You bloody idiot!' Flaky yells. 'What did you do that for?'

'Calm down, pencil dick. It was only a joke. I used the back of the blade. I thought it would lighten the mood.' I'm not sure Jerry's mood has been lightened. I think he may have soiled himself.

'I don't appreciate practical jokes,' he says, scowling at the oaf.

'Relax, man. No harm done.' Jerry turns and marches back to the ATV.

'Travis, I'll see you over at the Celebrity Chefs' camp once you've finished with this bunch. Brent, you come with me.'

'Very good, Jerry,' Travis says. 'Okay boys, if you'd like to grab your box and follow me, I'll lead you to your living quarters for the next month.'

⤜⤜⤜ ⤛⤛⤛

Our camp is a ten-minute walk inland through dense brush and jungle. There is a discernible track, but it is overgrown and will need cutting back if it's to be our main thoroughfare to and from the beach.

We arrive at a clearing that is about fifteen metres in diameter. The dense canopy of the jungle provides welcome relief from the heat of the sun. Four hammocks are already set up close to each other, strung between giant palm trees.

'The biggest danger on this island,' Travis begins, 'isn't from insects, snakes, or wild boars, it's from falling coconuts. If one hits you on the head, it's goodnight Vienna. We've made sure the hammocks are attached to trees that don't have any nuts on them, so at least you'll be able to sleep easy on a night.'

'How very thoughtful of you,' Geordie says. 'What's the number to dial for Room Service?' he sneers as he wanders off to inspect the camp. I pull a handkerchief from my pocket and wipe the sweat from my brow.

'I've never slept in a hammock before,' Flaky states as he tries to climb into one. After a few failed attempts, he manages it. 'Ooh, I like this. The distant sound of the ocean, the chatter of birds, the chirrup of insects—it's very relaxing and peaceful. I think I'm going to be happy here.' *Bloody buffoon! He's still living in a fantasy world of the Swiss Family Robinson.* Geordie sidles up to Flaky and lifts one edge of the hammock, sending him sprawling to the ground.

'You great, big, lumbering neanderthal!' Flaky yells. 'What the hell did you do that for?'

'This is my hammock,' Geordie growls. 'It's longer than all the rest.'

Travis leans into me and whispers. 'Is Geordie... you now... mentally stable?' He carries a worried frown. I stare back at him.

'It depends on your definition of stable. His behaviour at the moment is completely normal. However, when the shit hits the fan and things don't go his way, he has been known to become erratic and dangerous.'

Travis tries to smile, but the grimace remains. 'How did he pass the psychological assessment?'

'Damn good question, and one I've asked myself many times before, to no avail. I was banking on the psychological profiling to save us from this nightmare.' He eyes me suspiciously before he points up at one of the palm trees.

'There's a camera mounted about ten feet up,' he says. 'When it's live, you'll see a red light flashing. It will probably switch on in an hour or so once the techs at HQ are ready. It will only be a test to make sure it's working.'

'How many hours a day is it going to be on?' I question, alarmed at the prospect of having my every move monitored.

'I couldn't say exactly. Maybe an hour or two. It's merely to capture your environment and the mood of the camp for the viewers back home. Ninety percent of the show is all about the challenges. On the tree next to it is a loudspeaker. Whenever it's time for a challenge or team meeting, Gloria Gaynor's "I Will Survive" will play. That's your prompt to make your way to the games zone adjacent to Castaway Central. That was my idea,' he adds.

'You must be incredibly pleased with yourself. I'll tell you one thing though; I won't be attending any bloody team meetings. I thought this was a survival show, not the annual general meeting of Conglomerate Inc.'

'I'm not sure Jerry will be happy about that,' he replies with a frown.

'I don't give a fuck in a teacup what Jerry thinks. If he's not happy with it, he can put us on the next chopper out of here.'

'Ahem, yes, well... we can also speak to you directly in case of emergencies,' he adds.

'What sort of emergencies?'

'Oh, you know, bushfire, cyclone warnings, stingers.'

'Stingers?'

'Yes. Poisonous jellyfish.'

'Great. What about sharks?'

'Mainly reef sharks. They're not dangerous... usually. Let me show you the map of Crusoe Island.' We wander across the camp to a tree that has a laminated chart pinned to it. The southern part of the island has been split into five clearly marked rectangular zones of about equal size. To the southeast are the blue and red zones, labelled the Weathergirls and the Rock Stars, respectively. In the middle is the grey zone. This is where Castaway Central and the game's areas are located. To the southwest are the green and yellow areas, marked as the Entrepreneurs and the Celebrity Chefs. Behind the main zones is a plateau marked as Skull Mountain. 'This is your area, here,' he says as he taps at the large rectangle shaded red.

'You don't say.'

'You're the red team, the Rock Stars. You are not allowed out of your zone unless you're summoned to the grey zone where the challenges are held.'

'And how do we know where our zone ends?'

'When you see red triangles pinned to trees. They demarcate the edge of your boundary. For example,' he continues, tapping his finger on the red and blue areas, 'if you got to this point here, you'll see red triangles. On the other side of the tree would be blue triangles.'

'And if we're on the beach?'

'The entire shoreline is a free zone, meaning everyone can use it with impunity.'

'What happens if we abscond from our allotted zone?'

'If you're caught, you'll be punished and have some of your gear removed.'

'Such as?'

'Cooking utensils, hammocks, machetes. The things which make life bearable and liveable. Three strikes and you're off the show.'

'That's not punishment.' He frowns again. I study the map in more detail. 'How big is our area? Has it a water source?'

He chuckles. 'It's just over 80 hectares.' He may as well be speaking Double Dutch.

'What's that in acres?'

'About 200. And yes, there is a water source, although that's for you to find. All the team zones are similar in size and topography. There's plenty of food and water to sustain you if you know where to look and have the right skills.'

'If we find this water source, is it safe to drink?'

Travis looks puzzled. 'That's a naïve question. Did your team do the survival course with Hammer Harrington?'

'Yes. That's why we're naïve.'

'You can't mean that? Hammer is our senior consultant. He's one of the best survivalists on the planet.'

'Hammer is the biggest self-publicist on the planet.'

'The man's a hero.'

'The man's a twat.'

Travis appears mortally wounded and effects a pout. 'I'm sure Hammer would have pounded it into you about the importance of boiling water before you drink it.'

'I think Hammer was more concerned about pounding it into his personal assistant than teaching us basic survival skills. Okay, so the water needs to be boiled. I'll inform the numbskulls,' I reply as my weary eye falls upon my castaway companions who are all happily swinging back and forth in their hammocks doing sweet FA.

'Right, well, I better be going. Oh, one last thing, watch out for the leeches. If one latches onto you, don't pull at them. They need to be burnt off. That's another thing you should have learnt on Hammer's survival course,' he calls out as he heads back through the dense bush. A sense of foreboding swamps me. I gaze over at Flaky, Robbo and Geordie, who are now bickering about where the campfire should be located.

Poisonous jellyfish, sharks which may or may not be dangerous, wild boars, killer coconuts, snakes, stinging insects, leeches and three first-class fuckwits to contend with, not to mention Gloria Gaynor—what did I do to deserve this?

CRUSOE ISLAND

Somewhere in the South Pacific

Chapter 2

Privation

The campfire is crackling gently, not that we need it for heat, as the weather is warm and humid. We've had our first meal of the day; yams, roasted on a stick, and coconut. It was bloody lousy, and I'd swap my left testicle for a juicy burger smothered in fried onions and tomato relish. Flaky is snoozing in his hammock and Robbo has gone to fetch some more firewood.

Earlier in the day, we bumped into our next-door neighbours—the Weathergirls. We'd just finished slashing the overrun trail to the beach and were all hot and dirty, so we went for a refreshing swim in the sea. As we were splashing around, four bikini-clad women sauntered past, waving, and shouting hello. All I can say is they were a sight for very sore eyes. It could be interesting.

'What do you reckon, Bill? Not as bad as you thought it was going to be, eh?' Geordie says as he sits on a log opposite me.

'No. It's worse.'

He seems surprised. 'Aw, come on! It's not too bad. We've only been here half a day and we've already found food, a freshwater supply and cleared the path to the beach. We have plenty of firewood and tomorrow, at first light, we'll do some more exploring. We really need to figure out how we're going to catch some fish or crabs. We'll need protein if we want to keep our muscle mass. Yams and coconuts are okay occasionally, but not long term. We also need to build a shelter over the hammocks. If it rains, which it will, we're going to end up soaked.'

'Hmm...' I mumble as I prod at the fire with a stick. 'We'll discuss it tomorrow after a good night's sleep. I'm knackered.'

'Aye, I'm feeling weary myself.' We both fall silent. The sound of frogs chirping, the distant crashing of waves on the beach, and the cooing and warbling of a native bird soothes my frayed nerves.

'That's a nice birdsong,' I murmur. 'I wonder what it is?'

'No doubt David Attenborough will be able to identify it when he wakes up,' he replies, glancing over at Flaky, who is quietly snoring. He leans in towards me and lowers his voice. 'Hey, Bill, have you... you know... since you got here?'

'Have I what?'

'You know?' he says, peering around.

'No, I don't.'

He appears annoyed. 'You know, have you knocked one out yet? Bashed the bishop?'

I shake my head in disbelief. 'We've barely been on the island twelve hours. So, no, I haven't knocked one out yet. And as strange as this may seem, since setting foot on this tropical nightmare, accompanied by you lot, my normally overactive libido has gone on long-service leave.'

He nods thoughtfully. 'Hmm...'

'Why?'

Again, he looks shiftily around the camp. 'Well, I'm fit to bursting. I think it was the sight of those women today. My God! They were fine looking specimens. An encounter like that can do things to a man.'

'Fine looking specimens? You make them sound like pedigree dogs.'

'I didn't mean it like that. I'm just saying they were easy on the eye.' He pauses for a moment, deep in thought, before rising to his feet. 'Right, well, I'm away.'

'To bed?'

He appears a tad embarrassed. 'Erm, no. I thought I might have a little private time in the bush... you know... alone.'

'Christ! When a man's got to go, a man's got to go.'

'Not a word to anyone,' he adds, tapping his nose.

'My lips are sealed,' I say as I throw another branch onto the fire. He wanders off into the undergrowth with all the grace and stealth of a drunken rhinoceros on steroids. 'Oh, and Geordie! Keep away from the freshwater stream!'

'Aye, what do you take me for?' he yells back. As his crashing and bashing slowly fades from earshot, it's replaced by more crashing and bashing, and a few curse words, from the other side of the camp as Robbo emerges from the beach path.

'Exit fuckwit left—enter fuckwit right,' I mumble.

'That bloody track still needs trimming in places. I'm scratched to buggery,' he complains as he drops an armful of firewood onto the sandy And we also need to devise something to carry the firewood in. This is no stable. I have bloody ants crawling all over me.' He stops his whining as he surveys the campsite. 'Hey, where's Geordie?'

'He's gone for a wank.'

'Surprised it's taken him this long,' he yawns as he flops into his hammock. 'I hope you told him to keep away from the freshwater supply?'

'Of course,' I say, as I throw the stick on the fire and stand up for a good stretch. 'Right, I'm going for a little wander along the beach to cool off before bed.'

'Okay, Will. It's nice down there. A gentle breeze is blowing in off the ocean. Hey, how long has the camera been on?'

I peer up at the little red flashing light. 'Oh, great. Not sure. That thing's going to be a nuisance.'

'I'll look at it tomorrow. I'm sure I'll be able to fix it so it's only on when we want it to be on,' he whispers.

'Good idea. I'll catch you later.'

I amble in and out of the waves for a good fifteen minutes, thinking about things. I'm not in a particularly good frame of mind. It's just over forty-eight hours since I said goodbye to Fiona, Mary and Caesar and I miss them terribly. I'm used to being away from home for long spells. It's the nature of being in a rock band. But this is different. When I'm on tour, I can video call them each day and catch up on all the happenings. Things which when I'm at home I take for granted. What they had for dinner. How was Mary's day at school? How's my mother? Make sure you take Caesar out for ten minutes before going to bed; don't forget to lock and bolt all the doors. A whole month without seeing or talking to them is going to kill me. I sing a melancholy song as I walk on, troubled and feeling homesick.

'Why the sad song?' a female voice calls out from the sea, startling me. I turn to witness one of the women we encountered earlier in the day emerge from the water and walk towards me. The moonlight dances on her ebony skin as a wide smile reveals a row of pearly white teeth. Her eyes twinkle and shine.

'Oh, sorry. I thought I was alone.'

'You sounded like you were.' She holds out her arm. 'Hi, I'm Chloe Henry. We saw each other briefly this afternoon.' I shake her hand. It's soft and delicate, almost childlike.

'Pleased to meet you, I'm...'

'You're Will Harding, from The Shooting Tsars,' she says, cutting me off. 'I'm a fan of your music. I take it you're a contestant on the show?'

'No. I got lost on my way to the cinema.'

She laughs. 'So, who's your team? Have you been grouped with three other famous rock stars?'

'No, just the three muppets from my band.'

She giggles. 'You sound like you don't want to be here.'

'I don't.'

'Then why are you?' We saunter up the beach toward the jungle.

'Our band works as a democracy. On big issues, we all have a vote. The majority wins.'

'Ah, I see. And you lost three votes to one.'

'No. Our wives also have a vote. I lost six votes to one with one abstainer.'

'Why don't you want to be here, apart from the obvious reasons?'

'Because it's an exercise in futility. We don't stand a chance of winning. What's the point of taking part if you know you're going to lose? All it means is four long weeks of misery and deprivation.' She sits down on a log and pats it, indicating for me to take a seat.

'I'd say you already have an advantage over the other teams.'

'How so?'

'Take my group; we know each other professionally as we work in the same industry. But we don't know each other like friends know each other. How long have you lot been together? It would have to be nearly twenty years, wouldn't it?'

'Twenty-four... not that I'm counting.'

'There you go. You have established boundaries. You all know who the leader is, who the thinker is, who the doer is. There are three parts to this show; the physical and mental challenges but there's also one more.'

'Go on?'

'The social. The interaction between complex personalities. The annoying habits people have. With you lot living in one another's pockets for so long, you don't have to worry about those things. You're already a tight-knit group and each of you will know what your strengths and weaknesses are.'

'You don't know my bandmates. They could argue over what colour green is. What's the old saying, familiarity...'

'Breeds contempt,' she adds with a captivating grin. 'They can't be that bad?'

I pick up a stick and doodle in the damp sand. 'Yes, they are. And I include myself in that assessment. The fact is, we're not cut out for this sort of caper. We live pampered lives. We don't have the skills to survive on a tropical island.'

'Didn't you do the survival course with Hammer Harrington?'

I raise my eyes to the heavens. 'Yes. He was bloody useless. He spent a few hours with us on the first day, then we didn't see him again until we left.'

'Really? I'm surprised. He was most attentive and hands-on when we did the course with him.'

'I bet he was. Anyway, a two-day course in the Scottish Highlands is hardly good training for surviving on a tropical island in the South Pacific.'

'The skills you acquired are transferable. It's not the terrain, it's the knowledge.'

'And we're back full circle. As I said, we learnt nothing.'

'You'll be surprised what the brain stores away.' She smiles at me as her eyes lock onto mine. I suddenly recognise who she is.

'I know you, you're the weather girl off the TV,' I state.

She giggles. 'Yep, well done. That's what our team are called—the Weathergirls.'

'Your tone of voice tells me you're not enamoured with the name?'

'No, I'm not... we're not. When people hear the term weathergirl, they automatically imagine a bimbo with big tits, who points at fluffy clouds on a screen. We're not... we're meteorologists, with degrees, some with PhDs.'

'Well, it is a TV show. They've got to sensationalise it to beef up the ratings. A meteorologist doesn't conjure up the same image as a weathergirl to most people. We're called the Rock Stars. I'd prefer to be called the Hugely Successful and Talented Musicians. But you get what you're given.'

She rises to her feet. 'Yes, I know. I better get back. The others will wonder where I've got to. Nice to have met you and I guess we'll be seeing a lot more of each other.'

'I suppose we will.'

'Night, hope you sleep well,' she says as she turns and heads off across the sand. I watch her depart. After a few yards, she turns and throws me a cute smile and a little wave. I'm not sure I will sleep well after this brief encounter.

Back at lazy hollow, all is peaceful but Geordie still hasn't returned. Robbo is slurping juice from a coconut.

'That must be the longest wank in history,' I remark. Robbo rubs his arm across his lips.

'No, he was back a few seconds after you left.'

'Where is he now?'

'Gone for a dump.'

'From the sublime to the ridiculous,' I mutter to myself thinking of Chloe. 'Hey, I just met one of the contestants,' I announce as I clamber unsteadily into my hammock.

'Really? Whereabouts?'

'In the fucking supermarket carpark! Where the hell do you think I met her?'

'Oh, it's a her, is it? The chicks we saw earlier?'

'Yes.'

'What's she famous for?'

'She's a meteorologist,' I say as I lean on my side and stare at him. He scratches his head.

'A famous meteorologist? I didn't know there was such a thing. What's her name?'

'Chloe Henry.'

His eyebrows arch upwards. 'Oh, the weathergirl! Eh, she's a bit of all right, is Chloe. Who's she here with?'

'Three other weathergirls.'

'Did you ask her what the forecast is for tomorrow?'

'No. Call it a stab in the dark, but I think it could be hot and humid, with a possible afternoon shower, accompanied with a slight smattering of idiots.'

Chapter 3

Peep Show

Surprisingly, I had a relatively good night's sleep. When I awoke, I was looking forward to a two-course breakfast; a strong cup of black coffee accompanied with a cigarette. I had to settle for a drink of tepid water and a nibble on a piece of bloody coconut. I'm already sick of the damn things.

After our breakfast, which lasts about a minute, we decide on a course of action for the morning. Flaky and Robbo are heading to the beach to do a bit of foraging. Anything useful they can find they are to bring back to camp. Old rope, plastic bottles, netting, or even a discarded cleaning lady, may come in useful. Geordie and I are going to explore the jungle, mainly as a reconnaissance mission but also to find more coconuts. Apparently, the ones attached to the trees contain more milk than the ones on the ground.

We pick up a trail obviously made by an animal... possibly wild boar. It makes walking a little easier. Geordie brandishes a machete whilst I clutch a spear I made from bamboo. There's always a chance we could get lost, but all we need to do is listen for the sound of the ocean then head to the beach, then west... or possibly east.

'Hold up,' Geordie says raising his arm as though leading a regiment of light infantry. 'Red triangles dead ahead.'

'That's the end of our boundary.'

'I wonder what's on the other side?'

'The blue zone, the Weathergirls patch.' Geordie tiptoes gently across the demarcation line as if he's going to be miraculously transported into another world.

'Come on, let's head north,' I suggest.

'Wait, I can hear running water.' I sidle up beside him and cock my head. He's right, there's a definite burbling in the distance. We walk on for a further five minutes deeper into the blue zone until we come to a clearing. A small waterfall is cut into a small cliff. It deposits its precious cargo into a beautiful, crystal clear lagoon. 'Fancy a quick dip?' he says.

'You know the rules. Anyone caught in another zone will have privileges removed,' I say with a sigh.

'We don't have any privileges.'

'What about the hammocks, knives, mess set?'

'You're not chicken, are you?'

'No. I just want an easy life... although, the lagoon is enticing.' We drop our implements and run headlong into the refreshing waters.

'It's warm!' Geordie exclaims.

'You know what that means?'

'What?'

'We're on a volcanic island. This lagoon is a thermal spring heated from deep underground.'

'Aye, you could be right. I bet the waterfall is cool though,' he says as he immediately heads towards the cascading torrent. He stands beneath it singing loudly as water splashes over him. We spend an age cavorting like children before we lie on our backs, spreadeagled, and float.

'This is bloody paradise,' he murmurs. 'But...'

'But what?'

'I'm starting to get an aching in my belly. I'm a big man and I need a lot of calories to keep me going throughout the day.'

'You're right. I'm bloody starving. We need to catch some fish or a wild boar. Flaky reckons he's going on a vegetation hunt this afternoon, but I can't live off bush vegetables for a bloody month.'

'Aye, bollocks to that. Hey, look,' he says as he stands up out of the water. He points at a coconut tree which is listing at a precarious angle. It carries a heavy cargo of precious fruit near its canopy.

'At that angle, it's definitely climbable. A lot safer than going straight up. Come on, let's harvest the nuts.'

'Good thinking, Bill.'

'Who's going up?' I ask.

He gazes at me with a sneer. 'You English are weak as piss. Look at you... quaking in your underpants.'

'I'm not quaking. I'm merely asking the question; who's going up? Only one can cut the coconuts away.' He bends down, picks up his machete and dramatically thrusts it into his scabbard.

'Stand back, wee man. I'll scale the tree like a mountain puma. That's the difference between the English and the Scots.'

'What? Brains?'

He throws me a withering glance. 'No! We know no fear.' He climbs the tree, not quite like a puma, but more like a heavily pregnant warthog with three legs, and a fear of heights. After ten minutes he's about halfway up.

'Come on, Geordie! Get a move on!' I encourage. He stops for a breather.

'What's the bloody rush! It's not like we're short of time.'

'Yeah, I know, but we are in illegal territory. If we're caught here, there'll be repercussions.'

'Oh, quit your gibbering, man.'

'Why don't you come down and I'll go up... if you're scared?' Although the tree is at an advantageous incline, it's so tall he's already about fifteen feet above the ground. My deliberate counterbluff works its magic.

'Scared, am I? I'll show you who's scared!' His legs straddle the trunk as his arms pull him upwards. His new motivation makes him accelerate at the pace of a slug. I become bored and explore beneath the canopy. A faint, slightly unpleasant smell assails my nostrils.

'Christ, Geordie! I can smell that from down here.'

'What are you talking about?'

'You've let one of your carpet bombers go.'

'I can assure you I have not farted.'

'The smell certainly didn't come from my bottom.' I wander off to where the edge of the lagoon finishes. 'Well, I never!'

'What is it?'

'There's a volcanic mud bath. It's sulphur I can smell.'

'Apology accepted. Right, another few feet, and I'll be within striking distance of these bloody nuts.'

'You'll have bloody nuts after shuffling up that trunk for twenty minutes. I thought you were like a puma?'

'Below!' he cries as a bunch of coconuts narrowly miss my head and land with a damp clunk in the sand.

'You dickhead! You could have bloody killed me!' I yell up at him.

'Your problem is, you're not aware of your surroundings. A serious failing when you're pitted against the wild. Now stand back, you big Jesse, I'm about to cut the next bunch.' I quickly remove the first batch from the area and stand well back as another clutch of nuts falls to the ground.

'I've just had a thought,' I say while counting the coconuts.

'What about?'

'There's well over a dozen nuts here.'

'So?'

'We can maybe fit two in our backpacks and one in each hand, but that's all. We need to find something to carry them in, like a carryall or a supermarket trolley.'

'We can get Flaky to make a carry bag.'

'Flaky?'

'Yes. Did he not tell you about the basket-weaving course he went on last summer?'

'No. Thankfully I was spared that fascinating monologue.'

'Aye, you're not wrong. I had to endure thirty minutes of it on the flight over here. I was ready to commit hari-kari.'

'Actually, it's a bloody good skill to have. There're all sorts of things he could make.' I hear something in the distance which is incongruous to the usual background noise of the jungle. 'Shush!' I hiss.

'What? What is it?'

'I thought I heard something.' There it comes again. It's the sound of female voices, and they're getting louder. 'Geordie, I think we have company. Keep low.'

'Pretty hard to do when you're twenty feet off the bloody ground.' I dart behind a bushy palm, spread the fronds slightly, and peer out towards the waterfall. Four women materialise, clad in bikinis. I immediately recognise the heavenly figure of Chloe and her three attractive companions. They navigate the steep incline and stand at the side of the lagoon, chattering excitedly. One of them dips a toe in the water.

'Oh, it's lovely and warm!' she exclaims. Chloe doesn't need another invitation and quickly rips her top off and shimmies out of her bikini bottoms.

'I don't know about you lot but I'm skinny dipping!' she cries as she rushes into the water. The other three follow suit, disrobing and shouting and squealing with delights as they do so. There's a deep groan from above. I feel like a voyeur and release the fronds to block the scene from my view... for a few seconds... until I take another peep. Well, we were here first!

Their laughter and frivolity last a good fifteen minutes as the girls complete their ablutions and have some fun. Another groan comes from up high.

'This is too much for a man to bear.' Geordies anguished whisper hovers in the air. I spot Chloe freeze.

'Hang on, did you hear something?' she quizzes the other girls.

'No, what?' one of them says.

'It sounded like a human voice.'

'Maybe it was a bird?

'Hmm... maybe,' she says as they resume their naked splashing. In the deepest recesses of my mind, I'm hoping for a lesbian orgy but I'm pretty certain it won't materialise. One lives in hope.

They eventually finish their larking, put on their bikinis, and head back the way they came.

'Hey, Bill!'

'What?'

'I cannae hang on much longer. I'm losing my grip.'

'You lost that a long time ago. Hold tight for another minute until the girls are out of sight.'

'Easy for you to say.'

'It's either that or one of two options.'

'What's the first option?'

'If you fall from that height—a wheelchair for the rest of your life and liquidised food.'

'Second option?'

'I'll throw in a few quid for a decent casket. Plus, I'm good at eulogies.' There's a loud scream followed by a "fuck it!" as I watch, horrified as his body plummets to the ground. It's met with a gloopy splat as he enters the mud hole and disappears from view. The women, who by now have navigated to the top of the waterfall, stop dead in their tracks and spin around.

'What was that?' one of them cries with a concerned expression... although, not as concerned as mine.

'I'm not sure,' Chloe replies. A squelching sound, accompanied by a long ghoulish groan, resonates around the idyllic setting. A grotesque and horrifying creature slowly emerges from the sludge. It stretches to its full height as splats of mud drop from its hideous frame. Wafts of steam rise from the fiend creating an ethereal, ghostly scene. Even the birds have stopped singing. To add to the spectacle, the monster is sporting a massive erection and it's pointing horizontally in the direction of the women. They are frozen in fear unable to grasp the situation. And who could blame them? As the monstrosity lifts one leg onto the bank, the women let out piercing screams, turn tail and bolt for safety.

'You daft twat!' I chastise. 'Get in the water, clean yourself up and let's get out of here.' As Geordie washes himself off in the lagoon, I round up the purloined coconuts and think about Chloe and my own aching erection. How the hell does one get rid of these things on a tropical island? Apart from the obvious.

Chapter 4

Stu... the Security Guard

The water has been boiling for a good two minutes. I grab a stick and gently hook the wire handle attached to the can and lift it onto the sand.

'We really need about three of four of these pans,' I announce. 'It takes forever for the water to cool down. If we had a few on the go, we could set up a rotation system.' Geordie's busy husking coconuts using an ingenious contraption designed by Robbo... you heard me correctly... designed by Robbo. He sharpened a heavy branch into an angry looking spear then jammed it between two large boulders. The coconut is slammed onto the spike which splits the husk making it easy to peel by hand.

Robbo and Flaky's beachcombing expedition was relatively successful. They returned with a dozen washed-up plastic drink bottles, a plastic bucket, various lengths of rope and twine and a large sheet of tattered heavy-duty plastic. Robbo is building an A-frame to cover his hammock and Flaky is cleaning the dirt from a bucket of yams. He's watched over by his new best pal—Dorothy. No, he hasn't got lucky with one of the contestants. Dorothy is an Imperial pigeon that has taken a shine to Flaky; there's no accounting for taste. It follows him around cooing adoringly as he feeds it titbits. I do believe they're in love with one another.

Geordie and I have already received a lecture from him when we mentioned our early morning misadventure. Although, we were deliberately light on the exact details of our exploits. The sound of bustling in the undergrowth distracts me. A male voice calls out in a strong Birmingham accent.

'Lads! Security!' A plump man materialises from the undergrowth. He's aged about thirty, average height with short, cropped hair. He smiles broadly and drops our four backpacks onto the ground. 'Hi, lads. I'm Stu, the security guard. Everything's checked and accounted for. Sorry I didn't get them back to you yesterday, but everything is behind schedule. Old Jerry is running around like a headless chicken.' Stu is wearing the same yellow and red garb as Brent and Travis with "Security" and the name "Stu" stitched into it. A walkie-talkie is attached to his lapel and a satellite phone is tucked into a holster on his belt. 'So, how are you lads coping?' he enquires as he holds out his arm. We shake hands with him.

'Yeah, good, how about you?' Geordie replies. Stu pulls a hanky from his pocket and wipes sweat from his neck.

'Bloody hot and sweaty. Damned humidity. A word of advice; keep off the beach during midday. It's brutal. It's a lot cooler here in your camp. Early mornings and late afternoon is the best time to search for food.'

'We'll bear it in mind,' Flaky says. 'Have you any experience in survival?'

He chuckles. 'Yes. I know it's hard to believe now,' he says as he pats his ample belly, 'but in a different life I was in the SAS for five years. By the way, I'm a massive fan of yours. I have everything you've ever released. I must have been to at least twenty of your concerts over the years. Last time I saw you was about eighteen months ago at The Valley Festival. Bloody cracking gig.'

'Thanks. It was a good night,' I reply. 'Have you any news about the show? We've been here over twenty-four hours and we haven't heard anything from anyone.'

The smile slips from his face. 'The plan was to begin shooting tomorrow, but the way things are, they'll be lucky. They're having technical difficulties with the cameras.' I gaze up at the camera attached to the tree. There's no red light.

'It was on last night for a few hours, but I haven't noticed it recording today. That will be the reason why,' I say.

'Apart from bringing your belongings I'm here on a more serious matter,' Stu says gravely. I throw Geordie a sideways glance.

'Oh, and what would that be?' Flaky asks.

'According to the contestants from the blue camp, the Weathergirls, they had an intruder in their zone. I was wondering if you boys had seen anything suspicious?' We shuffle nervously and exchange cautious glances.

'Suspicious? In what way?' I ask.

Stu appears a tad embarrassed. 'The girls say they were bathing in a lagoon early this morning when they saw a creature.' He pauses as he tries to hide a smile. 'A Yeti type creature emerged from a mud hole. It let out a blood-curdling cry. As you can imagine, the poor lasses were petrified. I've done a thorough search of the area but can't find anything untoward.'

'Poor women. It must have been a terrifying sight,' Flaky says as he eyeballs Geordie.

Stu continues. 'Apparently... ahem... the creature was sporting a large erection,' he says as he stifles a laugh.

'Really,' Flaky says. 'Sounds like a perverted, peeping Tom is on the prowl.'

'We haven't seen any wild looking Yeti type creatures with erections, have we lads?' I say.

'Not recently,' Robbo replies with a smirk.

'All quiet and tickety-boo around here,' Geordie adds.

'I thought as much,' Stu says. 'To be honest, I'm wondering if the women accidentally ingested some magic mushrooms, and they imagined the whole thing.'

Robbo's ears prick up. 'What? You mean there are magic mushrooms on the island?'

'I don't know whether there is or there isn't. I'm just guessing what may have occurred. I mean, come on, mud monsters in human form, sporting a hard-on?'

'Aye, it is a tad fanciful. Maybe they caught too much sun. Heatstroke can play havoc with your mind,' Geordie suggests.

'If we hear or see anything unusual, we'll be sure to let you know,' I say.

'Okay, thanks,' he says as he turns to leave. 'By the way, I'm security for the red and blue teams, so you'll see me around quite a bit. I'm mainly here to watch out for any paparazzi attempting to come ashore but also to ensure no one is breaking the rules by leaving their zones. I'll catch you later.' We watch him leave as Flaky huffs and crosses his arms.

'We've barely been here a day, and not only have you broken the rules by entering a forbidden zone, but you've also been caught indecently exposing yourself,' he says snippily as he glares at Geordie.

'It wasn't like that,' Geordie barks as he heads back to the coconut spike.

'Well, what was it like?' Flaky demands following him.

'I was up a tree harvesting nuts when the girls appeared out of nowhere. They went skinny dipping for fifteen minutes. I lost my grip and fell into a mud hole. That's all there was to it.'

'You saw them all naked?' Robbo asks, almost salivating.

'Aye. Not on purpose mind. But they were right below me in my line of sight. Where else was I to look?'

'Did you see them as well?' Robbo questions, turning to me.

I nod. 'Yep. They were certainly a remarkable sight.'

'You pair of jammy bastards! Do you mean to tell me I spent the morning with Miss Havisham, collecting shite off the beach, sweating my balls off, while you two had your own private peep show?'

'That's one way of putting it,' I reply as I take a swig of water.

'You two are sick perverts. I'm disgusted with the pair of you,' Flaky gripes.

'Oh, pipe down Peewee, it was all totally innocent.'

'And the erection?'

'You know what erections are like, you have no control over them. They're a law unto themselves. If you'd seen what me and Bill saw, you'd have had an erection as well.' Geordie stops ramming coconuts onto the spike and gazes at Flaky. 'Then again... maybe not.'

'And what does that mean?'

'Well, look at you, you don't have a good shag left in you.'

'How dare you!' I rise to my feet to intervene.

'Boys, boys, boys... let's all calm down, shall we. Flaky, it's true what he says. It was totally innocent. We just happened to be in the wrong place at the right time... erm... I mean wrong time. Plus, look at all these fresh coconuts we harvested.'

'Oh, what a lovely bunch of coconuts,' Robbo sings.

'If you'd been caught, we'd have all been punished. You didn't think of the team. If we're to survive for the full four weeks the team must always come first. I want you both to give me your assurances you won't pull a stunt like this again.'

I glance at Geordie, wearily. 'Okay. I promise.'

'Geordie?'

'Aye. Scout's honour.'

'Good. Now let's put the matter to rest.'

'I'd like to put you to rest,' Geordie murmurs under his breath.

***

Swinging in my hammock I lazily watch as the others pull items from their backpacks. I've already mounted a laminated photograph of Fiona, Mary, and Caesar to the tree opposite me. I pick up my book, The SAS Survival Manual, and flick through the pages. As part of the rules each contestant was allowed to bring a few personal items; one book, a photograph, toiletries, two towels, a set of spare clothes, a blanket, a notepad and pens and pencils.

'Hey, lads, what books did you bring?' I call out. Flaky shuffles about in his bag and pulls out his book.

'The New Testament,' he says brandishing it like a trophy.

'I brought Bob Dylan's autobiography,' Robbo replies.

'Geordie?' I quiz.

'I brought along an adult colouring book. It helps me relax in times of stress.'

Why am I not surprised! 'Well done, you three. Good choices. We should be able to glean a wealth of survival tips from your reading material.'

'My Bible gives me mental and spiritual nourishment, which is even more important than physical sustenance.'

'Aye, my colouring books do the same for me.'

Flaky glares at him, frowning. 'Are you actually comparing your colouring book with the Bible?'

'No, of course not. I wouldnae dream of it. My colouring book is far more important.'

⤜⤜⤜⤜

Robbo comes stumbling into camp griping. He set off for the latrine more than an hour ago.

'Hell, that must have been a big jobby,' Geordie comments.

'Nightmare!' Robbo declares.

'What's wrong?' I ask.

'Still can't go. Twenty minutes squatting and nothing.'

'You're constipated,' Flaky says. 'It's dehydration. You need to drink more liquids.'

'What have you been doing for the rest of the time?' I quiz.

'I got lost on the way back and fell in a bloody swamp. I went for a dip in the sea to get rid of all the muck.'

'Christ, you need a chaperone,' Geordie says as he relaxes in his hammock and picks up his colouring book.

'It's too hot to do anything,' Robbo starts. 'I'm going to have a snooze until it cools off.' The camp falls silent apart from the incessant twitching and scratching from Robbo's hammock. I study Geordie as his patience slowly bleeds away. He keeps throwing Robbo annoyed glares. I'll give him another five minutes before he explodes. And here we go.

'For God's sake man! What is wrong with you? You're worse than a bairn.'

'Right on cue,' I murmur.

'What?' Robbo says innocently, startled by the outburst.

'You're lying there playing bloody pocket billiards. If you need a swifty off the wrist, then bugger off into the jungle and find a quiet spot like the rest of us do,' he thunders.

'Speak for yourself,' Flaky says.

'Ditto,' I concur.

'I'm not playing pocket billiards. I've got a bloody itch if you must know,' Robbo says, affronted by the accusation.

'Scratch, scratch, scratch, scratch! You're like a dog with mange. Can a man have no peace and quiet?' Robbo pulls at his waistband and peers down his shorts.

'Shit the bed,' he whispers.

'What's wrong now?' I query.

'Oh no, It can't be.'

'What is it?' Flaky asks.

'I think I've got a leech on my old fellow. It must have been from the swamp.'

'Here, let me have a look,' Flaky responds. Robbo appears alarmed at the offer of assistance.

'Get out of here! I'm not having you ogle my crown jewels.'

'I can assure you the last thing I want to do is gawp at your tackle box. But if it is a leech it needs to be removed. Now stand up and drop your pants.'

'No way!'

'Don't be ridiculous. We're all men of the world. We share the same anatomy.'

'I wouldn't be too sure,' Geordie mutters. Robbo reluctantly slumps from his hammock and drops his shorts and jocks. It's met with howls of laughter from Geordie.

'Sweet merry Jesus! I didn't realise acorns were native to the island!'

'Piss off! It's not bloody funny,' Robbo snaps.

'Aye, that's what your missus says,' Geordie guffaws. 'Although they do say, mighty oaks from little acorns grow. I'm not sure that's true in your case, though.'

'What am I going to do?' Robbo whines becoming ever more panicked.

'Just yank it off, man!' Geordie advises. 'I'm talking about the leech, by the way.'

'Don't be bloody ridiculous. That will cause severe bleeding and it may leave the jaws or teeth behind,' Flaky states.

'Jaws and teeth!' Robbo screeches.

'It needs to be burnt off,' I suggest.

'Burnt off!' Robbo is teetering on the edge of a complete nervous breakdown.

'Just leave it,' Geordie begins. 'The leech will soon realise it's on fallow ground and leave for pastures new. Although, on a positive note, it has doubled your girth.'

'Ignore the buffoon,' Flaky advises as he pulls a small twig from the edge of the fire. 'Right, can you grab your penis and stretch it out a little? I haven't got much to work with.' His comment has Geordie in uncontrolled fits of laughter.

'You be careful with that bloody twig,' Robbo says.

'Keep as still as possible,' Flaky says as he kneels for a closer inspection. 'I suggest you look away or close your eyes.' Flaky blows hard on the end of the stick breathing new life into the red ember. 'Okay, here we go, brace yourself.'

'Hi, lads, only me, security,' Stu's voice bellows out as he plods into camp. He stops dead in his tracks. The expression on his face indicates he thinks he's stumbled upon a gay dogging area. 'Oh, erm... I'm sorry. I didn't mean to intrude. I'll call back later when you two have finished,' he says as he hurriedly turns to leave. Geordie is in danger of cracking a rib.

Chapter 5

I Will Survive

Blaring music stirs me from my slumber. I'm unsure where I am or even who I am. I stare up at a green canopy and filtered sunlight. As I roll over, I fall to the ground and realise I've slipped from my hammock. *Damn it!* My memory returns as I remember I'm on a tropical island as part of a stupid reality TV show. The song, "I Will Survive" ends abruptly.

"Morning happy campers! Your camp commandant, Jerry, here! I hope you all slept well. Apologies for yesterday's technical hiccups but we're all sorted now. I hope you're all settling into your new life on Crusoe Island. Today we have our first team challenge. We'll give you time to breakfast and complete your ablutions. Mid-morning, when you hear three loud beeps, make your way to the games zone next to Castaway Central. Until then... au revoir!"

The music blasts out again before rapidly fading. Peace descends, well, at least for a few seconds.

'Jesus H Christ with fucking bells on!' Geordie roars. 'I'm not putting up with that every morning. We'll need to nobble it.' He staggers from his hammock and makes his way to the water bucket where he fills a cup and swigs it down.

'Maybe we could ask them to turn it down a tad,' Flaky says yawning. I glance over at Robbo who has managed to sleep through the entire thing.

⇝⋙ ⋘⇜

I'm flabbergasted, gobsmacked, stunned, and dumbfounded. Castaway Central resembles a military mobilisation prior to launching an invasion. We are given a whistle-stop tour of the area by Jerry and Felix Cain the American presenter of the show. There are over two hundred personnel as part of the production team; camera and sound crews with drones and a giant boom crane; a doctor and four paramedics; a marine department including divers, safety swimmers, boats, and amphibious equipment; two chefs and twenty kitchen hands; joiners, carpenters, mechanics, and engineers.

The main resort site features luxury cabins mounted on wooden stumps above the turquoise sea. They are domed with a weathered thatch and have steps that lead down to the water. A walkway links them all. They snake out in a semi-circle, one on the west and one on the east. There must be over forty in total. The jewel in the crown is the giant complex known as Castaway Central which sits back from the water like a mothership. It's three storeys high, can house thirty and has everything you'd expect from a boutique 5-star resort: swimming pool, bars, Jacuzzis, saunas, even a bloody tennis court. Some wag has cobbled together a handmade sign which reads, "Welcome to Felix and Jerry's Penthouse!" Behind this, and out of sight from the beach, are about fifty demountable cabins, I assume it's the workers' accommodation. Even these are pretty swish.

'Shit the bed!' Geordie whispers. 'I knew there'd be a lot of behind-the-scenes action, but nothing on this scale.' For the first time since arriving on the island, I feel a tad anxious. Jerry waffles on with considerable pride about the show's international success. He throws out facts and figures about audience ratings like confetti.

Apart from feeling nervous, I'm experiencing another emotion—annoyance. The show must make hundreds of millions in profit, and I appreciate the cost of putting it all together, but still, the production company will be raking it in. What's grating with me is the fact the charity cash prize is a paltry one million. Even though I'm only one of sixteen contestants, I get a distinct feeling I'm being ripped off. Here I am, once again, making money for the "man". To rub salt into the wound, I'm also bloody roughing it while Jerry and his buddies live it up in the lap of luxury.

We are introduced to the other three teams: the Weathergirls, the Entrepreneurs, and the Celebrity Chefs. I obviously recognise Chloe and the rest of her team, even with their clothes on. Two of the chefs I can identify and the other two are vaguely familiar. As for the entrepreneurs, three of them I've never seen nor heard of before. But there is one of them I know very well indeed. We've butted heads a few times in the past when our paths have crossed at TV and radio stations. The man is a self-appointed know-it-all of the highest magnitude. He makes Mussolini look like a liberal-leaning chemistry teacher. His opinions, of which he has many, spew forth from his rubbery wet lips like a geyser of toxic diarrhoea. Where there's harmony, he brings discord. Where there's unity, he brings division and where there's peace, he brings chaos. He's a ballbag, an oxygen thief, a slack-jawed media slut, and he has a face like a workman's bench. We make eye contact. He sneers revealing a row of yellowish teeth and walks towards me holding his hand out.

'Well, well, well! If it isn't Will Harding and his band of dysfunctional dimwits.'

'Piers Conrad, what a thoroughly unpleasant surprise. Please excuse me for not shaking your hand, but I don't have access to any disinfectant.'

He nods, smiling sagely. 'I thought this was a celebrity version of the show. What are you plebs doing here?'

'I could ask you the same question. I'd hardly call you an entrepreneur. That's stretching the bow to breaking point.'

'Au contraire my dear man, au contraire. I'm CEO of a worldwide, multi-million-dollar business, as you're well aware.'

'You trade gold on the futures market. A business you inherited from your father when you left Cambridge University.'

He scrunches his face up in disgust. 'Please don't swear! It was Trinity College, Oxford.'

'Same shit—different bucket.'

He turns to leave. 'I shall watch with amusement as you bunch of half-witted rock apes make complete fools of yourselves,' he chuckles. 'It will be the biggest clusterfuck of the year, maybe the decade. Ha, ha, ha!'

Robbo saunters over. 'I see you've been jousting with your old sparring partner again?'

'Yes. The sleazeball. I never let anyone rile me, but there's something about him that makes my blood boil. I despise the git with a raging passion. Where's Geordie and Flaky?'

'Geordie's over there talking with Brody Buchannan,' he says, pointing towards a tall man with a similar frame to Geordie.

'Is he the Scottish chef who shouts and swears at everyone?'

'Yep, that's him. And Flaky is behind you chatting with Dick Honeyman.' I spin around and study him.

'Hmm... face is vaguely familiar. What does he do?'

'He's on that show, The Foxes Lair. Sunday nights, 8 pm.'

I shake my head. 'Never seen it.'

'It's where the general public come forward with their business ideas and four venture capitalists haggle to invest. He's one of the dudes.'

'Sounds riveting. How did he make his money, this Honeyman?'

'He got in on computers way back. Have you never heard of the Honeyman B1?'

'No.'

'Never mind. Eh, up, it looks like we're not far off from the first challenge. I saw underwater cameras being set up earlier and Jerry's rounding everyone up.'

I'm tired and hungry and the last thing I want to do is partake in a stupid bloody water-based game. The challenge is simple enough. We swim out to our "red" pontoon moored not far from the beach and wait for the starting horn. Underwater, about twenty metres from the platform, is a long rectangular cage containing numerous coconuts, painted in team colours. On each coconut is a letter. We have to retrieve all the nuts, one at a time, drop them in a net bag, then swim back to the beach and rearrange the letters to make a word... or words. The first team to decipher the letters wins the contest. What's wrong with the world? People are starving to death and here are sixteen adults playing silly bloody games. Robbo, Flaky and Geordie appear excited at the impending challenge.

As we pull ourselves from the water and onto the pontoon, we are given five minutes to discuss our strategy before the Klaxon is sounded by the show's smarmy presenter, Felix Cain. I don't like the cut of his jib. He's all shopfront and no stock. Plus, he's American, which adds insult to injury as this is supposed to be a British show. Not that I have anything against Americans.

'Okay, what's the plan of attack, boys?' Geordie asks.

'I'm not sure a plan is needed,' Flaky says. 'It's a simple enough task. Why complicate things?'

Geordie huffs. 'I've watched a lot of these shows and it's always the team which thinks creatively who get the upper hand.' He's met with silence. 'Right, thanks for your input!' he growls.

'The least we can do is sort out the starting line-up,' I suggest. We waste our five minutes bickering as no one can agree on who should go first. Before we know it, the Klaxon echoes out. As the other teams get off to a perfect start, we're still on the raft arguing. The matter is soon decided when Geordie picks Flaky up and throws him violently into the water. The whole thing is utterly embarrassing, especially as the cameras are rolling and in two days' time, about twelve million viewers back home will be witnessing our ineptitude. I suddenly realise why we're here. We're the clowns, the jokers, the light entertainment. Maybe Piers Condom was right about us.

It takes Flaky a good five minutes to return with a single coconut and drop it in the string sack attached to the side of the platform. As the nut hits the bag, Robbo dives... or should I say, belly flops into the sea. Above the racket of the other competitors, I can hear Felix Cain laugh loudly into his microphone and make some facetious comment about Robbo's entry into the water. Geordie yanks Flaky back onto the pontoon.

'You took your bloody time,' he grizzles.

'It's a damn sight harder than it looks. You have to push a coconut from one end of the cage to the other to access it. It sounds easy but you can only move it a few feet before you have to pull your hand out and stick it through another part of the cage to flip it along. The cage is quite far down and I'm not great at holding my breath,' he explains, panting hard.

Geordie swallows nervously. 'No, I'm not either. I get claustrophobic.' I glance over at the Weathergirls who are the next team along. Their second swimmer is already putting her coconut into the sack. The Chefs and Entrepreneurs are close behind.

'Christ,' I murmur, 'we're getting slaughtered.' In a surprising development, Robbo is back in half the time it took Flaky. He deposits the nut as Geordie dives in. I pull Robbo onto the deck. He's barely panting.

'Nothing to it,' he says nonchalantly. As Geordie reaches the flag, designating the far end of the cage, he dives underwater. He's out of sight for a few seconds before his head bobs back above the gently rolling waves. He takes a deep breath and disappears again. He repeats the process another four or five times. We are rapidly dropping further behind.

'Did you need to come up for air?' I ask Robbo.

'Just the once. I've been practising at the local pool holding my breath underwater. It's all about keeping calm and not panicking.' I notice Geordie resurface yet again.

'Unlike that moron,' Flaky says. Geordie eventually returns, gasping for air and bewildered. I dive in and swim to the end of the cage. Underwater I grab a coconut and push it forward. Flaky was right, it only moves a few feet before I need to reposition my hand and repeat the process. I come up thrice for air before I get the nut to the opposite end, where there's an opening. I grab the nut and swim back to the pontoon. Geordie and Robbo pull me up as Flaky takes off again. I bend double, hands on knees, as I gulp in air.

'It's a fiendish game,' Geordie says with a creased brow.

'I've had an idea,' I gasp. 'Robbo, you're by far the strongest swimmer and can hold your breath the longest. I suggest you move all the nuts in one go to the far end. It will take longer, and we'll lose time, but once it's done, we only need to swim to the end nearest us and grab a nut.'

'That's a bloody good plan, Billy Boy,' Geordie says with relief.

Robbo nods. 'Yeah, okay. I'll give it a go.'

The plan bears fruition. By the time I drop the last nut into the sack we are well ahead of the other teams. It's confirmed by Felix Cain as his cloying banter booms from the loudspeakers.

"And by some sort of miracle, the Rock Stars have powered into the lead! They've come from nowhere to possibly steal the challenge. All they need to do is get their coconuts back to shore, rearrange the letters in the correct order, and they'll be the first team in the brand-new celebrity season to win the reward challenge!"

The other three jump into the water and we unhitch the string sack then paddle towards the beach.

'We can win this!' Flaky exclaims. 'Me and Will are good at word games.' If the producers put us on the show to humiliate us, they can think again. As we near the shore, the incessant, feverish commentary from Felix attracts my attention.

"Oh no! Disaster has struck the Rock Stars. It appears two coconuts have slipped from their carry sack. Without all the coconuts, they won't be able to complete the challenge."

I glance behind in dismay and spot the stray coconuts bobbing about in the water near the pontoon.

'Shit the bed!' I yell. 'Flaky, you and me will swim back and get the nuts. Geordie, Robbo, you two get ashore and begin figuring out the letters.' I'm flagging fast. We swim back to the pontoon and each grab one nut, turn and head back. It's my first mistake. I should have sent the fuckwit twins to retrieve the nuts. Geordie and Robbo are already hauling the bag up the beach. I peek across at the other teams. The Weathergirls aren't far from shore. They're closely followed by the Entrepreneurs and the Chefs. We're about twenty metres away from the beach when I develop a painful stitch and have to stop. 'Flaky, here take this,' I say as I lob the coconut his way. 'I've got a stitch. I need a moment.' He looks at me, concerned, panting hard.

'Do you need help?'

'No. Just a little breather. You go!' He grabs the second coconut and holds them out in front of him like swimming aids, as his feet and legs propel him along. It takes a minute of treading water before my painful stitch subsides. I'm just about cooked. I lethargically swim to shore and drag myself out of the water. The noise is deafening. I can no longer tell who is in the lead. A camera crew swarms in, right up close, in my face as I stagger up the beach towards my team. They're arguing violently with one another... what a surprise. Flaky is apoplectic as he points at the coconuts in their shies.

Geordie turns and shouts to me. 'Bill, I think we're still missing one nut! Me and Robbo have nearly figured it out but we're missing a letter "R". Are you sure there's no more nuts in the water?' The harsh sound of a Klaxon horn and the whoosh and explosion of a rocket in the sky signals the end of the game. I drop to my knees exhausted.

"And the winner of the first reward challenge of Celebrity I Will Survive is the blue team! The Weathergirls. Although not first back onshore they *were* the first to unscramble the letters and rearrange them into—Warm Pancakes. Ladies, the win puts you on top of the leaderboard with thirty valuable points. Please make your way to the winners' marquee and we'll reveal your reward."

Dizzy and exhausted, I force myself to my feet and make my way to the shies where the letters are lined up. No wonder Flaky was going off his tits. I stare in disbelief at the two words the birdbrains of Britain have assembled.

"WANKERS C AMP"

'Fuck me blind! How could you turn, "warm pancakes" into wankers camp?' I ask accompanied with a hefty dose of dispirited fatalism.

'They're bloody unreal!' Flaky yells. 'I told them it's a family show, but they wouldn't listen.' I drop to my haunches and place my hands on my head as the Weathergirls are ushered towards a small marquee. The flaps are dramatically pulled back to reveal a chef in uniform, surrounded by an array of cooking utensils. Felix Cain joins the girls, as a camera crew circle.

'Ladies, you have won a feast of warm pancakes, with maple syrup, bacon and scrambled eggs. However, you have also won something else. Something, which in the long run, is far more valuable.' The girls are ecstatic as they all congratulate one another. Felix continues. 'What do you cook pancakes in?'

'Butter!' Geordie bellows, receiving a scowl from Jerry and Felix.

'A frying pan?' Chloe shouts.

'Correct! Not only do you get a slap-up meal full of much needed calories, carbohydrates, and protein, but you get to keep the frying pan. An essential item for any camp kitchen.'

Piers sidles over to me, smirking. He points at Robbo's and Geordie's cryptic handiwork.

'I think your teammates were correct. You weren't missing a letter "R", after all. Wankers Camp sums your lot up perfectly. Ha, ha, ha!'

Chapter 6

Back In Yorkshire – Part 1

Jackie, Julie, and Gillian are sitting comfortably in the living room of Fiona and Will's palatial house in the Yorkshire Dales. The TV is muted, and excited chatter reigns forth. The girls are in high spirits. Fiona bustles in carrying a tray of cheese and biscuits, a chilled bottle of champagne and four wine glasses.

'Has it started yet?' she asks placing the tray on a table.

'No. It's on after the adverts,' Jackie replies as she struggles with the cork on the champagne bottle. Julie grabs the remote control and unmutes the TV. There's a loud popping as the cork reluctantly gives up the fight. Jackie fills the glasses and hands them out as the theme music to the show begins. The presenter Felix Cain appears on screen to the backdrop of a majestic tropical island.

"Welcome to a new season of I Will Survive. This time it's a little different —it's our inaugural season of the celebrity version! We have taken sixteen celebrities from the UK and put them into four teams of four, then deposited them on a tropical paradise in the South Pacific—Crusoe Island! Although, it may not be paradise for our contestants. It will be hard, harsh, gruelling, and unrelenting. There will be reward challenges, elimination challenges, points on offer, delicious meals for winners, and essential survival equipment up for grabs. There's only one rule; survival at any cost! But now, let us meet the teams."

The energetic, smiling faces of the Weathergirls flash up on the screen, followed by the toothy grins of the Entrepreneurs then the dapper Celebrity Chefs. Lastly, and more downcast than smiley, are the four rather dour looking faces of the Rock Stars.

'Oh, my giddy aunt!' Fiona exclaims. 'Look at them! They've got faces like a row of slapped arses!'

'They must have had an argument just before they took the shot,' Julie says.

The show starts off with a quick flyover of the island highlighting the flora and fauna and showing a superimposed map of the contestants' zones. Felix Cain, in a state of hyperactive excitement, explains the dangers the celebrities will face. Wild boars, snakes, insects, sharks, falling coconuts and a large malicious crustacean called the robber crab. Felix appears genuinely thrilled at the prospect of someone dying or at least being permanently maimed. It would be good for ratings. Fiona and the girls chat excitedly as each cast member briefly answers unheard questions by an unseen interviewer in a darkened room. Chloe Henry is first up.

"I know it will be hard, a challenge, but I'm up for it. It's important we bond as a unit straight away and work as a team, not just for the challenges, but also to survive. There are no individuals anymore... only the unit."

'She's very pretty,' Gillian remarks.

Julie sniggers. 'Believe me, after a few days in the wild without her make-up artist she won't look so radiant.' The interviews continue.

'Oh, I hate this guy!' Jackie says. 'He's such a smug, self-satisfied bastard.'

'Who is he?' Julie asks.

'Piers Conrad.'

'Who?'

'You know, he's one of the judges on The Foxes Lair.'

'Oh, yes. I didn't recognise him. He's lost a lot of weight.'

Fiona giggles. 'Oh my! Will hates him with an absolute passion. He calls him the golden globule of piss. He'll be so angry. I'm not sure he'll know many of the other celebrities though,' she adds with a frown.

'He'll know some of the chefs,' Gillian says. 'Will's an excellent cook and watches cooking shows for inspiration, doesn't he?'

'Yes, true,' Fiona replies curtly, miffed that Gillian thinks she knows Will better than she does. 'He used to love watching Marmaduke Smythe, or the Duke as he likes to call himself.'

'Is he the one who was taken off air for always being drunk by the end of the show?' Julie asks.

'Yes, that's the one. Will used to say it was the best comedy on TV. Oh, look... it's Brody Buchannan. This should be fun.'

'Geordie actually knows Brody Buchanan,' Jackie says.

'You've never mentioned it before. How does Geordie know him?'

'From their schooldays. They go back a long way. He's been over to our house a few times.'

'Is he as rude and foul-mouthed in real life as he is on his TV shows?' Gillian asks.

'Not really. He's quite nice. I mean, he does swear like a trooper, but I'm used to that living with Geordie.'

'I thought our lot didn't stand a cat in hells chance but now I've seen the celebrity chefs, I'm not so sure. I can't see their personalities meshing too well,' Julie adds with a smirk. The suave sophisticated tones of Xavier Pompadour interrupt the women's chatter.

"I believe we will win. As chefs, we are all disciplined. I own two Michelin Star restaurants which means I won't settle for anything but perfection. Losing is not in my lexicon."

'Ooh, he makes me go all gooey,' Julie says as she involuntarily shivers.

'Ugh! I can't stand him!' Fiona remarks. 'That long greasy perm and arrogant attitude is a real turnoff.'

'It's the French accent that does it. I don't care what he looks like.'

Next up is another celebrity chef—Keith Patel.

"Yes, I think we have a slight advantage. As chefs, we have a collective wealth of knowledge about what food sources are safe to eat and how to cook them correctly to obtain maximum nutritional content. The games, challenges, will obviously be important, but in the end, it comes down to food. Without food, you have no energy and without energy, you cannot win."

'Poor man,' murmurs Gillian.

'What do you mean, poor man?' Julie exclaims. 'He's worth a small fortune.'

'Yes, I know, but it must be difficult being a chef with only one eye.'

'I'm sure his good eye compensates for his lost one,' Jackie says.

'Do you really think he's blind in one eye or do you think his eyepatch is a prop?' Fiona quizzes.

'It's definitely true. I watched a documentary about him where they interviewed his mother. He lost it when he was eight-years-old,' Jackie adds.

'How?'

'He got hit with a cricket ball.'

'Ouch!'

Felix Cain's blinding teeth make another brief appearance.

"We'll be right back after the break to meet our last team... the Rock Stars!"

'Right, girls tuck into the cheese and crackers. I'll be back with another bottle of champers and a lemon meringue pie,' Fiona says as she rushes out of the door.

With adverts complete and a brief blast of the theme music, the interviews continue. First up is Flaky.

"Win? Yes, I'd like to think we could win, otherwise what's the point of being here? But in my heart of hearts, I'm not so sure. Why? Let me just say there are certain members of our team who are not cut out for this sort of journey. One is bone idle, one's a psychopath, and the other has the uncanny knack of always leading us into trouble based upon his flawed decision making."

Geordie's giant head now appears.

"A month away from the missus and bairns? Come on, get serious—any man would jump at the chance!" he guffaws.

'My God!' Jackie shouts. 'They broke the mould when they made him.'

'He's only joking,' Gillian says reassuring her friend.

'Aye, *I* know that. But do the other twelve million people watching the show know it? Bloody wanker!'

Next up is Robbo.

"Survive? Four weeks? Together on a remote island?" He laughs like a drain. "Listen, mate, I'll be surprised if we survive the plane journey over there."

'They're unreal, aren't they?' Jackie says as she shakes her head.

'They're a bunch of bloody idiots. All the other contestants came on and talked about resilience, tenacity, working together as a unit, a belief in themselves and winning being the ultimate goal to help out a charity. And what do our boys say? They bloody embarrass themselves, and us,' Julie seethes.

'Let's hope Will can finish with something positive,' Gillian remarks as her cheeks flush. Will's deadpan face fills the screen.

"Win? It's possible, yes," Will says thoughtfully.

'At last!' Jackie exclaims. 'At least there's one of them with a bit of self-respect.'

"If the other three teams are poisoned en-masse, abducted by aliens, or partake in a murder-suicide pact, then I'd fancy our chances of winning. Although, it still wouldn't be a forgone conclusion."

>>>> <<<<

The girls relax as the champagne and lemon meringue pie work their magic. The TV now shows cleverly edited clips of each team as they settle in for their first night on the island.

'The Weathergirls look organised,' Gillian says as the mounted camera scans a well laid out campground.

'Hmm, they do,' Fiona agrees. 'They're also very cooperative and caring to each other.' The cameras cut across to the Celebrity Chefs who engage in five minutes of fierce verbal altercations about the optimal time to boil the yams they've unearthed.

'I told you,' Julie states, 'those lot are trouble. Too many egos in close proximity.'

'Shush, they're on,' Gillian says as the next shots are of the Rock Stars camp. Flaky is asleep in his hammock. Will is sitting on a log prodding the fire with a stick as Geordie mooches over and sits opposite him. They talk in whispers that are not audible as Geordie glances around the camp.

'He's acting very suspicious,' Jackie scowls.

'What are they saying?' Fiona asks.

'I'm not sure. I can't hear. And where's Robbo?' Julie says.

'Maybe he's gone to the toilet,' Gillian suggests. On screen, Geordie slinks off towards the undergrowth.

"Oh, and Geordie! Keep away from the freshwater stream!"

"Aye, what do you take me for?" A moment later Robbo returns carrying an armful of wood, complaining bitterly as he does so.

"That bloody path still needs trimming in places. I'm scratched to buggery." He drops the wood on the ground. "And we also need to devise something to carry the firewood in. This is no solid. I have bloody ants crawling all over me. Hey, where's Geordie?"

"He's gone for a wank."

"Surprised it's taken him this long." He climbs into his hammock. "I hope you told him to keep away from the freshwater supply?"

The show cuts away to the adverts. The four women are silent, mouths agape, as they pull their eyes from the screen and stare, horrified at each other.

Having recovered somewhat, with the help of another bottle of champagne, the girls are on the edge of their seats as the first team challenge gets underway.

'You know what,' Julie starts, 'I don't care whether they win or not. As long as they make a fist of it and put some effort in.'

'I agree,' Jackie says. 'Maybe it will eradicate the mental image that twelve million people around the country have of my husband skulking into the undergrowth to masturbate. I wouldn't mind so much, but we had sex the morning he left. That's less than forty-eight hours between drinks.'

As the horn sounds, three figures dive into the sea. The camera cuts to the Rock Stars pontoon where an angry argument is in full swing. It eventually ends when Geordie picks Flaky up and throws him, like a rag doll, into the water.

'That's a good start,' Julie says with pursed lips. The girls watch on in dismay as their husbands fall behind.

'As bad as it is, I'll say one thing, Julie,' Fiona begins, 'I'm surprised at Robbo. He's the fastest out of all of them and he didn't even appear puffed when he got back to the pontoon.'

'I've got to hand it to him, Fiona, for the last six months he's gone down to the local pool every day, even on weekends.'

'Pool or pool hall?' Jackie says, laughing.

Julie chuckles. 'No, it's true. I'm the muggins who has to wash his towel and trunks each day.'

'Have you not taught your man how to use a washing machine yet?'

'He's banned from using it. I can't tell you how many times I've had a nice white top that has come out pink. He has no concept of separating colours from whites.'

'Ah, that old chestnut; learned helplessness.'

'Robbo's been underwater for a hell of a long time,' Gillian remarks her brow creased.

'Hmm, I hope he's all right. They'll have safety divers standing by, won't they?' Julie murmurs.

'There he is, he bobbed to the surface and went back down again.' The underwater camera shows Robbo working calmly and methodically as he pushes and cajoles all the coconuts to one end of the cage.

'Oh, I see what he's doing,' Gillian says. 'They're losing ground now but will make it up later as the others won't have to swim as far. What a clever idea of his.'

'I can assure you, it won't have been Robbo's idea,' Julie replies. The women become increasingly excited as slowly but surely the boys catch the other teams, then overtake them.

'I cannae bloody believe it! They're in the lead and getting further ahead. They're in with a chance of winning this!'

'And Flaky and Will are good at cryptic crosswords so they should be able to unscramble the letters and find the winning word,' Gillian comments.

'Or words,' Fiona adds.

'Yes, you're right, Fi,' Jackie says. 'The presenter deliberately emphasised word or *words*. It will be at least two words long.' Fiona is rocking back and forth on the edge of her chair gently clapping her hands together as the Rock Stars unhitch their swag and begin swimming back to shore.

'Come on, come on,' she whispers. The other women are transfixed, barely able to breathe. They all let out a collective scream and clasp their hands to their faces as Felix Cain gleefully points out that two coconuts have come adrift from the Rock Stars sack.

'Oh my God! I can't bear to watch,' Jackie screeches.

'It's okay don't panic!' Fiona yells, panicking. 'Will and Flaky are heading back to get them and Robbo and Geordie are continuing towards the beach. The other teams are still way behind.' Silence falls over the room as the drama unfolds.

'Oh, no! Will's stopped swimming. He's grimacing,' Fiona murmurs.

'I hope he's all right,' Gillian says, wincing.

'He's probably got a cramp or a stitch. Look, he's thrown the coconut to Flaky.' Drone footage captures Robbo and Geordie arrange and rearrange the nuts on the shies, desperately hoping to compose the winning words. The Weathergirls are already sprinting towards their shies. The camera cuts to

Flaky as he leaps from the water and rushes up the beach. Another shot is of Will in the sea with a tortured expression.

'Christ! He looks completely knackered,' Fiona says, wistfully. With some expert video editing the viewer does not see what words Robbo and Geordie have constructed, but whatever they are, it's created a violent argument between them and Flaky.

'Don't be bloody ridiculous! That's not going to be the answer. It's a bloody family show and you're missing a letter.'

'Maybe there's another coconut that escaped the bag,' Geordie shouts back at him. He calls out to Will who is dragging himself from the water. 'Bill, I think we're still missing one coconut! Me and Robbo have nearly figured it out but we're missing a letter "R". Are you sure there are no more nuts in the water?' The sound of a horn signifies the end of the game as a camera swoops into the faces of the delighted Weathergirls and the winning combination of letters—WARM PANCAKES.

'Oh, no,' Gillian cries. 'They were so close. It's not fair.'

'I'd like to see how close they got,' Jackie says as the vision shows Will staggering up the beach. He reaches the shies, appears bewildered for a moment before a look of inevitability flicks across his face. He drops to his haunches panting hard and places his hands on his head.

'This doesn't look good,' Julie says. 'I know the expression on Will's face. It means, fuckwits ahoy.' Felix Cain is talking constantly over the proceedings. The camera eventually reveals the letters on the Rock Stars shies for a brief moment as the show's theme tune starts indicating another ad break. Fiona hits the off button on the TV controller as silence pervades the room. They stare at each other, lost for words, maybe even suffering from a mild bout of neurogenic shock.

'I think they were trying to make, wankers cramp,' Gillian says. 'That's why Geordie thought there was a letter missing.' More silence.

'I'm glad we didn't let the children stay up to watch it,' Jackie murmurs. 'It will either be a ratings disaster or the largest viewing audience in TV history,' she adds wistfully. Gillian starts to snigger, followed by Jackie, then Julie. Fiona tries desperately to keep a straight face. Within seconds, four women in a living room in the heart of the Yorkshire Dales are holding their sides as tears stream down their cheeks. The deafening laughter becomes increasingly uncontrolled.

Chapter 7

Hunger Games

Thankfully, I'm awake and out of bed before Gloria starts singing. But I can still hear the distant strains of her forlorn, anguished warbling as I amble along the beach with an empty aching in my belly.

There's a rocky spur in the distance, which I estimate to be a good two hours walk or more. It could be a potential food source full of crustaceans. Yesterday's water challenge has sapped my energy. All we've eaten in three days is guava fruit, yams, and a bit of duckweed—a slightly sour and salty plant which grows in abundance on the fringes of the beach. I'm feeling lightheaded and jittery.

I pull a bottle of tepid water from my backpack and take a gulp as I gaze upon the peacock blue ocean. The water will be awash with all kinds of fish and crabs, yet we have no way of harvesting any of them. We need to construct a fishing rod or lines with hooks on, but we have no materials. Better still, would be some netting.

Instead of splashing through the tranquil breakers, I head back towards the high tide mark to examine any detritus which may have been washed up.

After two hours of walking, I near the outcrop of rocks. My heart sinks. The tide is in, and the bottom ledge of the crag is swamped with water. I navigate inland and climb the spur from the back end. The basalt is sharp and craggy near land but as I move closer to the ocean, it changes appearance and is smooth and glass-like in places, a testament to the never-ending motion of the waves. I freeze as I hear two female voices heading towards me. Their heads appear above a ridge.

'Oh, hi, Will!' Chloe waves. Both women saunter towards me beaming. 'Will, let me introduce you to Lucy Beckett,' she says. We shake hands.

'Hi, Lucy.'

'Lucy works for the BBC, the morning news,' Chloe explains.

'Nice to meet you, Will.'

'Likewise.'

'I'll see you back at camp, Chloe,' Lucy says as she throws an enigmatic smile at her comrade.

'Okay Lucy, see you back there.' Chloe turns her attention to me. 'What brings you all the way out here?'

'Probably the same reason as you—food.'

She laughs. 'Crustaceans?'

'Yes.'

'Great minds think alike. Unfortunately, the tides in. What's the time?'

I glance at my watch. 'Twenty past nine.' She ponders for a moment.

'If high tide was at nine, then low tide will be at three this afternoon.'

'It will be too hot by then,' I say.

'Yes, which means it will have to be three in the morning.'

'That's a bit dangerous; clambering about on wet rocks in the dark.'

'Aha! But the moon is waxing. Another two nights and there'll be a full moon. Even tonight there'll be enough lunar light to explore safely.'

'I see. How were the pancakes?'

She pulls a sad pout. 'Oh, I'm so sorry. I feel terrible. Your team should have easily won. What went wrong?'

'Two plonkers named Robbo and Geordie.'

She giggles. 'Is it true what they put—wankers cramp?'

I nod. 'Well, almost. They were missing an "R", so it was wankers camp.'

'Come on, do you want to explore further along the beach? It seems a shame to have come this far and not see what's ahead.'

'Yes, why not.' If I had been asked the question ten minutes ago, I would have baulked at the suggestion. But now, I seem to have newfound energy and optimism. We clamber down the rock and pad our way across soft sands.

She grabs my hand, unexpectedly. I automatically tense. She senses it and comes to a halt.

'Oh, I'm sorry. I didn't mean anything by it. Holding hands is like a comfort blanket for me. It makes me feel warm and secure,' she explains smiling sweetly.

I relax. 'Ah, I see. I'm sorry. I'm a northern man; we're emotionally repressed. Holding hands is fine.' She gives my palm a little tickle with a finger. 'Go on then, tell me about the bloody pancakes!'

'No. That would be cruel. But the giant frying pan is a boon. We keep it on the coals permanently. Anything we catch we chuck it straight on there.'

'Catch? Such as?'

'Oh, mainly insects; crickets, moths, caterpillars and the like.' It appears the Weathergirls are an industrious lot.

'I'm starving but I'm not sure I could eat insects.'

'Half the world eats insects. It's only western countries which turn their nose up at the idea. They're very nutritious and they're quite palatable. You pull their wings and legs off, bite off their head then pop the body into your mouth. Nice and crunchy.' We stroll on for another twenty minutes talking about anything and everything. I check my watch again.

'We better head back. The sun is starting to have some bite.'

'Yes, you're right. Oops, wait. I need to pee.' I assume she'll scurry off into the scrub but no, I'm wrong. She drops her shorts and squats right where she is. I turn and gaze out to sea. Not an ounce of modesty. The girls got some brass, I'll give her that.

We pick up a good pace as we head back to our respective camps, paddling in the refreshing gentle breakers. All too soon, I spot the blue pole that designates the pathway to her camp.

'Right, I'll see you later,' I say.

'Yes, you will. I need to complete my chores for the day. Firewood from the beach and water from the lagoon.'

'I heard you had a scare the other day near the lagoon.'

She laughs. 'Yes, obviously a prank set up by some of the crew to scare the "women". Don't you find it ridiculous there are sixteen competitors and only four are women?'

'I haven't really thought about it, but yeah, it does seem a little unfair.'

Her eyes narrow. 'Oh, don't get me started. Anyway, I better go.' She releases my hand with one last squeeze and turns to me. I know the move well; she's homing in to give me a friendly peck on the cheek. I turn my head slightly, but her lips bypass my cheek and lock onto my lips. It's not a proper kiss, but neither is it a formal parting goodbye. She skips up the beach and disappears into the dense undergrowth, before immediately reappearing, pointing at the sky.

'What?' I ask as I follow her outstretched arm and gaze at large ominous clouds in the distance.

'Cumulonimbus, expanding at a steady rate. We're going to get a downpour in a few hours. Make sure you've got your hammocks undercover and some sort of protection for the fire.' She turns and melts into the cluster of trees and shrubs. Very shortly I'm going to have a decision to make about the two of us. But for the moment I'll let it ride. I enjoy female company. It makes a pleasant change from trying to get sense out of neanderthal fruit loops.

I turn and saunter along the beach. It's not long before I spot another figure trudging towards me. As he nears, I recognise him; it's the celebrity chef, Marmaduke Smythe, or the Duke as he's colloquially known. He cuts a rather sad figure. He appears absorbed, away with the fairies. His head bobs from side to side in an uncoordinated manner. I've seen him on the TV many times, but it's the first time I've noticed he has a severe limp.

'Hello,' I say smiling at him. 'I used to enjoy your cooking shows.'

He smiles wearily back at me. 'Thank you very much. It's always reassuring to meet a fan,' he says in his refined, upper-class accent.

'Oh, I didn't say I was a fan. I said I enjoyed the shows. They had a certain element of...' I pause as I search for the appropriate words.

'Panache? Originality?'

'No...'

'A certain joie de vivre? Au nonpareil?'

'No. Calamity is the word I was searching for. Yes, calamity and black humour. You're a naturally funny man, in the old-fashioned way of vaudeville and slapstick. Were all those disasters staged or did they really happen spontaneously?' He appears taken aback. If I've offended him, I certainly didn't intend to.

'I can assure you nothing was staged,' he states frostily. 'As for the one or two mishaps which befell me, well, to err is to be human. Don't you find?'

'Indeed, it is.' He loses interest as he gazes around the empty setting. He leans in towards me and whispers in my ear.

'You don't know where I can get my hands on any alcohol, do you? You know, whisky or wine, or anything, really.'

I assume he's joking. 'Yes, there's an off-licence a few miles south of that rocky spur,' I say with a chuckle as I point at the crag in the distance. His eyes light up as he licks his lips.

'Excellent! Well, I mustn't keep you.' He sets off at a brisk pace. 'Oh, good luck with the challenges, by the way. May the best man win, and all that ballyhoo. Pip, pip!'

'Wait, I was only...' He turns and waves again.

Chapter 8

First Blood

As I enter our camp, I'm surprised to witness a hive of activity. Robbo is putting together the last of the "A" frames to cover the hammocks. Flaky is sitting next to a vast pile of long, slender, dark green leaves, weaving what appears to be a canopy for the structures. Geordie is tending the fire and boiling water.

'Ah, the wanderer returns,' Geordie says sporting a gormless expression. 'Where'd you get to?'

'I told you last night. I was getting up early to check the rocky outcrop down the beach.'

'How d'you go?'

'Bloody tide was in. But I reckon it will be teeming with shellfish at low tide. Three in the morning will be the best time to explore it. We're heading towards a full moon so there'll be plenty of light.'

'Three in the bloody morning,' Robbo gripes.

'Have you got something better to do?' I snap at him.

'Yes, sleep.'

'You can sleep during the hottest part of the day. If we want to survive the next four weeks, we need to be able to adapt... and quickly. There'll be heavy rain in a few hours so we should all work together to erect the roofs above the hammocks. We'll also need a lean-to for the fire to offer protection from the rain.'

Chloe was correct. By early afternoon, the rain fell in biblical fashion. It pelted down for over an hour before stopping as abruptly as it started. We got the roofs over the hammocks just in time and I have to admit, Flaky has done an amazing job with the weaving. A few drips entered, but considering the deluge, it's more than satisfactory. We even knocked up a quick lean-to for the fire and although the flame went out, there were still plenty of embers left once the downpour had abated. But now there really is a more pressing matter—food. Robbo and Flaky have gone off together to forage for edible plants and fruit while Geordie and I are searching for animal life.

We follow an obvious track through the jungle. I cut and slash with the machete whenever the trail becomes too narrow. I'm sweating like a stuck pig. The monsoon we experienced cooled everything off for a while but now the humidity is intense. Geordie is behind me brandishing a bamboo spear. I notice he's not sweating half as much as I am.

'What sort of animal trail do you think it is?' he asks.

I stop and wipe my brow. 'Not sure. Could be a wild boar, or a big lizard or maybe a giant rabbit.'

'You've watched too many kid's movies.'

'We seem to be heading towards the ocean. I can hear the waves. Maybe the boar likes to do a spot of sunbathing in the afternoon. You know, under an umbrella, sipping on a pina colada.'

He laughs. 'Aye, while getting oil rubbed into his back by a large-bosomed sow.'

'That would make it a sexist pig.'

'Ha-ha... don't give up the day job.'

'I already have. Which is why I'm on this Godforsaken island.' We come to a fork in the undergrowth and bear right. After another ten minutes hacking and slashing, we emerge out onto the upper end of the beach.

'Christ! I could do with a swim to cool off,' Geordie laments.

'As attractive as the water appears, let's not get side-tracked. Remember, food is our only goal at the moment.' A strange rasping noise accosts me. 'Geordie, are you suffering from a life-threatening chest infection? Pneumonia, bronchitis?'

'Don't talk daft! I'm as fit as a butcher's dog.'

'I'm not sure how fit a butcher's dog would actually be. Overweight and lethargic in my opinion. Wait... there it is again.'

'Aye, I heard it that time. It's coming from that thicket up there.' We tiptoe towards the source of the noise. At first, it's hard to see but as our eyes adjust to the lack of light in the dark flora we spot a wild boar, fast asleep and gently snoring. It has made a little nest under a shrub to give it shade from the sun but also to welcome the ocean's gentle breeze. It's not a babe nor is it full grown, but a juvenile... maybe twelve months old.

'Well, I never,' Geordie whispers as he hands me the bamboo spear. 'Here you go, Bill. Dispatch it swiftly. I cannae stand to see animals suffer.'

I wipe a drop of sweat from the tip of my nose and hand the spear back to him. 'Fuck that,' I murmur. 'You were happy to carry the spear for the last hour while I've been sweating my cods off hacking through the brush.'

He glares at me. 'Come on, man! You spotted it,' he says as he pushes the weapon onto me.

'So?'

'First blood, and all that. I wouldnae want to steal your glory.'

'Steal away. I don't mind.' I push the spear back into his hand.

'I see. Typical Englishman. When it comes to the dirty work, you go missing in action,' he grimaces as he thrusts the spear back into my arms.

'You're always saying how you Scots are natural hunters and warriors. Now's your chance to prove it.' I hold the spear out for him. 'You're not scared or squeamish, are you?'

'Of course not,' he huffs in indignation. 'I just thought that...'

'I'd want to kill it?'

'Aye.'

'No. be my guest.' He snatches the spear from me.

'I see, same old story. If you want a job doing, ask a Scotsman. You realise Britain would have been a basket case without the Scottish?'

'What planet are you living on? It is a basket case.'

'Oh, that's right, you may mock. But without Scottish ingenuity, you English would have had no...'

'Yeah, I know, electricity, lightbulbs, sanitation, Tarmac, lighthouses, Irn-Bru, castles, the Loch Ness Monster, television, screeching teeth jangling bagpipes, The Dandy and Beano, Kenneth McKellar, air, water, oil, gas, and last—but by no mean's least—The Proclaimers. Been a while since you Scots produced anything new though, hasn't it? They all seem to be nineteenth century inventions. Apart from The Proclaimers of course. You know what, I'm not sure why you're not an independent nation.'

His eyes narrow to slits as he regards me with contempt. 'Weak as piss,' he hisses. 'I'll dispatch this beast using the three Qs technique.'

I'm intrigued. 'The three Qs technique? Please elucidate.'

He puffs his chest out. 'Quickly, quietly and on-cue.'

'You nugget. That's two Qs and an O. And for your information, that particular cue begins with a C.'

He ponders for a moment. 'Aye, well never mind about that. Stand back and let the hunter go about his business.' He grips the spear high up the shaft and edges forward.

'Straight through the heart,' I whisper. He softly sings a depressing Scottish dirge.

My heart's in the Highlands, my heart is not here, my heart's in the Highlands, a-chasing the deer. Farewell to the Highlands, farewell to the north, the birthplace of valour, the country of worth. Farewell to the mountains...

'Oh, shut the fuck up! What are you trying to do, get the pig to commit suicide?'

'I'll have you know that's Robbie Burns!' he huffs indignantly.

'I don't care if it's Robbie fucking Williams! Get on with it.' He lifts the spear above his shoulder ready for the kill. I wait, then wait some more. 'What's wrong,' I whisper as the soft snores of the boar grow louder.

'Aw! Look at the wee little beggar. It reminds me of when I creep into the boys' bedroom on a night to watch them sleep.'

'You're odd.'

'Do you not do the same with Mary?'

I acquiesce. 'Yes. I do, occasionally. There's something calming and magical about listening to a young one fast asleep. It's a kind of perfect. I miss her... as I'm sure you miss your lads.'

'Aye, very true. They can drive me bonkers, but these are the best days of my life. Do you know what I'm going to do when I get home?'

'Kill the pig!' I hiss.

'No, I was going to say...'

'Shut up and kill the Goddamn pig before it wakes up!'

'Oh, right, yes. Slay the beast.' He refocuses his attention on the prey. 'But it's nought but a bairn,' he murmurs mournfully.

'It's not a bairn. It's got tusks and have you seen the size of its plums. Christ, they look like two cricket balls inside a hairy pair of bellows. This is survival, Geordie. We're wasting away. Think of pork crackling and succulent belly fat.'

He licks his lips. 'Aye, you're right.' He pauses and shoots me a concerned sideways glance. 'But it's not full grown yet, is it?' I grab at the spear.

'Give me the fucking thing! I'll do it.' He yanks the spear back from me.

'Oh no, you don't. If you think I'm going to give you gloating rights back at camp, you can think again!' We push and pull at the spear, back and forth. As he yanks at the weapon for the tenth time, I release my grip. He stumbles backwards and stands on a branch which splinters and cracks. We freeze. The animal opens one eye, lazily, and studies us. I'm not sure if pigs dream, I assume they do. What it was dreaming about I'll never know. Perhaps snuffling for truffles or rolling about in mud. It's not dreaming anymore though. For a moment it appears confused, wondering what two upright hairy faced creatures are doing poised above it, one of them, the ugly one, clutching a long, sharp looking implement. Geordie makes a sudden rush of movement as he thrusts the spear into my hands. I drop it. The boar has now had a few valuable seconds to assess the situation, and it doesn't like the look of it one little bit. It jumps to its feet and lets out a piercing squeal. I turn tail and run as fast as my weary legs will go. I look over my shoulder. The damn thing is hot on my heels.

'Aye, that's right! You keep running you soft Sassenach bastard!' Geordie's guffaw echoes out. 'Scared of a wee piglet!' As the boar closes in behind me, I brace for the sickening pain I'm about to experience as it thrusts its razor-sharp tusks into my calf or hamstrings. I spot a low hanging branch a few feet ahead. The boar emits another violent squeal as he bears down on me. I grab at the branch. My forward momentum swings me up, like a gymnast on the parallel bars. I pull my legs up and part them landing safely on the top of the branch. The boar comes to a skidding halt and glares up at me, then paws at the sand. It wanders around in a circle a few times, snorting and grunting. I can hear laughter from twenty feet away.

'Oh my, oh my! That has to be one of the funniest things I've ever seen!' The pig stops grunting and stares back down the beach. It snorts again, disagreeably, and sets off like a whippet on steroids. Strangely enough, this coincides with the abrupt curtailing of Geordie's laughter. Now it's my turn to chuckle. Geordie bolts towards the sea with the pig in hot pursuit. As it's nearly upon him, he dives into the water like a Russian Olympic swimmer who's been told it's either gold or the salt mines.

If Geordie had swum like that in yesterday's water challenge, we'd have won by ten minutes. The boar halts and patrols the shore for a few moments before running into the bush, disappearing from view. I drop from the tree, completely exhausted.

∗∗∗

I'm hot, sweaty, and itchy as I toss and turn in my hammock. The three morons are all fast asleep. My mind turns to Fiona and Mary. A shot of guilt and homesickness momentarily overwhelms me. I think of Chloe and my little mate downstairs stirs. A noisy rustle from the undergrowth breaks my train of thought. *What the hell is that?* It could be a snake? Or a wild boar? Perhaps the juvenile hog seeking revenge. I lean over the edge of the hammock and peer into the gloaming. *Holy shit on a stick!* I carefully and silently grab the bamboo spear propped up against the tree. With the blunt end, I reach out and tap Geordie on the head.

'Uh, shomeozgut, cribbage,' he mumbles incoherently before rolling onto his front.

'Psst! Geordie, wake up,' I hiss. There's no response. I clonk him on the back of the head, a little harder this time. A hollow sound resonates around the camp. I'm not sure whether it's from the bamboo or his oversized melon. Still no response. I turn the spear around and jab him in the arse with the pointy end.

'Christ! What the hell was that?' he yelps with alarm.

'Shh!'

He lifts his head and stares at me bleary eyed. 'What's your bloody game,' he asks rubbing at his buttock.

'Over there,' I nod. His eyes focus on the pile of coconuts we've accumulated for future use. Puzzlement is etched into his features as his eyes bulge.

'Jumping Jack Flash in a bag of bees! What in hell's name is that bloody thing? Have the aliens finally landed?'

'It's a coconut crab, also known as the robber crab.'

'Sweet merciful shite with bells on. If that thing tried to rob me, I'd hand my wallet over straight away.'

'Light a torch,' I say as I slip from the hammock. I tentatively tiptoe over to the grotesque and frightening creature. It appears oblivious to our presence... at the moment. Geordie creeps over with a bamboo torch, lighting up the area. 'Don't get too close,' I say.

'Why?'

'Apparently, they can jump a good six feet in height. They've been known to rip a man's throat out in seconds.' Geordie turns a whiter shade of pale as the torch trembles. He takes a step back.

'Yer bum's oot the windae,' he stammers.

'I'm not joking. Travis warned me about them the other day.'

'What? And you didnae think to mention it?'

'It slipped my mind. In fact, he said they're very partial to Scottish flesh,' I add as I fail to suppress a snigger.

'Oh, very funny! That's right, you may mock, you bloody bampot! Can you eat them?'

'I suppose so. Look at the size of those claws. There'll be plenty of meat in those buggers.'

'Well don't hang about. Dispatch the damn thing and let's get him in the pot.'

'Why should I kill it?'

'Because I was the one who was going to kill the boar. Now it's your turn.'

'I'm not even sure how to kill a crab.'

'Don't talk daft! Take your knife and with the tip of your blade stab it through the head.'

'It hasn't even got a head. It's a tangle of legs beneath a body.'

'Its head is at the front, near the eyes. Now stop playing for time and get on with it. And watch your fingers—if it's claw clamps onto one of your digits, you'll never play the guitar again.'

There are two ways to tackle this; slowly and surely or a rapid attack. I decide on the latter. I pull my knife out, take a step forward and thrust the tip of the blade through the top of its shell. A sickening cracking is followed by twitching legs as I hold the knife in place. A few seconds pass until the creature is no more.

'Well done, Billy Boy. Like I said, there's nothing to it. Right, I'll get the water on,' he says in an upbeat fashion, clearly buoyed by the impending meal.

'I think you're supposed to cook crabs in saltwater. That's what the chefs do on TV.'

'Too bad. It may have escaped your notice, but we don't have any salt or any other condiments for that matter.' I pull my knife out of the crab and clean it on a coconut husk.

'You may have missed it, but the small body of water next to the beach is called the South Pacific. It's saltwater. Go grab a bucketful.'

'Oh, aye. I never thought of that.' He grabs the bucket but stops before he hits the trail. He gazes upon the lifeless bodies of Robbo and Flaky. 'Look at those two wankers. Bloody bone idle, the pair of them.' He picks up a cup, dips it in the water bucket and throws it over Robbo.

'Oi! What the...'

'Wake up, Noddy! Here, take this bucket and half-fill it with seawater.'

'What the hell are you talking about, man?'

'You heard. Me and Bill have caught a crab. We need to boil it in salted water. Now stop your blather and make yourself useful otherwise you'll get no supper.' Robbo wanders off cursing profusely under his breath.

We are sitting on logs around the campfire as we devour the sweet meaty flesh of the crab. The crackle of the fire and the faraway eternal rhythm of the sea is our peaceful soundtrack as we all enter our own private heavens. My spirits rise and a sense of well-being returns. Robbo has juice dribbling down his chin and is making sure there's not one scrap of flesh left in the crab leg.

'I was speaking with Stu this morning,' he lazily says.

'Stu, the security guard?' I quiz.

He nods. 'Yeah. Stu, the security guard. He was telling me about the accommodation at Castaway Central. He says it's top-notch, five-star. Most of the crew are staying in those luxury huts which stretch out into the water. The big wigs, Jerry and Felix, and a few others are in the main house which is apparently huge and state-of-the-art.'

'That figures. Bastards,' I grumble.

'He said the food was restaurant quality. Fillet steaks, smoked salmon, you name it and they have it.'

'I'll never take food for granted again,' Flaky whispers as he sucks on a claw.

'This is ambrosia,' Geordie says, wistfully.

'Ambrosia was a fruit of the Gods. I'm not sure meat qualifies as a fruit,' Flaky corrects in his pompous way.

'Oh, shut your great big geggie!' he replies angrily as bickering resumes its normal transmission. Oh, well, the peace was nice while it lasted.

Chapter 9

What Goes Up?

A warm breeze wafts down from the lush green hills behind Castaway Central. It carries a sweet scent of bruised Mediterranean herbs, oregano, basil, rosemary. The occasional perfume of wild garlic joins the trio and torments me with thoughts of a rich Bolognaise sauce, deep fried cheese, courgette fritters and barbequed aubergine sprinkled with olive oil and lemon. I spend most of my waking hours thinking of food. I'm even dreaming about it. Last night, after the crab, I fell into a deep and wondrous coma. I dreamt of fish and chips, eaten from the paper sitting on a bench overlooking Whitby harbour. They were lavishly sprinkled with salt and vinegar. The batter was a deep golden brown, the flesh of the fish—silky white, tender, succulent. Afterwards, I bought Mary and me a giant raspberry ripple ice cream. We sat opposite each other on the beach, staring at one another as we studiously licked our treat away. The next moment, I'm outside a country pub. It's summer in England. The sun's gentle rays caress my face. I lift a pint of beer to my lips and take a gulp. The taste is almost orgasmic. Sweet, comforting, nourishing and familiar.

'Will, are you listening to this?' Flaky's snippy voice prises me from my trance.

'What? Oh, yes.'

Jerry is talking to the camera crew as we await our next challenge. All the teams have been assembled for over forty minutes, mooching around, waiting. I stare at the production team; cameramen, sound recordists, tech guys, the medical people, and Jerry and Felix. They all look well fed and pleased with themselves.

I'm lazing in the shade offered by one of the many large totem poles which protrude up from the sand like giant stepping-stones. They're painted in wacky blue, red, yellow, and green colours—I'm guessing to represent the colours of the four teams. I suppose it won't be long before we're expected to climb the bloody things or chop them down with an axe.

The Entrepreneurs are sitting not too far away. I focus on Piers. He's the oldest of his group, probably about ten years older than me; late forties to early fifties. I wish he'd wear a shirt. The sight of saggy man boobs and a muffin top around his midriff is not a pleasant view. Bags under weary eyes tell me he's not coping too well. I take some comfort from this. An intense argument has broken out between the Chefs. I'm too far away to hear what it's about but they all seem pissed off with each other.

Jerry finishes his talk with the camera crew, has a quick word with Felix, then he makes his way over to the teams.

'Okay, gang, apologies for the delay. If you'd like to get into your teams and line up, we'll make a start.' We oblige as the camera crews move into position. A make-up artist puts one last flourishing touch to Felix's sickeningly healthy cheeks. He turns to a camera and begins his spiel, as though he's talking directly to us.

'Good morning teams, welcome to day five and our second challenge.' He waffles on for a few minutes, explaining what the challenge is, before informing Jerry he wants to shoot the intro again from a slightly different camera angle.

'Give me strength,' Geordie grizzles. 'What a prima donna wanker.' The challenge is asinine. There's no other word to describe it. We have to climb onto the totem poles embedded in the sand and wait. Yep, you heard me correctly. The person who can cling onto the pole, the longest is the winner, or at least the team they belong to are. It must be nudging 30 degrees and the prick wants us to hang off a pole in the baking sun.

The starter gun fires, and we all rush to our allotted poles and start to climb. Every couple of feet there's a thick band of cord wound around the pole, a resting place for feet, or toes. There's been no mention of how high you have to go so I do the least amount of work as possible and stop once I reach the first rope, about three feet off the ground. I give it five minutes then pretend to lose my grip and drop to the sand.

'And our first challenger is out!' Felix screams excitedly as if he's got the winning ticket to an all-you-can-eat brothel. 'It's Will Harding from The Rock Stars, who barely lasted five minutes.' He's soon in my face with a camera crew to the side of him. 'Will, what went wrong?'

'I tried to reposition myself and lost my footing on the rope.'

'That's all it takes. One misstep, one wrong turn and it's all over. It's rather like a metaphor for surviving in the wild, don't you think?'

'No.'

'Right, well back to the other challengers. I can see Brody Buchannan from the Celebrity Chefs is looking comfortable. He's scooted his way to the very top of the pole. And Dick Honeyman from the Entrepreneurs also appears relaxed, as are most of the Weathergirls.' I find a nice shady spot out of the way and sprawl out on the warm sand. I close my eyes.

A raging thirst wakes me from my slumber. My tongue is stuck to the roof of my mouth. I can hear the dickhead, Felix Cain, speaking in excited gibberish in the distance. I sit up and glance around. Geordie is lying next to me and across from him is Flaky sitting cross-legged engrossed in the non-action that's happening, or not happening on the poles. On the other side of us are three of the Entrepreneurs, the four Weathergirls and the four Celebrity Chefs.

'Where's Robbo?' I ask Flaky.

'He's still up the pole. You'd know where he was if you'd shown the slightest bit of interest.'

I glance at my watch. 'Christ! He's been up there two hours!' I exclaim, astonished. 'Who else is up there?'

'Cliff Zimmerman.'

'Who?'

'Cliff Zimmerman.'

'Who the hell's he when he's at home?'

Flaky turns to me clearly annoyed. 'Do you take no interest in current affairs? He's the guy who developed one of the first functional electric cars. Surely you've heard of the HS74-M276X?'

'Can't say I have. He may be good at building electric cars but when it comes to naming them, I'd employ a team of specialists.'

'Shut up! I'm trying to concentrate.' Jerry comes over and corrals the fallen challengers back towards the poles to get some good camera shots.

'Rock Stars and Entrepreneurs can you please occasionally shout some encouragement to your teammates. At least look like you're captivated.' I stare at Robbo who is halfway up the pole looking completely relaxed with his eyes shut. In fact, I think he could be asleep, or possibly dead and rigor mortis has set in.

'Go on, Robbo' Flaky shouts. 'Hang in there. You're doing great.' I glance up at Cliff Zimmerman who isn't as chilled out as Robbo. Sweat is pouring off him and he keeps baring his teeth in obvious agony. His full weight is bearing down on his toes which are bunched up, digging into the rope. I do believe we are about to win our first challenge.

'Keep it up, Robbo,' Geordie yells. 'This other guy with the beard and long hair, who looks like Jesus Christ, is not far off from quitting.'

Flaky snaps at him. 'That's Cliff Zimmerman!' he hisses.

'Who?'

He sighs. 'Give me strength.'

'Cool!' Robbo shouts down bearing a smile. The most boring challenge in the history of boring challenges goes on for another interminable twenty minutes. Cliff now looks like he's got a severe case of the essential tremors. If his head twitches anymore I fear it could snap off.

'Who'd have thought it,' I say to Geordie. 'Old Robbo clinging on for nearly two-and-a-half hours.'

Geordie isn't impressed. 'He's cut out for it.'

'What do you mean?'

'A game where you don't actually have to do anything. He's spent his whole life practising for this.'

'I heard that!' Robbo shouts down. Another ten minutes crawls by. Poor old Cliff now looks like he's clinging onto a high voltage cable. I think he may have developed the rapid onset of myoclonus epilepsy.

'Why doesn't he just throw the towel in?' I lament. 'Surely, he can see he's not going to win. We could come back tomorrow, and Robbo would still be up there.'

'Because some people aren't quitters,' Flaky snipes. Geordie raise his eyebrows and glances at me.

'Oh, no!' Robbo cries.

'What's the matter?' Flaky shouts up to him.

'Not good,' Robbo says with an element of fear in his voice. Gone is the sanguine expression replaced by a wild-eyed stare. 'I'm coming down.'

'Don't talk bloody daft. Another few minutes and you'll be the winner.'

'He's right, Robbo,' Geordie encourages. 'They've already gone to fetch the body bag for the other guy.' Robbo descends, hesitantly.

'What are you bloody doing!' Flaky screeches. 'Stop right where you are!' Meanwhile, Felix is giving a running commentary in the background as the other three Entrepreneurs offer encouragement to Cliff. 'I'm warning you, Robbo!' Flaky threatens. 'What's wrong? Speak to me?'

'I've got to go,' Robbo murmurs as the sweat cascades off him. He's still halfway up the bloody pole and is making very delicate and tentative progress down.

'What do you mean you've got to go? Go where?'

'For a shit. I haven't had one since I arrived. It must have been the bloody crab we ate last night. It's shifted something.'

'Can't you hold it in for another five minutes?' I implore.

'I've been baking this lot for five days and I reckon I've got about five seconds left until I shit myself on national TV.' When he's a few feet from the ground he drops to the sand and sprints—I use the term loosely—towards the safety of the jungle. There's polite applause and cheers behind us from the Entrepreneurs, accompanied by the feverish high-pitched banter of Felix Cain. The three of us forlornly watch on as Robbo disappears into the bush along with whatever prize we so nearly won.

'Weak as piss,' Geordie mumbles.

We are gathered around the winners' marquee as Felix witters on in front of the cameras.

'To the winners go the spoils!' he declares.

'Shouldn't it be, to the victor goes the spoils?' Flaky comments.

'Who cares,' Geordie mutters, sullenly.

Felix continues. 'The winners of the Totem Pole Challenge are... the Green Team! The Entrepreneurs!' It's followed by more mindless whooping and cheering, mostly from the assembled production crew. I thought this was a British show? Since when did the Brits ever whoop? We are well-known for a few polite handclaps and the occasional "here, here" but that's about as far as our emotive, congratulatory acknowledgements go.

'Get on with it, you shiny-toothed, pigeon-chested, knobjockey,' Geordie mutters under his breath.

'Twenty points were on offer. You have now jumped onto the leaderboard and are in second place behind the Weathergirls on thirty points. Make your way into the winners' enclosure, the magic marquee is awaiting you.' I've seen this film before as I wince at the thought of what food may be on offer. The flaps on the marquee are dramatically pulled aside to reveal the chef from a few days ago. He brings forward a large metal serving dish, covered with a bell-shaped cloche, and hands it to Felix who with a dramatic flourish, raises the lid to reveal four big juicy beefburgers in buns, a mountain of fries and a big bowl of salad and a side dish of relish.

'Fuck me sideways with a marrow,' Geordie moans, licking his lips.

'You've also won a Dauerhaft cauldron,' Felix elaborates.

'Bloody product placement,' I whisper to Geordie. 'I thought this was supposed to be about raising one million quid for charity?'

'I guess Dauerhaft are putting up some of the money.'

'This show goes out on commercial TV. Don't they pay for it by advertising revenue?'

'God knows how it all works. And frankly, at the moment I don't give a shit.' The Entrepreneurs are getting impatient for their burger and fries. If Felix doesn't wrap up quickly, he could be trampled to death.

'Some of the more eagle-eyed of you may have noticed a common thread to our first two challenges?' Felix says.

'I have; the show's shit,' I remark. Jerry glares at me as he waves his hands at the cameramen.

'Keep rolling! We'll cut it in the edit.' Felix clears his throat and repeats the question. The winner, Cliff Zimmerman thrusts his hand into the air.

'If you win a reward challenge, you win three prizes.'

'Cliff, you are correct!' Felix declares. 'You get points on the leaderboard; you enjoy a much-needed meal; and lastly, you get a valuable piece of survival equipment for your camp. I'd like to say a special thank you to one of the show's sponsors, Dauerhaft—experts in the finest kitchen cookware for over eighty years. German engineering at its best.'

'It gets worse,' I grumble. 'There was nothing said about this when we signed the contracts. I'm not here sweating my frigging gonads off to promote a German company which makes frying pans!' I receive another fierce glare from Jerry who again waves at the cameramen to continue filming. The Entrepreneurs troop into the marquee. Piers Conrad turns and smiles at me as he rubs at his bloated belly whilst licking his lips. The flaps close and the production team disperse.

'That man is beginning to piss me off.'

'Do you want me to put him on his arse when the cameras aren't around?' Geordie offers.

'Nah. He's a litigious prick. Anyway, I want something special for old Piers. Something far worse than a biff on the nose.'

'Such as?'

'Total humiliation.'

As I enter the camp, I'm accosted by a familiar but out of place smell. I assume it must be the fire. Robbo's hammock is swinging gently back and forth.

'Did you refill all the water containers?' I ask.

'Yep. All done. Where's Flaky and Geordie?'

'They're both looking for seaweed.'

'That should go well. A marriage made in heaven.'

'I don't know what you've thrown on the fire, but it smells just like weed,' I say. Robbo lifts his head up. In his mouth is a giant reefer the size of a King Edward cigar.

'That's because it is weed,' he says with a cheeky smile.

'Good God! Where the hell did you get the joint?' I splutter astonished.

'Stu.'

'Stu, the security guard?'

'Yep. Stu the security guard. I told him I'll put him on our VIP email list, so he'll receive signed copies of all our new releases. Oh, and a backstage pass to any future gigs he wants to attend.'

'We don't have a VIP mailing list.'

'We do now. It has one member.'

'I see. A bit of bribery goes a long way.'

'It certainly does. It's all part of the survival process,' he says as his head disappears under a giant plume of smoke.

'You want to take it easy on that. You haven't had a spliff for over a week. It will go to your head.'

'That's what I'm hoping.' Robbo falls silent as I pick up my journal and begin scribbling. I use the front of the book as a diary, recording our daily events, as mundane as most of them are. In the middle of the book, I've developed a psychological profile on everyone I've had an interaction with. For example, next to the name Piers Conrad I have the following: narcissist; arrogant; entitled; lacks empathy; self-important; ugly both in looks and personality; yellow teeth. The back of the book is reserved for my own meandering thoughts, a free flow of consciousness without much structure. There are bits of prose, attempts at poetry, a few lines of possible song lyrics and a list of words that occasionally pop into my head without reason. Balderdash, incapacitated, hegemony, flibbertigibbet, flubber, Ralph Emerson, squib, and Cleckheaton are just a few examples. I have no idea why such words materialise in my mind for a few brief seconds. They must mean something.

Squabbling voices from the beach trail end my reverie. The peace and quiet was all too brief.

'You've eaten seaweed before when we were in the Scottish Highlands on Hammer's survival weekend,' Flaky argues.

'Aye, and it tasted like shit.'

'It's full of essential nutrients and roughage.'

'I don't care what it's full of. It's like chewing on rubber.' I put my journal away as they both saunter into camp. Flaky throws his backpack on the ground.

'Seaweed for supper,' he says with a grin.

'I heard. At least it's something.'

'Where's Robbo?' Geordie asks.

'In his hammock.'

'Lazy prick. Did he do the water run?'

'Yes.' Geordie ambles over to Robbo's hammock and stares into it.

'Oi, Noddy, why don't you get up and make yourself useful instead of lying in bed all day?' He gets no response. 'Oi, Robbo did you hear what I said?' He pokes at him. 'Robbo?' Geordie turns to me with a concerned look. 'Hey, lads, I think Robbo might be dead.'

'Don't worry. He's in a weed coma, that's all.'

'A bloody weed coma! You're joking, right?'

'I jest ye not. He snaffled a joint the size of a cruise liner from Stu.'

'Stu, the security guard.'

'Yes.'

'My God!' Flaky exclaims. 'If Robbo was the first man on Mars, he'd be walking around with a joint dangling from his lips within twenty minutes of touching down. I don't know how he does it.'

'Where there's a will, there's a way,' I reply.

'Aye, if he showed the same tenacity for finding edible food, we'd never go hungry again,' Geordie gripes.

Chapter 10

Oysters on the Rocks

Beeps from my watch wake me—2:45 am. I relax for a further ten minutes, then slip from my suspended cot.

'Hey, boys... come on... time to get up,' I say in a hushed but urgent whisper. There's no reply, just a few groans. 'We're going on the scavenger hunt to the rocks,' I say with false enthusiasm. 'We're meeting up with the Weathergirls. We don't want to keep them waiting.' There's no response apart from snoring, a whistle, and a half-hearted fart. *Christ!* What the hell, I can probably do it quicker without them and with less stress.

As I emerge onto the beach, I flick my torch on and off three times. Almost instantly, I receive the same semaphore back. It's a full moon, but the jungle is still dark and foreboding. I walk on for ten minutes until Chloe's voice calls out.

'Hey, Will!' She sprints from the undergrowth, beaming.

'Hi, Chloe. Where are the others?'

'Oh, I didn't bother to wake them. We've all had a tough day, and they were all worn out. I'll surprise them with a midnight feast. What about your gang?'

'Fast off. Anyway, if I had brought them along, it would have been four hours of whingeing and petty bickering.'

'Looks like it's just ye and me,' she says as she encircles her arm around mine.

'Yes... I suppose it is,' I reply nervously. We walk on for a good hour talking about how we are coping with the situation, the privations, the constant dirt, and hunger. Moonlight illuminates the rocky outcrop in the distance, and a long swathe of beach between it, and the water. The tide is out.

'How do you write songs?' she asks unexpectedly.

'Erm... all sorts of ways,' I reply, not wanting to elaborate.

'For example?'

'I just noodle around on my guitar, playing chord progressions and humming along. Sometimes a melody will stick, or a lyric.'

'It all sounds rather haphazard. What if you don't get anything?'

I laugh. 'It is haphazard, and most of the time I draw a blank! It's like fishing. You can spend a week with your line in the water and not get a nibble. Then one day, same location, same time—bang! You've hooked something. The best melodies are the ones that come to me whilst I'm asleep.'

'Really?' She sounds sceptical.

'Yes, really. The hard part though is forcing yourself awake to record it. I have a tiny micro-recorder on my bedside table. I can't tell you the number of times I've had a great melody, convinced myself I'll remember it in the morning, don't record it and then...'

'You've forgotten it when you wake up?'

'Yes.'

'Have you children?'

'Yes. Four... well, I'm the stepdad to Fiona's three boys and I have a daughter of my own, Mary.'

'That will keep you busy.'

'It used to. The youngest lad is nineteen now. They all live in Dorset, near their grandmother. They're all mad surfers. The Yorkshire Dales doesn't offer much excitement for lads of that age.'

'Your wife must miss them. How old's Mary?'

'Six.'

'I bet she's a daddy's girl and can wrap you around her little finger.'

A stab of homesickness and guilt gnaws at my innards. 'She can, and she does. Fiona's always lecturing me for spoiling her. Enough about me, what about you? Are you married? Kids?'

'No and no. I have a long-term partner, Trevor. We've been together fifteen years, which is probably five years too long.' Her honesty takes me by surprise.

'Oh,' is all I can muster.

'I don't love him anymore. He's become quite boring, as I have too.' We walk on in silence for a while. 'My truthfulness unnerves you, doesn't it?'

'No, of course not.' I try to laugh her question off, but it doesn't sound convincing.

'Liar.'

⇢⠀⇠

The rocky outcrop is discouraging.

'I think one of the other teams got here before us,' I say. There is still an abundance of shellfish clinging to the crag, but they are so small it wouldn't be worth the effort to prise them from their home.

'I think you're right. And I bet I know who it was,' Chloe says, her disappointment obvious.

'The Chefs?'

'Yes. You know how much celebrity chefs like their bloody shellfish.'

'Greedy bastards. They could have left some for other people.'

'You can't blame them. We'd have done the same.' I explore the rock hoping they may have missed some, but they've completely plundered anything worth eating. I jump down to the wet sand and pick up a cluster of brownish seaweed.

'Looks like we'll have to make do with algae again.'

'Yes. There's no point going back empty handed. Although we didn't have to walk this far to get our hands on it. The beach is strewn with the stuff.' I dump the weed into my backpack and skirt the perimeter of the rock, still in the hope the Chefs missed some crustaceans. About halfway along there's a narrow fissure carved into the basalt. It runs along at a horizontal angle for about ten feet before dropping away. I kneel and stick my torch in the gap.

'Bastards!' I exclaim.

'What is it?' Chloe says as she leaps onto the sand and joins me.

'I can see some good-sized mussels and what look like oysters and they're exactly just over an arm's length away. If that lazy Scottish git had got out of bed, I bet he'd have been able to reach them. He's got arms like rubber man.'

'Geordie?'

'Yes.'

'Here, let me have a look.' She drops to her knees and peers into the crevice. 'You know what, I reckon if I lay on my side, I'd be able to shimmy my way in.' She is slight, but I think she's being overly optimistic.

'Don't be silly. You'll cut yourself to ribbons and if you get stuck, Christ, it doesn't bear thinking about.' She pays absolutely no heed to my warnings as she throws her pack to the ground and slides into the crack.

'It's as smooth as glass,' she says with a laugh as she quickly wriggles away from me. 'You were right. They are oysters. I'm going to go further and see what's at the end.' She quickly disappears from view as she gets to the end of the fissure and drops down.

'Chloe, are you all right?' There's silence. 'Chloe, speak to me.' More silence. I experience a dizzy rush to the head. If she's knocked herself out, then it's curtains. It would be a good two hours to Castaway Central, by which time the tide, which is already on the turn, would have swamped the rock. 'Chloe!' I shout, becoming increasingly alarmed. Her grinning head pops back into view.

'What's wrong?' she asks with a giggle.

'Christ! Don't do that. You scared me to death. I was worried about you.'

'I didn't know you cared,' she replies with a mischievous smile. She tosses something my way. It slides along the glazed rock like a curling stone on ice, shoots from the crevice, and plants itself into the sand. I pick it up.

'Nice one!' I call back, admiring a generously sized oyster. She repeats the process another dozen times. I'm so engrossed in proceedings I take my eye off the incoming tide. It's not until I feel water splash against my ankles, I'm aware of how fast the water is rushing in.

'Chloe! Start making your way back now. The tide's on the move.'

'Just another minute,' she shouts back as she disappears again. I quickly gather the shellfish and drop them into my bag along with my torch. Another wave rushes up the beach.

'Chloe! I'm serious! The tide's coming in at a bloody gallop. Get back here right now!' Thankfully, she reappears, clutching what appears to be more seaweed. She throws it in front of her then wriggles forward. Her progress is slow and at one point she grimaces. 'What's wrong?' I ask, perturbed.

'I'm snagged on something.'

'Hell,' I curse, as another wave hits me on the knees.

'I think it's my belt.' She's still about eight feet away from safety. The next surge sends a ripple of water along the crevice. My heart's thumping against my breastbone. She fumbles with her belt and rips it from the buckles on her shorts as she shimmies forward again. I let out a nervous sigh as I turn my gaze towards the ocean.

'Shit the bed,' I murmur.

'What's wrong?'

'There's a big swell which is breaking into a cluster of angry looking waves.' She becomes wedged again as she pushes the seaweed forward. 'Forget about the bloody seaweed!' I yell.

'It's full of mussels,' she puffs as she lobs them my way. I grab the haul of seaweed, stash it in my bag, and throw it up onto the rock as a barrage of waves hit the shore.

'Chloe, hold your breath!' I dart up the beach, away from the incoming flood. The first wave completely swamps the fissure and as it retreats out, it's hit by another, then another. It feels like a lifetime for the water to recede. I race back across the sand and stick my head into the gap. I can no longer see her as the coffin shaped gap is underwater. Panic sets in. I scoop at the seawater as a torrent of violent bubbles rises to the surface. She lifts her head and gasps for air, coughing and spluttering. The belt has washed along the narrow tunnel. I stick my arm in and grab it.

'That was fun,' she says with a cheeky grin as she sucks in air.

'Grab the belt!' I scream. She reaches out and grips the belt as I heave with all my might. She slides along, slowly. I'm blindsided by a wave which knocks me off balance and tumbles me up the beach. 'Fuck!' I cry as I stagger to my feet, race back down into waist-high frothing water, and stick my arm into the crevice. I feel her fingers grab mine. They interlock, and I pull with every ounce of strength I have left. I don't even see the next wave. All I know is I'm now underwater, clinging desperately onto Chloe's delicate hand. My senses are overwhelmed. There's only darkness and a sleepy swooshing throb around me. Another wave breaks harmlessly above. I can't hold my breath much longer. A tickling sensation on my palm brings clarity. It's Chloe's fingernail. She's saying goodbye. As she tries to release my hand, I give one last heave. Something gives. Her body collides against mine as we rise to the surface, only to be pummelled back under by a giant swell. It picks us up and tosses our exhausted bodies further up the beach. We scrabble along on our hands and knees to safety and collapse.

➤➤➤ ⬅⬅⬅

We are sitting on a high ledge of the rock as the waves harmlessly crash far below us. The moonlight skips and dances over the turbulent water as Chloe uses her knife to shuck a large oyster.

'Open wide, ' she says as she turns to me.

'No. You have it,' I reply.

'If it hadn't been for you, I wouldn't be having anything ever again. I insist. Open wide.' I part my lips as she gently coaxes the oyster in. The sensation is bliss and I take a moment to savour and celebrate the elaborate flavours as they kindle my taste buds.

'My God! I know it's a cliché, but if you could take the very essence of the ocean and reduce it into one mouthful, the oyster would be it.' She opens another one and pours it into her mouth. Her eyes close in ecstasy. It's a perfect moment on a perfect night, despite one of us nearly dying. Near-death experiences always heighten the senses for a fleeting time afterwards. We sit in relaxed silence and gorge on the oysters for ten minutes.

'I hope they don't cause you any problems,' she eventually murmurs cryptically. I'm confused.

'What?'

'The oysters. They're an aphrodisiac... full of zinc.'

'Oh, I see what you mean.' She shucks the last one. 'You have it,' I say.

'We'll share it,' she replies with a glint in her eye. I'm unsure how one shares an oyster. 'Open your mouth, nice and wide.' I obey her instructions as she moves the shell towards me. Just as I think she's about to drop it in, she slurps it into her mouth and clamps it shut. Her head moves towards me as her hand carefully cradles the back of my head. As our lips touch, she opens her mouth. The slippery delicacy begins to slide from her to me. She bites down on it so it's now half in her, half in me. I gently suck at it for a moment until she releases, and it slips down my throat. It's the most erotic experience of my life. My little friend downstairs, who never misses a trick, immediately wakes from his long slumber, and pushes against my damp shorts. I'm embarrassed and lift my leg to hide the protuberance. 'How did that feel?'

I cough. 'Ahem... it was nice.' I reply as I fix my gaze back out to sea.

'No. It wasn't nice. It was hot, sexy, sensual... wasn't it?'

'Erm... kind of,' I say as my erection hardens to excruciatingly, painful proportions which could end in a heart seizure or my head vaporising.

'For a creative person—a singer-songwriter, you aren't particularly good at showing your genuine emotions, are you?' she says with a wicked giggle.

'No, I'm not. My upbringing... I guess. I put all my innermost thoughts, my truths, my feelings, into my songs.'

'Maybe that's why you write songs, to get your emotions out in the open.'

'Perhaps. Come on, we better head back and hand out the mussels to our fellow campers. They'll only get half-a-dozen each, but better than nothing. I feel guilty for eating the oysters.'

'Don't. We were the ones who put life and limb at risk. We deserved our prize.'

'Yeah, you're right,' I say as I rise to my feet and throw my backpack on. She follows suit but before I can move away, she leans in close and pecks me on the lips.

'Thanks for tonight. I'll never forget it.' Her arm brushes against my crotch. I'm not sure whether it's accidental or intentional, but it doesn't help matters either way.

By the time we near Chloe's beach trail back to her camp, the sun is rising as the full moon stubbornly refuses to go to bed. There's an awkward silence between us and I try to make some small talk, as though nothing really happened.

'Right, well... I'll sleep well today.'

She gazes at me. 'We don't get many of them.'

'Sorry? We don't get many of what?' I ask, trying not to appear baffled.

'Times like these. Times we've just experienced. It's a kind of perfect.' I clear my throat again. She smiles, sad, yet happy, a blissful melancholy. 'You're sweet.'

'Am I?'

'Yes. And you don't even know it, which makes it all the sweeter.' I lean in and give her a quick peck to the cheek.

'Right, better go feed the fuckwits. I'll see you at the next challenge,' I state as I turn to leave.

'Will,' she calls out, 'if you ever need a change—I'll be waiting.' I wave at her as I wander off, unsure exactly what she meant.

Chapter 11

Hammered

We've been on the island for ten days, participated in four challenges and not won any of them. We are sitting on the bottom of the leaderboard with o points. Actually, that's not true—we are joint bottom with the Celebrity Chefs, who appear to be as incompetent and dysfunctional as my gang.

We are perpetually hungry. Our recent diet of coconuts, guava fruit, yams, and duckweed are wearing extremely thin—rather like our bodies. A week has passed since I slurped on oysters with Chloe and I'm desperately in need of some carbs and protein, as are the others. But that will have to wait as Gloria has started singing again. The blasted song lasts about fifteen seconds before Jerry's plummy accent summons us to the games zone for another challenge. We trudge wearily from our camp.

'I don't like the look of this,' Geordie grumbles. All four teams are lined up close to the ocean, which means another water-based challenge, hence Geordie's gripe. The big man does not have a natural affinity for the water. The production crew are preparing their equipment and are in buoyant spirits, which is not hard to do when you have a full belly. Jerry peers at his watch as his two-way radio crackles into life. He pulls it from his safari jacket, murmurs something into it and smiles broadly. With one raised thumb he signals to Felix, and the camera crew start recording.

'Hello teams and welcome to another beautiful day in paradise! Before we progress with today's challenge, we have a special surprise in store for you all!' Felix announces with a suave professionalism which makes me want to vomit.

'Let's hope this surprise involves a slap-up steak and chips dinner, a few lines of speed, and the chorus line from the Moulin Rouge,' Robbo says.

Felix continues. 'We have a VIP guest dropping in to give you some survival tips.' I notice one camera is positioned pointing up at the sky.

'Oh, fuck,' I mutter.

'What's up with you?' Robbo asks.

'I've got a sneaking suspicion who our VIP visitor is.'

'Oh, aye, who?' Geordie asks.

I focus my attention on the sky as a single-engine plane comes into view. The rattle of the prop eventually reaches us like an angry swarm of bees. 'Who's the most vainglorious, self-absorbed, wank-goblin you can think of?'

'Christ, there's so many to choose from. Can you narrow it down a touch?' Geordie says scratching at his shaggy beard. A dot falls from the sky as Felix swings into a paroxysm of crass adulation, worthy of any arse sucker. 'Oh, no. It's him, isn't it?' Geordie moans.

I nod. 'Yep, it's him all right. He couldn't have just arrived quietly by boat, could he?'

'Look on the bright side,' Robbo says grinning.

'What bright side?' I reply.

'His chute might not open.'

'One lives in hope.'

'I have no idea who you're talking about,' Flaky says, puzzled.

'You'll see soon enough.' The dot grows in size as it plummets towards the ocean.

Geordie throws a sneering glance at Felix, who has gone red in the face with his exultations. 'Felix needs to calm down otherwise he's going to ejaculate into his boxers.'

'I think it's too late for that,' Robbo says.

'A man who served king and country in the SAS for five years...' Felix continues with his crass fawning.

'What does he mean, king and country? We haven't had a king for well over sixty years. Bloody idiot,' Geordie mumbles. I pull my eyes away from the tumbling wonder boy and gaze over at the Celebrity Chefs who are engaged in yet another intense argument with one another.

'They make us appear almost normal,' I comment, slightly pleased there's another group of people in the world who are complete tools. Gasps of awe ripple across the beach. I peer back up to the gargantuan airborne ego. As his chute deploys, he's yanked upwards. 'Well, there goes the chute theory.'

'He's well-off course,' Flaky says. 'He's going to fall way out to sea.'

'Whatever happens, I can assure you this whole brazen spectacle will have been choreographed to within an inch of its life.' As superman nears the water, he unclips his harness and jettisons his chute. The parachute accelerates violently away as its former occupant does a few somersaults then plunges into the water with a textbook swan dive. Shrieks and cries erupt from the more gullible amongst the teams and crew.

'What a first-rate wanker of the highest magnitude,' Robbo drawls.

'Oh, I know who it is,' Flaky exclaims. A few seconds pass before the sound of a high-powered jet ski appears amongst the waves, accompanied by a film crew in a speed boat and an overhead drone. He's standing tall on the ski, the wind blowing his curly dark locks back over his head, dressed in a black wet suit. A maelstrom of sea spray is left in his wake.

Robbo chuckles. 'All because the lady loves... Milk Tray.'

'Bloody hell!' Flaky starts. 'I don't think he's going to stop. He's going at a hell of a pace.' The jet ski leaves the water at the speed of an aquatic missile. It slides up the beach with alarming alacrity, as the man in black gives a dramatic salute to the cameras strategically positioned. Unfortunately, even the best-laid plans can go awry. The nose of the jet ski ploughs into a slight sand ridge and comes to a bone-jarring halt. Its occupant, whom I can only imagine was feeling mighty pleased with himself a second before, is catapulted like a human cannonball in a distinctly horizontal angle.

'This will not end well,' Robbo notes. Alas, one cannot defy the laws of physics for long. Gravity was always going to win this contest. With a certain amount of glee, I watch on as the flying bighead face plants into the sand, and yet the velocity of his unexpected flight still carries him forward, face first. Eventually, the visual spectacular comes to a natural ending.

'Hammer Harrington has landed!' Geordie proclaims.

'I think Hammer Harrington might be dead,' Robbo adds, rather drily. Screams and shrieks abound as all manner of people rush to the aid of our fallen hero. Unfortunately, I cannot offer my assistance as my legs buckle at the knees and I drop to the ground.

⋙ ⋘

We're on the pontoon awaiting the launch of the flare to start the challenge.

'Will, can you stop laughing and focus your attention on the job at hand?' Flaky lectures me.

'S... s... sorry,' I stammer. 'Oh, oh, oh. I need to catch my breath.' I glance at the bucket and two oars on the pontoon then out at the ocean. About fifteen feet away is the unmistakable sight of a submerged rowing boat anchored to the ocean floor with metal weights. The object of the game is to dive down, remove the weights and somehow pull and push the boat back to the pontoon where we can bail it out with the aid of the bucket. We then row back to shore collecting a flag from another pontoon along the way. The first team to ignite the flare at the finishing line is the winner. I gaze up at our team flag which flutters gently in the breeze. *What am I doing here?*

'I think it's Dorothy,' Flaky says pointing towards a bird skimming across the ocean heading towards us. 'It is!' he exclaims as the damned pigeon perches on top of the flagpole cooing softly. 'It's a good luck sign. She's come to watch us win.'

'You know, Flaky,' Geordie begins, 'you have an unnatural obsession with that bird. It's most unbecoming. If you were a child, I could understand it, but you're a fully grown man or at least a variant of one. It's time you started acting your age.'

'Oh, be quiet you killjoy. I much prefer Dorothy's company to yours.' He refocuses his attention on the contest. 'How are we going to tackle this? We need a strategy,' he says, taking the challenge extremely seriously. 'Remember, there will be a meal waiting for the winner.'

The thought of food clarifies my thoughts. 'Okay,' I start, 'we'll all swim out to the boat and dive down. I know you're not keen, Geordie, but we'll need your muscles to help lift the weights. Once the weights are out, you head back to the pontoon. Me, Robbo and Flaky will somehow manoeuvre the boat back. Bugger bailing it out with the bucket... it will take forever. We'll try to lift the nose of the boat...'

'The bow,' Robbo interrupts. I throw him a filthy look. 'Just saying, that's all.'

'Thank you, Captain Hornblower. We'll lift the bow of the boat onto the platform then Geordie can drag it up and flip it over, emptying the water out. Then we climb aboard. Geordie, you sit in the middle to give the boat a bit of ballast. Robbo, sit at the pointy... towards the bow and me and Flaky will sit at the stern with the paddles.'

'Are you sure it will work?' Flaky asks.

I rub at my thick beard. 'No, I'm not. If we work together, we can give it a damn good try, though. We need that meal.' The annoying voice of Felix booms out through the speakers. A few seconds later a red flare erupts into the turquoise sky. We dive into the water and swim towards the submerged boat. It's about ten feet down and I'm already out of puff as I tread water above it. Flaky and Robbo immediately plunge beneath the waves as I suck in air. I glance at Geordie who looks extremely uncomfortable.

'What's wrong big man?'

'I'm not cut out for this water malarky. Anything else I can handle, but water scares me.'

'I've never known you to be scared of anything.'

'You don't know the half of it.'

'I remember you once telling Wallace that brave beats scared every day of the week.'

He nods. 'Aye, come on, let's do it. Fortune favours the brave.'

'But not the foolish.' We swim down and manhandle the weights from the bottom of the boat. They weigh a bloody ton but at least they have a U-shaped handle attached to them. Flaky and Robbo pull at one together as Geordie grabs another with both hands and pulls it up to his chest and drops it over the side as I help Robbo and Flaky. Within thirty seconds we've removed all the weights. I give Geordie the thumbs up and signal for him to head back to the platform. The rest of us return to the surface and refill our lungs before heading back down. The boat has already lifted itself from the ocean floor a little. We swim beneath it and push it upwards. It's surprisingly easy to get it to the surface. Geordie is back on the pontoon shouting his encouragement. We take a good three minutes to navigate the boat back to base. I glance over at the other teams. We appear to be neck and neck with the Chefs and Entrepreneurs. The girls are way off the pace, hardly surprising if their weights weighed the same as ours. Flaky and Robbo grab the bow and lift it out of the water as I push at the stern. The tip of the boat wobbles and slips onto the structure as Geordie grabs it and heaves with all his might. His lean, taut, muscles ripple and strain as a grimace takes up residence on his face. The other two now join me at the stern and all three of us push together. As the boat slips onto the pontoon Geordie flips it onto its side with gargantuan effort. The water cascades from the hull as he pushes it back into the water. I hold it in position as the other three climb in. Geordie leans over, grabs my arm, and physically yanks me from the sea. I position myself at the back with Flaky and grab an oar as Robbo takes his place at the front. The Chefs and Entrepreneurs are still bailing their boats out, as the girls push and cajole their vessel back to the pontoon.

'We've got this, boys!' I scream.

'Today we eat like kings,' Geordie shouts. We're still about fifty metres from shore as I glance behind me. The Entrepreneurs have set off and not far behind are the Chefs.

'Lift the tempo, Flaky!'

'Don't stress. We've got this one in the bag,' he shouts.

'Nevertheless, let's get to the bloody beach as quickly as possible.'

'Shit the bed!' Geordie cries.

'What? What's wrong?'

'There's water coming in.'

'Where from?'

'There's a bloody plug hole under this middle seat.'

'Find the plug and bung it up!' I yell.

'I'm looking. There isn't one.'

'There must be.' As the water enters, the boat sinks lower into the ocean until the inevitable happens and waves breach the sides. We're only in about six feet of water but we're all completely spent and don't have the strength to raise the boat. The Entrepreneurs soon pass us, laughing and throwing insults. Twats! A moment later the Chefs pass by, arguing violently with each other. They're a nightmare! We stare in exhausted disbelief as the Entrepreneurs beach their boat, trundle up the shore, and release the flare. Gloria begins to sing.

⟫⟫⟫ ⟪⟪⟪

Felix goes through the usual rigmarole but instead of the flaps to the marquee being dramatically drawn back, where undoubtedly a wholesome meal and a set of kitchen knives are awaiting the winners, the whole production team appear to stand down. Jerry steps forward.

'Okay, gang. I'm afraid we need to reshoot the arrival of Hammer Harrington on the jet ski. It will only take thirty minutes, then we'll do the winners presentation.' I'm fuming, and not just because of the imposition of having to hang around as the walking ego reshoots his landing. No, I suspect we are being set up. Twice we were in the winning position and some malfunction with the equipment scuppered our glory. I smell a rat. We drop onto the sand beaten and deflated as Hammer Harrington comes screaming into shore. For some peculiar reason, this time he doesn't attempt an amphibious landing but instead does the equivalent of an aquatic burn-out before jumping into the water and jogging up the beach.

'Hells bells!' Robbo exclaims. 'He looks like he's had a laser skin peel.' It's true. Hammer's face is sore and angry. He has a red strip from his chin, all the way up his Roman nose, ending near his hairline. Even this moment of schadenfreude does not lift my mood. Jerry, Felix, and Hammer are now in fierce discussions as to what the best camera angle is to minimise horrifying the viewers back home. I stand and pace up and down the beach awaiting the conclusion of the farce. I want to get back to my hammock and the campfire. Piers Conrad saunters over.

'What do you want, Condom?' I snap.

'Came to say hard luck, old chap.' There's not an ounce of authenticity in his voice. 'Don't worry, I know for a fact you lot are going to win something soon.'

'Really?' I reply not wanting to engage with the oily bag of sputum.

'Yes... the wooden spoon!' he says as he breaks into guffaws. Normally, I ignore pricks like him, but today I'm in a combative mood.

'When the games rigged, it's hard to win.'

He chuckles, melodramatically. 'It's always the same with your type—bad losers. You're always a victim. That's what's wrong with the country. Too many bloody victims crying into their beer.'

His words sting me. 'Our type? And what type is that, exactly?'

He sucks air in through his yellow teeth and stares thoughtfully at the ocean. 'Oh, you know, the lower demographics. You can't help it I suppose. Hundreds of years of genetics are at play. You can't fight nature. You're part of the woke snowflake brigade which blights the western world.'

'Woke? Past tense of wake. I don't see being awake to inequality and prejudice as a flaw, it's a good thing. As for being a snowflake, you're the biggest snowflake doing the rounds.'

His face crinkles with disdain. 'Don't talk bloody stupid man! I'm the antithesis of a snowflake.'

'I think you need to look at a modern dictionary. A snowflake is someone with an undeserved sense of entitlement, an inflated sense of self-worth, a person who is unable to handle opposing views. I bet you still wish we had slavery.'

He gives me a slippery smile. 'Slavery never went away it merely changed its name. Zero hours contract workers is the term we use today. Bit of a mouthful but it's a similar thing.'

'How do you sleep at night?'

'I sleep fine and, in this world, it's dog eat dog. And I'm top dog. What people like you will never understand is it's nothing personal, but you must always put your own interests first.'

'So why are you on a show where the winners donate one million pounds to charity?'

'Nothing to do with the charity. I couldn't give two hoots about raising money for disadvantaged children in Africa. It's all about my profile. I want people to see a different side to me.'

'There isn't a different side to you. You're a two-dimensional figure in a three-dimensional world. You're black and white. To you, it's us and them.'

'Yes, but I'm a damn fine actor. Once this circus of a show is finished, the Great British public will see me as firm but fair and caring.'

'Oh, I see. Do I detect a future tilt at becoming a member of parliament?'

'My, oh, my! Whatever gave you that idea?' He turns to leave.

'Enjoy your meal. I hope you choke on it.'

'I will enjoy it. I will savour every delicate morsel. I've heard on the grapevine it's steamed trevally with boiled new potatoes swimming in butter. Pip, pip, old chap.'

As we trudge back to camp Geordie notices my simmering silence.

'Come on, Billy Boy, at least we made a fist of it. I'm sure it wasn't sabotage. We can hold our own we've just had a run of bad luck. We're bound to win a challenge, eventually.'

'It's not just that,' I snap.

'What else is it?'

'The slimeball, Piers Conrad.'

'Got under your skin again, has he?'

'Yeah, like scabies.'

'Ignore him. He's full of wind and piss.'

'No. I'm going to take the bastard downtown before I leave this island. I'll rub his face in the dirt.'

'Bill, don't waste your energy on people like him. We have more pressing matters you should be focussing on, like getting some bloody decent food into our guts.'

'Hmm... you're right. Piers Conrad can wait for now. I'll cook that inbred, elitist, snob slowly.'

Chapter 12

Stealth Invader

We've been summoned to the games zone even though there are no challenges for a couple of days. The cameras are rolling as Felix begins.

'You may wonder why we called you all here today.' I'm not wondering at all. The great man is standing directly next to Felix. This is all about Hammer. 'As you know, Hammer Harrington is one of the greatest survivalists on the planet.'

'We only have his word for it,' I murmur.

'Over the next two days, he'll be observing how you operate as a unit, as survivors. I'll hand you over to Hammer to explain in more detail.' Hammer takes a stride forward dressed in his standard head to toe black. The idiot must be boiling.

'Gang,' he says with arms folded, biceps bulging. 'As you know I'm a stealth invader.'

'A what invader?' Robbo whispers to me.

'Stealth invader,' I repeat.

'It sounds like a giant dildo.'

'It is.'

'I'm also known as the White Shadow,' Hammer continues as people scratch their heads. 'I'm here, there, everywhere and nowhere all at the same time.'

'He gets around a bit,' Flaky comments.

'I'll be watching you. You won't see me; you won't hear me; you won't smell me; and you won't sense me. I'm Will-o'-the-wisp, the Invisible Man, Bilbo Baggins.'

'Don't forget the Mad Hatter,' Robbo says. 'He's got more personas than an asylum full of schizophrenics.'

'I am omnipresent, omniscient and impotent.' A few titters emanate from the crew and competitors as Jerry shouts cut and whispers into Hammer's ear. Hammer looks confused.

'What did I say?' he asks Jerry.

'Impotent. Okay, take it again from the omni bit. Roll.'

'I am omnipresent, omniscient and omnipotent.'

'And an omni-twat,' Geordie adds.

Lucy from the Weathergirls raises her hand. 'Ahem, Felix, Jerry, I'm not sure that as four women we want to be spied on by a man,' she says. I have to agree it's a totally legitimate concern. The peeping Geordie and I did was purely circumstantial. Before Felix can answer, the Hammer intervenes.

'Ladies, I can assure you I am a man of honour. If you are in a state of undress, I shall avert my eyes.'

'Likely story. Bloody perv,' Flaky says. The Weathergirls don't appear convinced, nor does anyone else.

'When I was in Desert Storm, surrounded by the elite Iranian Guard...' Everyone begins to disperse.

'It's a wrap, everyone,' Jerry shouts.

⇝⇜

We are taking our late afternoon dip in the ocean. It's something we usually do as a group. It refreshes us before the last stretch of the day. The temperature has dropped a little, and the water is cool and invigorating. It's a time to unwind, have some fun, forget our privations, our petty grievances and bond as a unit. We have a leather football we found washed up on the shoreline a few days ago. It's been named, Wilson. We've invented a game called uppity. It's a bit like volleyball. We count the number of times we can keep the ball in the air without it hitting the water. Each player can only hit the ball once before another player must hit it. Our highest score is ninety-seven.

As we near our record, Robbo completely misinterprets the trajectory of the falling ball. It bounces off his head at an acute angle and squirts off into the water. I swim after it as Geordie and Flaky playfully chastise him. As I gather the ball, I notice an angular shaped periscope watching us. Call it a hunch but I suspect it could be the Hammer. I retrieve the ball and paddle back to the others. With a nod and a wink, I make them aware of my discovery. We are only chest high in water.

'Hey, Geordie, why don't you change positions with Robbo? You know what a short arse he is. Robbo, you move nearer to the shore.'

'Aye, good idea, Bill.'

'Is everyone ready?' I yell. There's an uproar of cheers. 'Geordie, I'm going to tee this one up for you to get us started.' The periscope moves dangerously close to Geordie. I throw a nice gentle lob in his direction. He leaps from the water like a magnificent marlin as his long arm slams down on the ball with terrific force. The ball hits the tip of the periscope like a guided missile. It disappears, followed a few seconds later by a torrent of violent ruddy coloured bubbles. There's a moments silence. The distinctive nozzle of a snorkel appears followed by the slap of black flippers. They head away from us into deeper water.

•»»› ‹«««•

With the aid of Flaky's palm woven carry bags, we haul a large load of fresh coconuts back to camp. As we tip them out in the designated area next to Robbo's improvised husk remover, Geordie taps me gently on the calf with the toe of his shoe. I turn to him. He nods his head slightly to the left. I lift my arms above my head and yawn as I spin on my heels. With eyes narrowed, I scan the surrounding bush. About five metres away is a small screw pine. It's roughly two metres in height. Peering out from between the leaves is the gawping face of Hammer, the Stealth Invader.

'Fuck me blue, he stands out like the dog's plums,' I murmur under my breath. 'Hey, Geordie, have a quick check of the nuts to make sure none of them have gone off. Nothing worse than going to the trouble of de-husking and splitting only to find it's rotten.' For a second, he appears confused until he twigs.

'Aye, okay, leave it to me.' He bends down and carefully assesses a few, placing them to one side as he does so. 'Hello, hello, this one is iffy,' he declares sniffing at a coconut, then shaking it from side to side.

'If there's any doubt, throw it away.'

'Yep, will do.' He picks the nut up by a strand of fibres and tosses it in the direction of the screw pine. There's a loud clonk, followed by a "fuck" and the crackle of twigs and leaves.

>>>> <<<<

We saunter into camp laden with wood, water, and yuca tubers. I immediately spot the omniscient and impotent White Shadow in a tree, nestled in the branches about fifteen feet up. The knobjockey is directly above the gently smouldering fire.

'Don't look now,' I say under my breath, 'but the invisible man is in a tree, the one which overhangs the fire.' We quietly and efficiently go about our business and complete our daily chores for the next twenty minutes. Flaky peels the yuca tubers and dices them before dropping them into a pan of cold water.

'I suggest we head to the beach and do some scavenging,' I say. 'The sea was rough last night. It may have thrown up some goodies for us.'

'Good idea, Billy Boy.'

'What about the yucas?' Flaky says.

'We'll get them on the boil when we return.' We hoist our backpacks on and set off for the beach track.

'Oh, wait,' Geordie says. 'Those damn midges have been driving me mad. I reckon it's time they were fumigated.'

'Good thinking,' Robbo agrees. We head back to the fire and scrape up a vast pile of leaves and jungle detritus then dump it onto the embers.

'That's the ticket,' Geordie says. 'It will smoke nicely. Hopefully, it will get rid of the bugs.' We hang around for a minute until the dry tinder ignites, sending a billowing tunnel of smoke heavenwards.

'Okay, let's go,' I say. We hit the trail and walk on for a few feet before we melt into the undergrowth and wait. First, we hear a cough and a splutter followed by silence. Next comes a few expletives, violent coughing, and another torrent of curses. A dull thud, which sounds uncannily like Bilbo Baggins falling from a tree and hitting the ground hard, is accompanied by a long painful groan and more obscenities.

⇒⇒≫ ≪⇐⇐

We are again summoned to the games zone. In front of us is Hammer, Felix, and Jerry. Hammer appears a tad worse for wear. His arm is in a sling, he's missing a tooth, sports a black eye and has a lump on his temple which resembles a rampant brain tumour. His face is a violent pink colour with flakes of skin hanging on by a thread. No longer the handsome rakish boy wonder, he looks more like a burns victim who has just crawled from a train wreck. Three different camera crews are strategically positioned to capture the same bullshit from different angles as the White Shadow takes centre stage. Jerry yells at a camera crew who have moved in for a close up.

'Damn it, no! I told you no close ups. I only want long shots, very long shots. Move to the back and get some footage from there,' he barks at the crew. You know you're having a bad day when the back of your head is your most attractive feature.

'I'm sorry to say, after my two days on the island, it's time for Hammer to love you, and leave you,' the Hammer begins, referring to himself in the third person. It's followed by deafening silence, mixed with a healthy dose of apathy and a flurry of buttock scratching from the competitors. 'I've watched each team, incognito, for the last forty-eight hours. Not once have I been observed.' This is greeted with muted coughs and sighs from the teams plus one less than muted "bullshit" from Geordie. Jerry calls cut, and we have to listen to the verbal tripe all over again as they do a retake.

'I'm awarding twenty points to the Weathergirls as they displayed to me their four Vs; vivacity, vitality and vigour.'

'Hang on,' Robbo exclaims, 'that's only three!' There's another cut as we go through the whole laborious sequence again. I'm ready for a smoke, a pint of Guinness, and a pickled egg.

'Roll,' Jerry commands.

'To the Weathergirls, I'm awarding twenty points as they displayed to me their four Vs; vivacity, vitality, vigour and verve.'

'Those words all mean the same thing,' Flaky notes with puzzlement.

'To the Entrepreneurs, I award ten points for their three Es.'

'Eh up, is there a drug dealer on the island?' Robbo exclaims excitedly. Shooting is brought to a halt again.

After ten minutes of lecturing by Jerry and Felix, filming resumes.

'As for the Rock Stars and The Celebrity Chefs... I'm sorry but I cannot award you any points! Both teams are a complete shower. You are argumentative, slovenly, lazy, and worst of all... there's no teamwork. Remember Hammer's old adage—united we stand, divided we fall.' He does a military salute towards the camera, followed by a wink. 'Before I go, I'd just like to remind viewers my new series, The Bermuda Triangle—Hammered, will be airing in early February. Same channel, same time.'

'Sweet Jesus,' Flaky whispers shaking his head.

'Good luck teams but it's time for me to leave. I can hear the call of the wild. Adios amigos! Adios Crusoe Island!' Hammer declares as he leaps from the platform and stumbles awkwardly.

'Cut!' Jerry shouts. Another ten minutes lapses as my life ebbs away.

'Adios amigos, and kon'nichiwa, Crusoe Island,' Hammer shouts as he carefully lowers himself from the platform and sprints towards the sea. A high-powered speedboat is waiting for him in the breakers. He leaps aboard and pulls at the motor's ripcord with his one useful hand. It emits a farty noise but appears a tad reluctant to get on with its one job in life. After five excessively violent attempts, Jerry yells cut.

'Fuck me backwards over a bacon slicer,' Geordie laments. 'This is longer than Gone with the Wind, and not nearly as entertaining, and that was as boring as bat shit.' I tend to agree.

The scene is shot again, this time with the speedboat motor primed and purring like a cougar beforehand. The Hammer reverses the boat then swings it around and powers out over the waves tracked by drones, and camera crews in similar boats. He gets about one hundred metres offshore then pulls the boat around and heads back to the beach. A helicopter is waiting for him.

'What a wanker,' Robbo reflects as the chopper thunders away.

Chapter 13

Crackling

The bamboo is tied up into four large bundles. They are approximately twelve feet in length and each bundle contains eight poles. Travis and Brent have dragged them along the beach, from Castaway Central, with the aid of their all-terrain vehicle.

'Thanks for the firewood, guys,' Geordie says. 'It's very thoughtful of you.'

'It's for your challenge tomorrow.'

'Really,' I say. 'Let me guess. We have to build a scale model of the Eiffel Tower?' Brent, who is not the sharpest hook in the tackle box, is surprised.

'No. You have twenty-four hours to build a raft. You will be summoned to the challenge tomorrow.'

'What does the challenge involve?'

Travis laughs. 'You know the rules, Will. We're not allowed to divulge any information. And as it so happens, Brent and I don't know what the challenges are until you do. '

'Let me take a stab in the dark. We paddle our raft from point A to point B to point C, carrying all of us, grab a flag and the first to cross the finish line wins.'

'How could you possibly know that?' Brent exclaims appearing concerned. Travis kicks him in the shin.

'Like I said. We don't know what the challenges are. Right, we'll be off, ciao.' The ATV starts up, does a sharp U-turn and heads back down the beach. I hear the crunch of sticks behind me and glance around to see Robbo and Flaky walking towards us.

'What did they want?' Flaky asks.

'They dropped off a pile of sticks to build a raft with,' Geordie replies.

'Anyone had any raft building experience?' I quiz knowing the answer. I'm met with silence.

We sit down for a good hour and discuss what the best design would be for the raft and scribe our ideas into the sand with a stick. We produce a couple of feasible blueprints, but it's all too hard. Robbo yawns and slumps onto his side. His yawning sets off Geordie who has heavy bags under his eyes. The perennial gnawing in my guts visits me again—it is an unwelcome visitor who always outstays my frosty welcome. I gaze upon the ocean as Flaky's voice rambles on in the background. The pastel turquoise swirls up and down like a gigantic piece of silk. Once refreshing and inviting it holds no allure for me now. I rise slowly to my feet and turn to head back to camp.

'Will, Will, did you hear me?' Flaky badgers.

'No. I need to eat and have a sleep. We'll discuss it later and come to a collective decision.' There is no disagreement as they all follow me. As we make our way towards the brush, a noise makes us stop.

'What the hell is it?' Robbo asks. I nervously glance at Geordie.

'Shit the bed,' he whispers.

'It sounds like grunting,' Flaky says, his eyes narrowing as he peers into the jungle. Geordie and I edge back.

'Don't go any further,' I advise. An ear-splitting squeal sends a glug of adrenalin into my veins. We turn tail, screaming, shouting and dash towards the safety of the water. Hot on our heels and gaining fast is the juvenile wild boar. He obviously doesn't care much for human company. I can't say I blame him. We dive into the sea and swim out a few metres as the boar paces up and down on the sand.

'Can they sw... swim?' Robbo stammers.

'Not sure,' I say.

'I assume so. Most animals can,' Flaky adds.

'What are we going to do? We can't stay here forever,' Geordie says. The boar patrols the beach for a good five minutes emitting deep grunts and the occasional squeal. It stops at the water's edge, shivers violently then keels over with its legs up in the air. Puzzled glances are exchanged.

'I think it might have had a coronary,' Robbo whispers.

'You could be right,' Flaky says. I creep out of the water and make my way to the stricken animal.

'Watch out, Billy Boy, that pig could be playing possum. He's a wily bugger.' I peer over my shoulder at my three fearless friends. I grab a stick and give the boar a gentle poke in the ribs. There's no reaction. I bend down and place my ear on its side.

'It's not breathing,' I say. 'This is definitely an ex-pig.' I stand and smile at the three gallant heroes as they wade out of the sea.

'It must have been born with a genital defect,' Robbo says.

'You moron! You mean congenital defect,' Flaky corrects.

'No, I don't. Have you seen the size of its ballbag? They're like two avocados inside a hairy purse.'

'You know what this means, boys?' I say. 'Pork crackling is on the menu. Let's get it back to camp and gut it.'

'Hang on, shouldn't we gut it here? We don't want all the blood and gore back at camp. It will stink the place up,' Geordie says.

'Yes. Good point. Okay, Geordie, if you'd like to do the honours,' I say nodding at the animal.

'No way! You found it; you gut it.'

'Typical! You won't be as reluctant when it comes to eating it, will you?' I realise how completely unprepared I am for this sort of thing. All my meat comes in shrink-wrapped polystyrene containers. I've seen it done on films and documentaries but to gut an animal, which was alive a few minutes ago, is another matter. 'I'm not sure what to do,' I mumble.

'My grandad had a smallholding,' Robbo says.

'Poor man. We can't all be over-endowed in the trouser department,' Geordie replies.

'A smallholding is a farm, you dipstick,' Robbo retorts.

'Really... how interesting. My grandad used to wear a flat cap. Anymore riveting family history you'd like to regale us with?'

Robbo pulls a face. 'He used to keep a few pigs. Do you know you can eat every single part of a pig?'

'What, even its arsehole?' Geordie queries.

'Best part,' Robbo says with a chuckle. 'We'll save it for Flaky. They do say you are what you eat.'

'I'll have you know I won't be eating the flesh of an animal,' Flaky huffs.

My impatience is on a par with my hunger. 'You were saying?' I say, glaring at Robbo.

'Oh, aye... pigs. First of all, you have to bleed them.'

'How?'

'Cut its throat. Then you need to split it open and pull the guts and offal out. Normally, you'd save the offal but as we don't have a fridge freezer handy, I suggest you toss it into the sea.'

'Oh, that's right! Pollute the ocean. Dump whatever muck you want into it,' Flaky lectures.

'Shut up, you big tart. The crabs and fish will eat it,' Geordie grizzles.

'It's a hairy little bugger. How do we get rid of the hair?'

'Simple. My grandad used to lay it down on a good bed of straw. He'd place the pig on top of it and completely cover it with another layer of straw, then set fire to it. It burns hot and fast. It removes most of the hair but doesn't cook the meat. Then it's just a matter of scraping the skin with a sharp blade. Any remaining hair will singe off as we spit roast it.' I pull my knife from its sheath and hold the handle towards Robbo.

'As you're the pig expert, maybe you'd like to show us how it's done.'

'Oh, no, not me. I'm squeamish. Just because I know what to do, doesn't mean I can do it.'

I sigh. 'Fine! As usual, it's muggins here left to do the dirty work. Geordie, hold the bloody thing up by its back legs and wade out into the water a little.' He picks the beast up and stands in the shallows. 'I'm guessing pigs are no different to humans. They must have a jugular on the side of the neck,' I say as I run my fingers across the pig's throat.

'If they're the same as us, they'll have two jugular veins. One on the left and one on the right,' Flaky says, looking pallid. I take the knife and stick it firmly into the neck above the breastbone, then slide the blade to the left and right. There's a sudden gush of blood which catches me unaware soaking my shorts and running down my legs.

'Oh, you dirty bastard,' Geordie moans. There's a dull thump as Flaky collapses on the sand. Geordie stares at him with disdain. 'Weak as piss!' It doesn't take long for most of the blood to drain out. The turquoise water turns a ruddy colour as gentle waves stain the sand. As I split the beast down the middle, the intestines spill out with a gloopy splat into the sea. Nausea is threatening to overwhelm me. I place my hand inside the opening. It's warm and wet. I have no idea what I've got hold of, but I yank it out and toss it into the water, dry retching as I do so. After a few minutes of feverish, uncoordinated pulling and slashing, the carcass is empty.

'I think that's everything,' I say, swallowing hard.

'Well done, Bill. Good job!'

'Are you okay to carry it back?'

'Aye, no problem,' he says as he lifts the pig up and throws it across his shoulders. 'What about Calamity Jane?' he says staring down at Flaky.

'Robbo, throw some water over him.'

'My pleasure.'

Chapter 14

The Raft

We build a roaring fire and wait for it to burn down leaving a bed of hot coals. A spit, fashioned from bamboo, holds the pig a few feet above the glowing embers.

'How long should we cook it for?' I ask the swineherd expert.

'Fucked if I know,' he replies.

'You need to be careful with pork,' Flaky says. 'It's a dangerous meat if not cooked properly. You could end up with severe food poisoning.'

I turn to Geordie. 'How much do you think it weighs?'

He wrinkles his nose. 'About ten kilos, at a guess.'

'Okay, we'll give it five to six hours to be on the safe side. It will need turning to get an even temperature. Robbo, you can be spit master. I'm going for a swim to get rid of all this blood and shit off me.'

As I make my way back to the camp, the usual wafts of smoky firewood greet me. This time it's a little different. Infused with the smoke is the sweet aroma of pork. I salivate at the prospect.

There's a calm hush about the camp. The only disturbance is the hiss and crackle as pork fat drips onto the coals. The waiting is torture. It doesn't take long before an argument breaks out between Robbo and Geordie. According to Geordie, Robbo is turning the spit wrongly. His technique seems okay to me.

'You're turning the thing too bloody quickly. It needs to be slower.'

'If I do it any slower, the skin blisters,' Robbo shouts back.

'Aye, it's supposed to! What do you think crackling is? You numpty!'

'The whole thing's barbaric,' Flaky moans as he lazily rocks in his hammock.

After five hours and many arguments later, I take my knife and slice a chunk from the pig's shoulder. The skin is crispy, and golden brown, the flesh, moist and white. I take a bite and hand it to Geordie. An explosion of flavours saturates my taste buds as I become lightheaded. Geordie rips a chunk off and passes it on to Robbo. They both drop to their haunches and fall silent.

'I cannae find the words to express how good it tastes,' Geordie eventually purrs.

'It's like it's the first time I've ever eaten meat in my life,' Robbo says as he closes his eyes and chews slowly, savouring every last morsel.

'Okay, boys. This little beast is ready for eating. Flaky, come and get some.'

'Don't talk ridiculous. You're well aware I'm a pescatarian.'

'I'm well aware you're starving, have little energy left and if you don't get some calories into you soon, you're going to be bloody useless to the rest of us. Now's not the time to stand on your principles. This is survival. You can go back to being a pescatarian when you get home.'

'Leave him, Bill. In the land of the blind, the one-eyed man is king,' Geordie says, cryptically as he carves a huge chunk of meat from the beast and retires to his hammock. 'There'll be more for us.'

I need to try a different tack with Flaky. 'Give me your reasons for being a pescatarian?'

'You know full well why,' he replies sulkily.

'You don't like the inhumane treatment of animals?'

'It's not just that, but it's the main reason. It's also far healthier to be a pescatarian.'

'This animal lived a happy life, well, until it met me and Geordie. It wasn't raised in a battery farm. It wasn't cruelly killed. It died of natural causes. As for being healthier, I agree with you. But this is different. You can't just nip out to your allotment or supermarket and load up on vegetables and fruit. We spent over an hour on the beach trying to figure out how to build a raft earlier, with little success. Do you know why? Because our energy levels are depleted. Our blood sugar is low. Our brains are starved of sustenance. This isn't a game anymore, it's for real. We need to survive, and it doesn't matter what we eat as long as we eat. We're not four individuals, we are one unit. If one of us fails, we all fail. Now put your pride and principles to one side and eat.' I slice off another juicy piece from the shoulder and walk over to his hammock. He sits up and stares at the offering.

'It will probably make me sick,' he grumbles.

Robbo is still on his haunches hoeing into a slab of meat ripped from the belly. Fat drips down his chin. 'This is a hundred times better than the best joint I've ever smoked,' he says with a wistful look.

'There you go,' I say as Flaky grabs the meat. 'You'll never get a greater endorsement.' He slowly nibbles at the pork in silence. Within five minutes he's wolfing down meat like a ravenous carnivore. I take a spot near the fire and fill my plate. I can already feel a surge of endorphins flood my body as my spirits lift. There's something completely natural about the whole experience. For the first time in ages, I feel connected with the environment and alive, unlike the pig. This is how cavemen must have felt.

⟫⟫⟩ ⟨⟨⟪

We're back on the beach staring at the bamboo poles. We spent a good hour gorging on the pig. Then another two hours in deep sleep. Now, we are energised, in good spirits and good humour.

'I've been pondering on this,' Robbo says. 'Perhaps we're overthinking it.'

'You've never overthought anything in your life,' Flaky replies.

I turn to Robbo. 'Go on?'

'Before we get into any elaborate designs, why don't we tie the four bundles together, side by side, and see if that works. Bamboo floats, right? What does it matter what the design is.' I glance at Geordie who raises one eyebrow.

'You know what, for a dim-witted space cadet, it's not a bad idea.'

'Thanks,' Robbo replies.

'Let's give it a go. What have we got to lose?' Geordie says.

We drag the bundles to the edge of the water and with the aid of the rope we were given in our essential items' chest, lash the bamboo together. Once it's in the water we attempt to climb aboard. All is well until Geordie tries to get on. The raft lists to one side sending us sprawling into the sea.

'Well, it was worth a try,' Flaky says.

'Hang on,' I begin, 'let's apply some physics to this. Geordie, how much do you weigh?'

'Before I came on this bloody island, I weighed ninety kilos of solid, lean muscle.'

'His head must weigh at least half that,' Robbo says.

I ignore him. 'And how much do you weigh?'

'Seventy-five kilo but I reckon I've lost at least five.'

'Flaky?'

'Sixty-eight.'

'And I weigh seventy-three. Okay, how about this—Geordie, you get on the raft first and lie flat out, longways, with your head and shoulders hanging over the side. Your weight is now distributed evenly. Robbo, you sit on the opposite end to Geordie, and me and Flaky will sit in the middle either side of Geordie.' After a few failed attempts, the plan works. The raft is stable and floats. We paddle with our hands and ride a few gentle waves laughing and joking as the sun melts slowly into the horizon.

⤙⤚ ⤙⤚

We're back around the campfire as the day wanes. We adjusted the height of the spit, so the pig doesn't burn. There's still a hell of a lot of meat left on it as we tuck in for seconds.

'I'll sleep well tonight with a full belly,' Geordie says.

'Yep, me too,' Robbo agrees. A crunching sound from the beach trail has us all nervously glancing at each other.

'What was that?' Robbo whispers.

'I'm not sure,' I reply.

'Maybe it's the pig's mother looking for her bairn,' Geordie begins. 'She'll not be too pleased when she sees the state of the little blighter.'

'Don't be ridiculous!' Flaky scolds.

'Psst, Geordie,' a disembodied voice calls out from the track.

'Fuck me! A talking pig,' Robbo says.

'Psst, Geordie, over here.' Geordie stands and heads off into the trail. He's back a moment later and glances at the camera on the tree; it's recording. He nods at Robbo who disappears, and a few seconds later, so does the camera's flashing red light.

'Okay, Brody. The coast is clear,' Geordie calls out. Brody Buchannan materialises out of the darkness sporting a wide grin. He slaps Geordie on the back, as he stares at the pig and licks his lips.

'I was taking a brisk constitutional along the beach when I smelled the pork,' he says.

'Help yourself,' Geordie says. 'There's too much for all of us to eat and it will only go to waste.' Brody pulls his knife out and edges towards the fire.

'How's that gorgeous wife of yours and your bairns?'

'They're all good,' Geordie replies. 'I'm missing them.'

Brody grins. 'I know what you're missing, you lascivious old perv. She's a feisty one is Jackie, I'll give you that. They're always better in the sack, though.'

'Hang on! You can't just wander into our camp. It's expressly forbidden in the rules,' Flaky says. As Brody slices a piece of flesh from the beast he glances over his shoulder at Flaky.

'Pull your neck in, pipsqueak,' he says as he stuffs the meat into his mouth and carves another slice.

'I beg your pardon!'

Brody wipes his mouth on the back of his hairy arm. 'I take it, he's Flaky?' he says to Geordie.

'Aye.'

'Every group has one, you're not alone. Ours is Xavier Pompadour. The pretentious Gallic twat. Today has been a nightmare. I need a long walk on an evening just to calm down otherwise I'd end up killing him. If I say black, he says white; if I say left, he says right. He's insufferable.'

'I hear you, brother, I hear you,' Geordie says with sympathy. Brody turns to me.

'And you're Will Harding,' he says as he slaps me on the shoulder so hard, I nearly fall into the fire.

'Y... yes.'

'I've always wanted to meet you but whenever I drop in to see Geordie, you're never there.'

'How do you two know each other?' Robbo asks as he climbs into his hammock carrying a loaded plate of meat. Brody and Geordie laugh.

'Oh, we go right back to our schooldays,' Brody says. 'Me and Geordie used to lock horns during the regional school sports carnivals. Geordie represented Banereed Grammar, and I was the top athlete at Canockmore Comprehensive.'

'Aye, good times. If I remember rightly, you never once beat me. You always ended up second.'

'Not true. I once beat you in the javelin and caber tossing contest. I think it was our final year.'

'I'm surprised,' Robbo says with a chuckle. 'Geordie's the master at tossing his caber.' Brody stops chewing and eyes Robbo warily.

'You must be Robbo, the pothead, correct?'

'I like a quiet smoke once in a while but I'm no pot...' Brody interrupts him.

'One of our team is an addict as well,' he states as he cuts another hunk of meat from the pig.

'Who?' Geordie asks.

'The sniper's nightmare—Marmaduke Smythe. Upper class twit.'

Geordie laughs. 'Why do you call him the sniper's nightmare?'

'Because of his limp. Haven't you noticed how his head rocks from side to side? He's an alcoholic. The first week he suffered from terrible shakes. Sad, really. It's ruined his career. He's hoping this little stint on the show will resurrect it. I told him he's dreaming. He's bloody useless around the camp. He even went looking for an off licence the other day. Daft old bugger. Keth Patel's all right, if a little moody.'

'You mean Keith Patel, the chef with the eyepatch,' Flaky corrects.

'We call him Keth.'

'Why?'

'Because he has one eye missing. This meat is exquisite. I can't tell you how much better I feel already. Have you any salt?'

'No. The shops were shut,' Robbo says as he crunches on a piece of crackling.

Brody throws him the evil eye. 'Are you taking the piss?' he snarls at him aggressively. Robbo stops chewing and shuffles uncomfortably. 'Where do you think salt comes from?'

'Saxa?'

Brody guffaws. 'My God! You lot are dumber than a bag of bolts! It comes from the sea, you clown.'

'Oh,' Robbo murmurs.

'Fill a bottle with seawater then boil the liquid off and you're left with sea salt.'

'Won't it have sand in it?' I enquire.

'You don't fill it from the shore. Find a tranquil spot. Then let the water settle for a few hours and slowly and carefully pour three-quarters of the water into a pan.'

'Thanks for the tip,' I say. 'I reckon it's why I've been getting cramps—a lack of salt.'

'Too much salt is bad for you,' Flaky chirps in.

'He's a laugh a minute, your mate, isn't he?' Brody says to Geordie. 'Listen Beaky, in this humidity you lose salt from your body faster than you can replace it. And it makes you drink more water. Right, I better get back before it's too dark.' He cuts off another massive chunk of pork belly and turns to leave.

'Take some back for your team,' Geordie suggests.

'Nah, no way. I'm not feeding Xavier Pompadour.'

'Hey, Will?' Brody calls to me. 'Loved your last album, by the way. You, me, and Geordie should hang out together sometime. I have a villa in Tuscany by the edge of the sea. We must organise a week or two there next summer. We'll have a ball. What do you say?'

'Sounds great, Brody. I'd love to.'

'Good. Good man.'

'What about me?' Robbo chips in. Brody stares at him, silently.

'He's okay,' Geordie says vouching for him.

'Aye, all right. You can come along as well.'

'Don't I get an invitation?' Flaky says, wounded by the snub.

'I'm not sure I could put up with you for a day, never mind a fortnight.' Flaky appears crestfallen. Geordie winces at Brody. 'Oh, what the hell! You can all come. Let's make it happen. Good luck with the raft challenge tomorrow. Catch ya!'

Chapter 15

Keeping Afloat

Felix is explaining the rules to the four teams as Jerry coordinates the camera crews. When we arrived, pulling our raft through the shallows, we were greeted with much mirth and merriment by all. Our aquatic mode of transport is the butt of numerous jokes. I must admit, compared to the other rafts, it does look like the runt of the litter. Of course, the Entrepreneurs have built one that could probably circumnavigate the globe, without them getting their feet wet. It's more like a catamaran than a raft.

'Two of your team will swim out to the two pontoons painted in your team colours to await rescue. The other two will paddle out and collect your teammates. On the way back grab your team standard from the pole in the water then head to shore. The first team to cross the finishing line will be the winner of today's Reward Challenge. And you all know what that means... fifteen points, a nourishing meal, and a piece of survival equipment. Is there any part of this challenge you don't understand?' he yells with way too much enthusiasm. 'Okay, good. You have five minutes to decide who your paddlers are going to be and who's going to be rescued.' As we discuss our options, Piers Conrad sidles over to us sporting a cheesy grin.

'My oh my! You lot certainly bring some entertainment value to the show. How long did it take you to build your raft? A minute? Thirty seconds? Hopeless,' he scoffs as he walks away.

Flaky and I pick up an oar each and await the starting gun.

'Feeling full of vim and vigour?' I ask him.

He smiles. 'Surprisingly, yes.'

'Good. We're going to win this.'

'Hmm... I wish I shared your enthusiasm.'

'Flaky, just for once can you try to be positive, it's half the battle.'

He winces. 'Yes. Sorry. Okay, let's win this stupid bloody challenge.'

'That's the spirit.'

Our raft may appear like discarded driftwood, but it's fast and efficient and skims through the water. We make it to the first pontoon where Geordie's standing. We're a whisker ahead of the Celebrity Chefs. We lose ground getting Geordie into position as we have to take it slowly, so he doesn't capsize the raft. As we collect Robbo, we are neck and neck with the Chefs, but the Weathergirls are closing in fast behind both teams. The Entrepreneurs are well out of contention despite their over-designed catamaran. We paddle the raft around and head back towards the pole which holds the team standard. The Chefs edge slightly ahead as we are in danger of being pipped at the post again.

'Geordie, lean forward a tad and use your arms to push water under the boat,' Robbo suggests.

'Aye, okay.' As he shuffles forward the nose of the raft dips violently beneath the waves and I fear we are about to be swamped. But as he starts to scoop at the water it buoys the boat and increases our speed. We near the pole holding the flag.

'Robbo, brace yourself. You only get one chance at this. We're not stopping, so make sure you grab it first go.'

'You can rely on me,' he says. I'm starting to believe I can. The Chefs reach their pole first but make a fatal error and stop paddling as one of their team reaches out for the flag. We speed past our pole as the raft lists heavily on Robbo's side as he leans out.

'Got it!' he yells. Flaky, Geordie and I paddle for all we're worth. I have a rush of energy as I realise we are going to win. As we enter the shallows, we jump from the raft and haul it up onto the beach then sprint across the finishing line to the sound of Gloria's dulcet tones.

'At least we don't have to worry about what's for dinner tonight,' Robbo says. 'Who'd have thought it? Out here on a tropical island and they serve us fish and chips with mushy peas and bread and butter.'

'A nice pot of tea wouldn't have gone amiss. Not sure why we couldn't have a cuppa,' Geordie moans.

'Caffeine. It could be classed as an artificial pick-me-up and give us an unfair advantage,' I say as I throw more fuel onto the fire.

'Christ, I'm talking about a cup of tea, not methamphetamine.' I pick up the fishing rod and purse of hooks we also won in the challenge.

'This is a Godsend,' I mumble. The others are all lazing in their hammocks as night-time closes in.

'Hey, Robbo, I have a question for you,' Geordie says.

'Go on?' This should be interesting.

'When you pull a jumper on, do you go arms first or head first?' Well, I never! And I thought he was going to ask him about astral travel or the lead-up to the Napoleonic wars.

'Oh, definitely head first. It stems from my childhood. I had a few harrowing experiences with the arms-first method. If you get your head stuck in the neck hole and you've gone arms first, then it's like being trapped in a straitjacket. '

'Aye, me too. I'm a head first man. Flaky what about you?'

'Arms first.'

His reply seems to infuriate Geordie. 'You always have to be different, don't you!'

'Well, you asked. What do you want me to do, lie?'

'Right, as much as I'd like to participate in this stimulating conversation, I'm going to test the rod out. I'll see you three nut jobs later.'

'Going arms first is inherent with danger! Can you not see that, man?' Geordie continues, oblivious to my comments.

'Only if you're a moron!' Flaky shouts back.

I stroll along the beach looking for shellfish to use as bait but I'm not having much luck.

'Hi, stranger!' Chloe's voice calls out, as she ambles out of the bushes.

'Oh, hi Chloe.'

'Well done on winning today's challenge. How were the fish and chips?'

'Awesome. I wish they'd served them in butcher's paper though. They always taste better that way.'

She chuckles. 'You're such a northerner, aren't you?'

'You make it sound like a crime.'

'Have you had any luck with the fishing?' she says as she sits down on the damp sand.

'No. I haven't got any bait. To be honest, I just needed to get away from the camp. I'm going a bit stir crazy.' I drop down beside her. 'How do you get along with your team?'

'Like a house on fire. I've made three new best friends.'

'Do you ever argue or bicker?'

She pouts and wiggles her cheeks from side to side. 'No, not really. We do occasionally disagree on the way something should be done, but it's always conducted in a logical and polite manner.'

'What do you talk about?'

She laughs. 'You'd think we were all really boring. We talk about our families, husbands, and partners. Annie and Carol have children, so they talk about them a lot. And of course, we spend a lot of time talking shop.'

'Shop?'

'Yes, meteorology, weather patterns, that sort of thing. Occasionally, we'll talk about deeper things, you know, spirituality, life, and death. Annie's quite religious.'

'We've got one of them. Is she painful?'

'No, not at all. She doesn't try to convert anyone. She explains what it means to her. How it brings her a degree of comfort to believe. We also spend a lot of time planning for the next day. Where we should forage for food, who's in charge of the fire and replenishing the water, practical things. Why, what do you boys talk about?'

'Jumpers and the best technique for putting them on. Fascinating subject.'

She offers me an inquisitive smile. 'You're joking, right?'

'I jest ye not.'

'I bet you talk about sex a lot, don't you?'

'Normally, at home, yes. But not out here.'

'Why?'

'If you talk sex, then you think sex and considering there's no chance of sex, then it's a form of self-torture.'

'Do you miss it... sex I mean?'

'I'm a man; what do you think?'

She giggles. 'I'm sure there are some men who aren't interested in sex.'

'If there are, then I've never met one.'

'Are you good at it?'

Christ! What a question. 'I'm not sure. You'd have to ask my wife. She's never complained yet, but then again, she's never given me a standing ovation once we've finished.'

'You said you were going stir crazy, earlier. Why?'

'You certainly ask a lot of questions.'

'It's the only way to get answers.'

'Being stuck with those three 24/7 is trying at the best of times.'

'Do you love them?'

I'm appalled at the question. 'What!'

'You heard; do you love them?' I shuffle uncomfortably in the sand and feel myself blush.

'Well... I... I mean...'

'What are you embarrassed about?'

'I'm not embarrassed.'

'Yes, you are. You've gone red in the face. What is it with men and expressing their emotions? You must know whether you love them or not.'

'I'm fond of them... no, I'm not fond of them. They annoy the shit out of me. But, still, I guess. Well... they're like brothers, yes, annoying brothers. Does that answer your question?'

'It does. Although it would have been quicker for you to say yes.' She jumps to her feet. 'Hey, come with me, I have a little hideaway to show you. It's where I sometimes go when I need some space for myself. It's my meditation spot. You can use it if you like when you need some time alone.'

'Where is it?'

'In the jungle—out of bounds. Actually, it's in your zone.'

'You're naughty.'

'I know. I like being naughty. It gives life an edge.' She leads me along a trail which starts off in the Weathergirls area but soon hangs a left and it's not long before I notice blue triangles on the trees marking the boundary. We walk on for another ten minutes until we come to an oval clearing. The canopy above us is tightly enclosed apart from one perfectly shaped round hole in the epicentre. It's like a planetarium offering a perfect view of the stars above. It's also eerily quiet.

'Wow!' is all I can utter.

'Do you like it?'

'Yes. It's peaceful and cool, as in the temperature, I mean.'

She sits down on a log and pats at it. 'Here, sit next to me.' I lay the fishing rod down and take a seat. She holds her finger to her lips. We sit for a good ten minutes in absolute silence. After a while, I relax as the fog in my head clears. She reaches out and places her hand on top of mine. It's warm and soft. Her short fingernails scrape across my skin. It's delicious and sensual. She turns and stares into my eyes. My heartbeat is racing as she leans in and rests her lips on mine, barely touching. I try to fight it but I'm weak. The air from her nostrils tickles my shaggy beard. Her lips press harder as she slips her hand around the back of my head and pulls me into her. She kisses me passionately. I'm wrapped up in such an onslaught of emotions my conscious mind only absent-mindedly hears the crackle of twigs and rustle of leaf litter.

'Oh, sorry. I didn't mean to interrupt,' Geordie's voice booms out. Chloe pulls away and stares at the ground.

'Oh, Geordie... ahem, Chloe was just showing me her meditation spot.'

'Aye, it looked like it,' he replies, curtly.

Chloe stands. 'Well, I better get going. The others will be wondering where I've got to. I don't want them sending out a search party.' She skips off through the bushes until she's out of sight. Geordie glares at me.

'What's wrong with you?' I ask as I get to my feet and pick up the rod.

'I think that's a question you should be asking yourself. Have you no scruples, no loyalty?'

'I'm not sure what you mean.'

'You know damn well what I mean. You're a married man. What about Fiona?'

'Christ, Geordie. It was one little kiss between two lonely people. It's hardly a crime.'

'A little kiss, you say. And what would have happened if I hadn't stumbled upon you both?'

'What are you implying?'

'You have previous.'

'What does that mean?' I shout becoming angry.

'You know what I mean,' he sneers.

'No, I don't! If you've got something to say, then say it!'

'Okay, I will. Gillian... there, I said it.'

'Gillian?'

'Oh, don't come the innocent with me. Yes, Gillian, Flaky's missus!'

'Oh, piss off.'

'Are you denying it? It's obvious to everyone apart from Flaky that Katrina is the double of your little Mary. Can you look me in the eye and tell me you're not Katrina's biological father?' I'm shaking with rage. I'm angry with Geordie but even angrier with myself. 'Well, come on, out with the truth.'

'Yes, Will, out with the truth,' Flaky says as he steps from the shadows.

Chapter 16

Conflict

Flaky marches up to me until our noses are inches apart. His face is hard yet emotionless.

'Well, I'm waiting? What's happened between you and Gillian? I demand to know,' he says, coldly.

I stare at the leaf litter for a few seconds before raising my head, reluctantly. Our eyes lock onto each other. It's time for some truth.

'It was one kiss, a long time ago.' His face is thunder. He takes a step back and swings a fist which slams into my right cheek sending me sprawling to the ground. I rub at my split lip with the back of my hand and inspect the crimson stain as he turns and runs off, whimpering. I could die.

'Nice one, Billy Boy,' Geordie growls as he storms off in a different direction. I flop down onto the log I was sharing with Chloe. It seems like a lifetime ago. After fifteen minutes, I've gathered my thoughts and my lip has scabbed over. With hollow legs, I wearily rise and follow in the direction that Flaky took.

I find him on the beach, sitting with legs pulled up to his chest. I drop down beside him.

'What do you want?' he says, sniffling.

'To say sorry. It should never have happened, but it did, and I can't change the past.'

'Is it still going on?'

'Is what still going on?'

He erupts. 'Don't you dare play games with me! I want answers and you're going to damn well stay here as long as it takes. You and Gillian, is it still going on?'

I let out a long sigh. 'It was never "going on" as you put it. It was a one-off, I swear on my life.'

'I see. Where?'

'It was the time you and Gillian came to stay with me and Fiona. You arrived on the Saturday, and we arranged to go for a walk up Inglegor Pike on the Sunday. You came down with a cold and pulled out. Fiona was three or four months pregnant with Mary, so me and Gillian went alone.' I pause hoping it's enough information for him.

'Go on. Whereabouts did this treacherous deed take place?'

'The foothills, before we went up the pike.'

'And who initiated it?'

'Flaky, this isn't going to...'

'I said who initiated it?' he screams in my face. 'I'm waiting!'

'I did.'

'I see. And what did she do... Gillian?'

'She was hesitant.'

'You forced yourself upon her?'

'No of course not. What do you take me for?'

'That's a damned good question I've yet to find an answer to! You were saying; she was hesitant?'

'Yes, at first. It was just one kiss, that's all.'

He ponders for a while, troubled, suspicious. 'Hang on a minute, if Fiona was three months pregnant that means this all happened about nine months before Katrina was born.'

'I suppose.'

'It was more than a kiss, wasn't it?'

My memory drifts back to that fateful day. Gillian and I had reached the summit and stood on the edge surveying the majestic verdant Yorkshire scenery below us. We'd both shouted "freedom" at the top of our voices to listen to the echo. It was exhilarating, cathartic, liberating. As we returned to the windbreak, she suddenly stopped. In excited agitation, she suggested we should get naked and make love, right there and then, on top of the peak.

'Well?' Flaky badgers.

'No, I swear to God.'

'You don't believe in God. Swear on Mary's life.'

'Don't be stupid.'

'You can't, can you? Because you had sex with my wife, and you are possibly Katrina's father. Of course, it all makes sense now. We were trying for a child. Gillian wouldn't have been on the pill.'

'You're letting your imagination run amok. I'm telling you; it was one, short, brief kiss. And I won't swear on Mary's life because... well, it's tempting fate. But I swear on my life, it's the truth.'

'And since then?'

'Nothing. It was a moment of foolish madness.'

'Do you both love each other?'

'No, of course not... well, I mean of course I love her, you know, like a sister.'

'Hah! You'd stick your tongue down the throat of your sister if you had one, would you?'

'No. You're putting words in my mouth.'

'Better than someone else's tongue. You realise this changes everything... forever! It not only means the possible break-up of my marriage and family but possibly yours too. Is Fiona aware of what happened?'

'No.'

'Well, she'll be aware when I get back home. You can be damned sure of that. Now, if you don't mind, I want to be alone. I can't bear to be around you. Some friend you turned out to be.' I rise to my feet and trudge back to camp.

Robbo is sitting next to the fire reading his Bob Dylan biography.

'Is there anything you need to tell me?' he drawls.

'What?'

'Do I smell really bad or something? First, you leave, then Geordie goes, then Flaky disappears. Then Geordie comes storming back, grabs his colouring book, and pencils and buggers off again. Then you show up looking like you've lost sixpence and found a penny. An hour ago, we were all as happy as pigs in shite after the fish and chips and winning our first challenge. What's going on?'

'Do you really want to know?'

'Not really, but I've reached a boring part in the book.' I slump down next to him.

'Geordie caught me kissing Chloe.'

'Where?'

'On the lips?'

'I meant, whereabouts?' he huffs as he closes his book.

'Oh, some spot in our zone she found. She calls it her meditation place. It's peaceful.'

'Until tonight?'

'Yes, until tonight. '

'Well, she's an attractive woman and you're... a man.'

'Thanks.'

'No problem.'

'Anyway, after she hurriedly left, Geordie takes the moral high ground.'

'Geordie?' he says with incredulity. 'Since when did he grow a moral spine?'

'You don't know him like I do. He has scant regard for societies rules and conventions, but when it comes to loyalty, he turns into a zealot. He started on about Fiona.'

'This is better than a soap opera. Carry on.'

'He accused me, in not so many words, of sleeping with Gillian.'

He exhales, deeply. 'Katrina?'

'Yes. The fact Katrina and Mary look alike. Then he asked me whether I was the father.'

'And?'

'Flaky appears out of the fucking shadows like Dick Turpin about to rob a stagecoach. He heard everything.'

'Ah, I see.' He picks up a stick and prods at the coals sending a shower of embers flickering skyward. 'And did you sleep with Gillian?'

'No. We kissed... once.'

'So, Katrina isn't yours?'

'No.'

'And you and Gillian, now?'

'It was a one off. One mistake I deeply regret.'

He stares at me. 'You've got a bust lip.'

'I deserve it, I guess.'

'Flaky's getting a bit aggro in his old age. That's two punches he's thrown in twenty-five years. The first time he's drawn blood though. Go on, what happened next?'

I get the distinct impression Robbo is actually enjoying the drama unfold. 'Flaky ran off, then Geordie stomped off. I caught up with Flaky on the beach. He said he's going to tell Fiona when he gets home. He's going to burn everyone's playhouse down. Sweet revenge.'

'It's a bit over-the-top. I mean, one kiss. What will Fiona do if he does follow up on his threat?'

'I'm not sure. She'll probably disappear down to her mother's for a week or two and let me stew in my own juices. But she's not going to leave me over one kiss, is she?'

'I don't know. To her it's not just one kiss; it's about trust. If it had been with a complete stranger, she may have been more forgiving. But when it's with one of her best mates... well, that's a firecracker.'

'He'll probably leave the band.'

He sniffs. 'Flaky? So what? Hey, don't get me wrong, he's my brother in every way apart from blood, but we can get a better replacement than him on the skins.'

'I don't know how many times I've got to tell you and Geordie; if one of us leaves the band—there is no band.'

'Fine. We get a new drummer and set up a new band. Leave the Shooting Tsars in the past and move on. Making music is what makes me get up in the morning. It's electric. It makes me feel alive. And the money's not bad. I'm not giving up music because you had one snog with his missus.'

'I don't see how it can work anymore. There'll be bad feeling all the time; simmering resentment and mistrust. I've stuffed it up good and proper.'

'I think you're getting your knickers in a twist.'

'What do you mean?'

'I've hung out with all those old guys from the sixties. They've got some tales to tell. They were all hopping in and out of each other's beds with their bandmates' wives or girlfriends all the time. It was almost expected. No one batted an eye. You're dealing with a one-off pash. It's hardly Caligula and the fall of the Roman empire, is it?'

I'm riled at his casual take on events. 'No, it's not. But this isn't the summer of love. And it's not what *I* think that matters, it's what Flaky thinks.'

'Give him time. He'll come around as long as you've told him everything there is to know,' he gazes at me enquiringly.

'Gospel.'

Robbo has become something of a revelation to me since we arrived on the island. I automatically assumed he'd be the weakest link—I was wrong.

Four days have passed since my highly personal and guarded secret became common knowledge to my bandmates, and everything has turned to shit. The camp is in disarray and Flaky and Geordie have sent me to Coventry. If you've ever visited Coventry, you'll know how miserable it can be. There's only Robbo and I who are trying to maintain some sort of schedule. All the chores are conducted by the two of us, and it's a lot of arduous work. Our team competed in two further challenges and were abysmal coming last in each one. We're now joint bottom on the leaderboard again after the Chefs won their first reward challenge yesterday.

I've finished my jobs for the day. The water containers are full, and the fire is stoked. It's close to dusk and the mood in the camp is oppressive. Flaky is sitting opposite me. He spends his time either reading his Bible or sat with Dorothy in his lap stroking her as he stares forlornly into the fire. Geordie is lying in his hammock with his coloured pencils and colouring book. Robbo has been gone for a good two hours. He said he needed some air, which is not like him. I grab the fishing rod and my backpack.

'Right, I'll see if I can catch us some fish for our supper,' I say, in an optimistic tone. I get no response. I slink off like a cowed dog and head to the beach. As I emerge from the jungle, I meet Robbo coming the other way.

'What's it like back there?' he asks.

'I've seen more life in a morgue.'

'Maybe we should pull the pin. We can say Flaky has mental health issues. It could get us off the island.'

'I think he genuinely has got mental health issues, and who could blame him, and I'm not far behind.' I ponder for a moment. 'I think you're right. I'll see Jerry tomorrow and have a talk.'

'Oh, here, I salvaged these from a piece of driftwood.' He pulls a few live limpet shells from his pocket and hands them to me.

'At last, some decent bait. Christ, I hope I catch something, my belly's aching again.'

'I'll see you back there,' he says as he plods away.

I call out. 'Oi, Robbo... thanks.'

He halts and turns around. 'For what?'

'For not casting me adrift.'

He grins. 'Everyone needs a mate when they're in a spot of bother. You'd do the same for me.'

My line has been in the water for a good hour without so much as a nibble. A familiar voice calls out as I cast in again.

'Will! Will!'

'Oh, fuck me,' I mumble glancing over my shoulder as Chloe comes trotting out of the undergrowth. It's not that I don't relish her company... it's just... well... you know.

'Hey, what's happened to the Rock Stars over the last two challenges? It looked like you weren't even trying. Is it hunger? Are you lacking energy?'

'Yes. But that's not the reason,' I say as I reel in the slack on my line.

'What's the problem?'

'Our kiss the other night. That's the problem.' I spend the next ten minutes going over the whole gory story. She stands silent, mouth agape, until the end.

'Oh, my! This is all my fault.'

'No, it's not. I shared one quick kiss with you, a stranger. That's not the issue. The issue is the kiss with my best friend's wife.'

'Surely, she has to share some of the blame?'

'You don't know her. She's naïve, innocent, a wallflower... no I don't mean that. She's a great lass, but she's not experienced in the ways of the world. I've been around the traps. I knew what I was doing—she didn't.'

She laughs, in an ironic manner. 'Really? You'd be surprised at how devious women can be. Even the wallflowers.' I put fresh bait on my hook, wade into the shallows and cast in. Chloe sidles up beside me and rubs her hand across the bare skin of my back.

'I'm terrible at fishing,' I murmur.

'My dad taught me how to fish. He used to say you have to think them onto the hook.'

'Who's your dad? The Dalai Lama?'

She sniggers. 'So, what happens now?'

'Are we talking about fish or Flaky?'

'Flaky.'

'Not sure. Everything is up to him. But if there's no change by tomorrow, I'm going to see Jerry and tell him we're quitting the show.'

'The contracts we signed are watertight. The only way off the island is through a significant and life-threatening injury.'

'Mental health can be a life-threatening injury. I'm worried about his mental state.' She places her hand on my cheek and pulls it towards her.

'I'm sorry,' she murmurs. The temptation is irresistible but as luck would have it, I get a twang on my line.

'Whoa! I'm on!' I strike as the tip of the rod twitches and quivers. The rod bends double as I reel in.

'Hell, it's a big one!' she exclaims. A familiar silver flash appears in the gently frothing waves. I pull the fish onto the beach and watch as it flips and twists trying to escape capture.

'You're right, it is a big bugger. Damn, I don't have anything to knock it senseless with.' She rushes off towards the bush and returns with a short, heavy stick. I watch on as she swiftly administers three hefty clonks to the head, removes the hook then pulls her knife from its sheath.

'You re-bait and get your line in. They could be on the bite,' she commands with some urgency. She takes the knife and thrusts it into the gills on either side. Blood oozes out. 'You need to bleed them straight away unless you keep them alive in the water.' As I re-bait my hook I watch on as she grabs the fish and runs her thumb and fingers down the body, from tail to head. 'I'm squeezing the main arterial.' I cast in as she guts the fish, rinses it in the ocean, then expertly fillets it.

'Your dad did teach you well. What species of fish is it?'

'A trevally. Beautiful eating. You're lucky.' For the next twenty minutes, I'm on a roll as the fish commit suicide and launch themselves onto my hook. As I beach them Chloe stuns, bleeds, guts, and fillets them in a fraction of the time I'd have taken, and more expertly. Adrenaline is buzzing through me, along with an unwanted amount of testosterone as I watch her at work. By the time the fish go off the bite, we have sixteen handsome fillets.

'Go!' she shouts. 'Get them back to camp while they're still fresh. Wrap each one in a palm leaf and put them over semi-hot coals for ten minutes, turning once. It's like steaming them. They'll be wonderful.' I give them another quick rinse in seawater and drop them into my backpack. *Where are my manners?*

'Hang on. You're as much a part of this as I am. Here, you take half,' I say as I pull eight fillets out and hand them to her. She's about to refuse. 'Not a word, I mean it. If you hadn't been here, I wouldn't have caught half as many.'

She relents. 'Okay. It's very generous of you.' She gives me a quick peck on the cheek. Our hunger outweighs our ardour as we both hurriedly depart in opposite directions... which is probably for the best.

Chapter 17

Fishy On A Dishy

As I hold my torch out in front of me to illuminate the camp trail, I run headlong into Geordie as he rounds a dark corner.

'Oh! It's you,' he says with an element of surprise.

'Who were you expecting? Bill Gates?' He stares at me for a moment as an awkward silence swallows us. His face softens as I sense he has something to say but doesn't know how to begin. It doesn't last long. A hardened frown returns.

'Aye, well, I'm away for a walk. The campsite is overbearing at the moment.' He turns to leave.

'Geordie, I'm surprised at your reaction to what happened the other night.'

He stops and slowly spins in the sand. 'And why's that?'

'Come on mate, we've been through thick and thin together. I fucked up but you don't need to throw me under the bus. It wasn't your wife I kissed. How many times have you stuffed up and I've always been there for you? I've got to say... I'm disappointed in your behaviour.'

He stiffens, aggressively. 'Oh, is that right? You're disappointed in my behaviour... now there's a joke.'

I sigh wearily. 'For God's sake! It was one bloody kiss. It didn't last longer than a few seconds. The reaction, especially from you, is disproportionate to the offence. It's not the end of the world.'

'Try telling Flaky that. Anyway, I don't believe it was only a kiss.'

I puff air out into the dark night. 'Go on?'

'The fact Mary and Katrina could pass as sisters, or half-sisters, leads me to think you're lying about events.'

I take a step closer and glare into his brown eyes. 'I am not Katrina's father. Even if I were, which I'm not, what business is it of yours?' His eyes widen as they flick back and forth across his face.

'Because I'm your best pal. If you had told me the truth after it had happened, I'd have been more understanding. But to bury it away like a coward, well... it's hard to take. You know the unwritten rule of a band; wives and girlfriends are off limits. It's family.'

'Not in the summer of love.'

'What?'

'Nothing. So, that's it then? You've abandoned me. And when I think of all the times I've been on hand to help you out of the shit. The time I saved you from hanging yourself. The fights, the altercations, dealing with police at 2 am in the morning... always me. It was only last year you thought Jackie was having an affair. Who came to your assistance to find out the truth?'

'I didn't hang myself. It was an accident,' he mumbles as he drops his gaze to the ground.

'Nevertheless, I was there for you.'

'Aye, you're right, and I appreciate it. But this is different.'

'No, it's not. It doesn't matter what the misdemeanour or indiscretion is. Best pals forgive one another.' The awkward silence returns as my patience takes leave of absence. 'Suit yourself. By the way, I have eight juicy fillets of trevally in the bag. Come and eat, I think our hunger is affecting our judgement.'

He smacks his lips. 'No, you guys have them. I'm away for my walk.'

'Stop being a martyr. You can go for your walk and sulk after you've eaten. You need food. You're wasting away.'

He scratches his shaggy beard. 'Aye, maybe you're right,' he says slowly. 'But this doesn't change anything,' he adds as an afterthought.

I'm surrounded by many pleasant sounds. Bird and insect clamour, the ceaseless percussion of the ocean, the swish of the canopy, the crackle and snap from the fire, the arthritic creak of the hammock ropes. But by far the best noise is the occasional "oh, yes" of human voices as we pick at our fish. It's sweet, slightly salty, smoky and above all tasty and nutritious.

'I could have eaten double,' Robbo proclaims. I don't have the balls to tell him I split the swag with Chloe.

'Yes. It was delicious,' Flaky agrees. 'Thank you, Will.' *It's the first time in four days he's spoken to me.*

'Perfect,' Geordie says as he sucks noisily at his fingers. 'Not sure how you managed it, because I know you're shit at fishing, but you did us proud. Cheers! I'm going to put some more fuel on the fire. It's getting chilly.'

'The problem is,' I begin, 'it's feast or famine. We find a food source and eat well, then we go a day or two with virtually nothing apart from coconut. What we need is a basic but constant supply of staples to sustain us. If we do catch some fish or crabs, it's a bonus.'

Flaky picks up his Bible and takes up position near the fire as he wraps a blanket around himself. Robbo and I clear up the plates and wash them in silence as Geordie stokes the blaze. Peace erupts. Things may be returning to normal; I can feel it in my water.

A hush has fallen over our site. I never fail to be amazed at the difference heartening food can make to one's mood when you're perpetually starving. Flaky flicks at the pages of his Bible as I give the fishing rod a wipe down with a damp rag. Robbo swings in his hammock, humming a tune to himself. Geordie is sitting opposite me staring wistfully into the coals. I assume he's wrestling with his conscience.

'I can't do this anymore!' Flaky screeches, shattering the serenity and making the rest of us start. His blanket falls to the ground as he leaps to his feet, tosses the Bible into the fire, grabs his torch, and scurries off into the undergrowth. Robbo and Geordie stare at me, horrified. The incident paralyses us as time grinds to an abrupt halt. My eyes swivel to the hot embers. The leather-bound, gold embossed Bible lies silently in the incandescent coals as hungry flames lick at the edges of the paper. The symbolism is not lost on me. The book was the blueprint for Flaky's life. It's been his guidance, his mentor, his comfort since he was a small child and now it has failed him, as I have failed him. He didn't just throw the Bible into the coals, but our friendship as well. I jump to my feet and step into the fire.

'Billy, you daft bugger!' Geordie exclaims. 'Get out of there!' I reach down and grab the smouldering tome. Searing pain shoots across my palm as I come into contact with fierce embers. With a quick flick of my arm, I lob the book into the sand. Geordie gathers up a pile of dirt in his giant mitts and dumps it on the Bible, as I hop from the scorching cinders gripping at the wrist of my blistered hand.

'Here, put your hand in the water,' Geordie shouts as he pulls a bucket forth, grabs my arm and plunges it into the liquid. 'Robbo, get the first-aid kit!' I wince as the cool liquid attacks the pain. It's throbbing like hell as Robbo hurriedly pulls some ointment and a bandage from the first-aid kit.

'You stupid bastard! What did you do that for?' he cries.

I force a grin. 'Surely, you've heard the story; his grandmother gave him the Bible when he was six years old.'

'I must have dodged a bullet. I've never heard that one,' Geordie cackles as he pulls my hand from the liquid and inspects my palm. 'Not too bad. It will blister and you'll need to keep the bandage clean.'

'Not an easy task considering our situation,' Robo notes.

'Rinse it out in seawater three or four times a day. That should stop any infection.' Robbo squeezes a thick glob of petroleum jelly from a tube and daintily spreads it across the burn with the tip of his finger. Geordie takes me by the wrist and applies a tight gauze bandage. He attempts to fasten it with a safety pin but jabs the needle into the ball of my thumb.

'Aargh! You cack-handed cretin!'

'Ah, stop you blethering man. You're worse than a bairn.'

'Here, let me do it,' Robbo says as he seizes my angry, pulsating hand.

'Back off, man! I know what I'm doing,' Geordie yells.

'Not from where I'm standing you don't. Pass me the safety pin. Ouch! You bloody moron. You've jabbed me in the end of the finger,' Robbo cries as he stumbles back stamping heavily on my foot.

'That was your fault. You've never been the most dexterous of people.' I wrest my hand from the bumbling, bungling, birdbrains and grab the pin off Geordie.

'I appreciate your efforts, boys, I really do. But I'll take care of it from here before someone loses a fucking eyeball!' I quickly secure my bandage, pick up the Bible and grab Flaky's discarded blanket. 'I best go see him.'

'He might want to be alone,' Geordie advises.

'I'm sure he'll tell me if he does,' I reply as I set off.

As I emerge from the jungle, I spot Flaky sitting cross-legged close to the water's edge. He flicks a quick glance over his shoulder before returning his gaze to the ocean. I walk up behind him and drape the blanket over his shoulders.

'Geordie was right; it has got chilly,' I mutter. 'I retrieved this for you.' I hold out the Bible for him.

He gives it a cursory glance. 'I don't need it anymore. It has no use,' he replies morosely.

I sit alongside him. There's a fraught silence. After ten minutes of nothing, I finally think of something to say to break the impasse.

'When I was about ten-years-old I was given two guinea pigs for my birthday. At first, I loved them. I'd clean out their cage twice a week; make sure they always had plenty of food and fresh water each day and built a pen for them outside which was cat and dog proof. As time went by, the novelty wore off. It wasn't long before I saw them as a nuisance, a chore. Initially, we kept their cage in the front porch of our house, until my dad told me to move them out into the shed in the back garden. They were quite smelly, so he had a point.

That year we had a freezing winter. I'd taken to feeding them every second day, then third day, then... well, I can't really remember. One morning, when I walked into the shed, they were dead. It had been a bitterly chilly night. Their little teeth were stuck in the grille of their cage. They must have been trying to gnaw their way out. They'd frozen to death. I buried them in the garden and stuck a little cross in their grave.

I can't express the amount of guilt I felt... feel. Even now, thirty years on, I'll sometimes wake up in the middle of the night in a cold sweat, hyperventilating, thinking of them. I have to get up and go outside and have a smoke to calm myself down. Occasionally, I'll shed a tear.

What I did, or didn't do, was wrong. Even though I was a boy, I knew the rules, the responsibilities. The guilt will never go away. It will stay with me forever, as a reminder to keep trying to be a better man.

I'm flawed in so many ways. I don't mean to be... but I am. I'm never going to be perfect. It's a cross I have to bear. But... although I can regret the past... I can't change it.' I pick the Bible up and hold it out to him again. He notices the bandage.

'You burnt yourself.'

'A mere flesh wound,' I say smiling at him. He takes his Bible and I turn to leave. 'Don't stay out here too long; you may freeze to death.'

<hr/>

Flaky strolls into the campground. He pauses for a moment, removes his spectacles, and rubs them against his shirt.

'I'd like your attention.' We stop what we are doing, which isn't much and focus on him. 'I have a statement to make; tonight, I have spoken with Jesus!'

'Eh up!' Robbo exclaims. 'I didn't realise he was on the show. What team's he in?' I drop my head and throw him a glare as Geordie stifles a long overdue smirk.

'I was speaking figuratively!' Flaky snaps. A deep intake of breath appears to calm him as he continues. 'Not less than an hour ago, I was a lost lamb aimlessly trudging through a snowdrift of sand.' I exchange glances with Geordie and Robbo who appear as confused as I am at his terrible metaphor. 'I threw my Bible onto the fire. Do you want to know why?' Responses are not forthcoming. 'I'll tell you why; for all the years it has helped me out, in times of crises, this time it failed. As I sat here tonight, reading the New Testament, Christ's teachings, I could not find the answer I was searching for.' I wish he'd get a hurry-on as I need to take a leak. 'When Will came to the beach and handed me the Bible, a copy my dear, beloved grandmother gifted me as a small child, I believe it was Christ who guided him.' *No, it wasn't!* 'His selfless act of sticking his hand in the fire to retrieve the Good Book was courageous... if foolish. However, when he left, I flicked through the pages wondering what passage I could read to give me fortitude. I could find none. That's when I asked the Lord for his help. He pointed at his book and said, it's in the whole.'

'What was in the hole?' Robbo quizzes rubbing his head. Flaky closes his eyes, clearly annoyed at the interruption.

'Whole with a "W". As in, total, entire, complete.'

'Oh, I see.'

'I pondered his words for a moment, confused, perplexed, bewildered.' *He's not alone.* 'Then it came to me in a blinding flash. What is the one overriding message of the New Testament?' I wish he'd stop throwing these questions out there. He gazes, with a slightly disappointed countenance, at three atheists. 'Forgiveness!' he shouts making the rest of us flinch. 'Even on the cross, as he sat dying, he asked Our Father, who art in heaven, to forgive the sins of mankind for they know not what they do.' *Sat dying... on a cross? I think he has lost his marbles.* He turns to me. 'Will, when you say it was only a kiss, it was still infidelity.'

'Yes. I know.'

'A betrayal.'

'Yes.'

'Duplicity and disloyalty.'

'Yes,' I sheepishly reply.

'A treacherous act of perfidy carried out by an unscrupulous scoundrel without morals or accountability.' He's laying it on with a trowel now.

Apparently, I'm Casanova on a Viagra overdose rampage. I have no other option but to nod contritely.

'Yes. You're right.'

'However, I have found it in my heart to forgive you.' I feel relieved. 'I will not tell Fiona about this dastardly episode. It can bring no good to anyone and may do irreparable damage to your marriage and Fiona's and Gillian's friendship.' He now fixes his attention on Geordie. 'And as for your scurrilous assumptions that Katrina was fathered by Will, I find them hurtful, gossip-mongering nonsense.'

'Hang on a minute!' Geordie fires up. 'I'm not the one on trial here.'

'If you'd allow me to finish!' Flaky demands as Geordie huffs but keeps quiet. 'I agree, Katrina and Mary do look alike. However, if you hadn't already noticed, Will and I are not a million miles apart in our appearance.' *Cheeky bastard!* 'We are of similar stature and looks. Both fetching men in our prime.' I notice Robbo snigger. 'I dare say when the girls reach their teenage years they will change.' He coughs, embarrassed, as he reflects on his words. 'I meant in their appearance to each other... not their, ahem, their... well, the changes teenage girls go through.'

'You mean tits and bums,' Geordie offers.

'I wouldn't have put it as crudely as that, but yes. Geordie, as I've found it in my heart to forgive Will, I'd like you to find it in your heart to do the same.' Geordie purses his lips as his head slowly rolls from side to side. He stares into the fire for a second before we both lock eyes.

'Aye, okay,' he smiles as he takes a step towards me and holds his arm out. 'But you're on Last Chance Avenue. Another stunt like this and we're finished. Do I make myself clear?'

I nod and smile back. 'Yep. Hearing you loud and clear.' He grabs my hand and shakes it vigorously, which under normal circumstances would have been welcome. However, as it's my blistered hand, the experience is less than enjoyable. I'm wondering if he did it on purpose.

'Okay, to finish off I'd like us all to stand in a circle and join hands as I offer up a prayer.'

'Shit the bed twice,' Robbo mutters under his breath. As awkward as it feels, we oblige. As we join hands Flaky closes his eyes and bows his head. We reluctantly follow suit.

'Dear Lord, I ask you to forgive William Harding for his sins, as I have forgiven him for his sins. He knows not what he does... quite often. I also ask forgiveness for my wife, Gillian, even though I believe she was led astray, coerced, and manipulated into this unholy alliance.

May I also ask for courage and fortitude to help us progress in the competition for the good of charity... my charity. Please bless Geordie and show him the light, and also help him reduce his flatulence emissions. May you lead Robbo back onto the path of righteousness and if you could recommend a drug rehabilitation clinic with a good conversion rate, it would be appreciated. And lastly, please provide us with an abundance of food to maintain body and soul.' I squint through one eye at Robbo and Geordie.

'This is all your bleeding fault!' Geordie mouths at me. I shrug.

'Oh, Lord, who art in heaven, hear my prayer. Amen.'

'Amen,' we chorus as we quickly release hands.

'Okay, I'm glad that's cleared the air. No more rancour. But one last thing,' Flaky continues. 'I know we don't have a cat in hell's chance of winning this competition, but please, don't let us be the first one's eliminated from the island. I think from tomorrow onwards we need to buck our ideas up and make a bloody fist of it. Let's take some pride in ourselves. Right, well I need to take a visit to the latrine then get my head down for the night. These last few days have been very trying.' He picks his torch up and disappears into the brush.

'Holy shit and thunder!' Robbo gasps. 'That was painful.'

'Aye. He's definitely lost the plot,' Geordie concurs. 'But he did make one good point; we need to lift our game.' We flop onto our hammocks, emotionally and physically exhausted.

'The problem is, Geordie, Will is right,' Robbo says.

'About what?'

'This feast and famine loop we're constantly in. We have a couple of good days with food, then a couple of days with barely anything. It's taken its toll. If we want to progress any further in the comp, we need to find a sustainable nutritious food source.'

'Maybe Flaky's prayer will be answered,' Geordie says with a heavy inflection of sarcasm as he kicks off his sandals and climbs into his hammock. 'Bill, I suggest you atone for your sins by coming up with one of your master plans. Right, I need some shut-eye, so if you two could pipe down, it would be appreciated,' he says as he releases a blistering fart.

'Are they still testing atom bombs in this neck of the woods?' Robbo asks. 'Anyway, Geordie, make the most of it as you won't be getting much sleep tomorrow night.'

'Why's that?'

'Have you forgotten? It's Jerry's belated 60th birthday bash and they're holding a massive party. That's why there's no filming for two days.'

'Oh, aye. What with all the excitement it slipped my mind. Miserable, mean spirited fuckers. The least they could have done was invite all the competitors to it.'

As I swing lazily in my hammock, I ponder Geordie's words. He's right, we need a plan, and a bloody good one at that... but what?

Chapter 18

Survival At Any Cost

I throw the shovel on the ground and wipe the sweat from my brow with the back of my hand.

'That should do us,' I say surveying the three deep holes. Robbo peers into them.

'Hellfire! There's water at the bottom of that one.'

'Job's a good 'un', Geordie says as he wipes himself down with a towel then pulls his shirt back on. I turn around as Flaky comes clomping through the undergrowth carrying three mats woven from palm leaves. He places each one over a hole.

'Perfect fit,' he comments, pleased with his handiwork. 'You do realise the first downpour we get, these holes are going to fill up with water?'

'Yes, that's why black bin liners are on our shopping list. We'll call the holes Tom, Dick and Harry.'

'Why?' Flaky asks.

'After the tunnels in The Great Escape. This will be *our* great escape.'

Flaky rubs at his chin. 'Didn't they all get shot at the end of the film?'

'Not all of them... just some of them,' Geordie says as he eyeballs Flaky suspiciously. Our larders are situated in an area a few metres behind our main camp safely out of sight of the camera, but near enough for easy access. The boom of music and clamour of laughter and shouts began a good two hours ago. I glance at my watch.

'Come on, let's do it. The party's in full swing.'

>»>> «<«<

We follow the trail we cut earlier in the day to the very edge of our western perimeter. I spot a few trees emblazoned with a red triangle as we emerge from the scrub and wander a few feet into the grey zone. We can see the party in the distance. There must be a dozen marquees set up near the games zone. High-powered temporary lighting illuminates the scene. The music is now much louder and distant shrieks and loud guffaws drift to us on a warm lazy breeze.

'I'm not sure about this, Will. If we get caught, we'll all be sent home in ignominy. We'll be the pariahs of the country. It could have a detrimental effect on our career,' Flaky says with a furrowed brow. It's at least the tenth warning I've received from him since I first explained my plan.

'Oh, shut up, you big Jesse and grow some balls... and a spine to go with it,' Geordie snarls.

'Excuse me, but this isn't about me being scared or not. I'm merely pointing out the possible consequences and ramifications of our actions. It's called being an adult,' he snaps back, indignantly.

'We have the perfect defence,' I repeat, yet again. 'The show's motto is survival at any cost. And that's what we're doing tonight. You can't have a show with that catchphrase then impose multiple rules which must be obeyed. It's a contradiction in terms. If we get rumbled, I'm sure the British public will sympathise with our predicament. They may even be on our side —the anti-heroes. Anyway, I can guarantee you, our fans won't give a flying fuck in a teacup if we're booted from the show.'

'He's right, Flaky,' Robbo begins. 'We're a rock 'n' roll band. People expect us to break the rules. We're not the King's College boys' choir on a day trip to the Queen's annual garden party.'

Flaky huffs. 'Okay, fine. On all our heads be it. But don't say I didn't warn you.'

'We won't. Now quit your snivelling. I've had enough of your griping for one lifetime. I've been flat out like a lizard drinking all day, and I'm not in the mood for it,' Geordie adds.

I stare at him. 'Have you been hanging around with your Aussie mate—Downunder Dave, lately?'

He pulls a defiant expression. 'And if I have, is it any business of yours?'

'No, but you do realise Downunder Dave is a serial bore-a-thon and a campanologist?'

'I don't care what his sexual preferences are, as long as it's consensual, over the age of consent, and doesn't involve small furry animals... or the mentally insane. I'm open minded.'

'The Renaissance Man cometh forth,' Robbo chuckles.

'Give me strength,' Flaky huffs as he rolls his eyes to the heavens. 'Come on, let's get on with this farce.'

'Okay, we'll go over the plan one more time,' I state. 'Flaky and Geordie, you make your way down to the sea but keep to the edge of our boundary. It will give you cover. There's barely any moonlight so you shouldn't be observed. Me and Robbo will head north for a kilometre or so until we're sure we can't be seen from the party. Then we'll make our way West to Castaway Central. When we're in position, I'll flash my torch on and off three times. That's your signal.'

'And what if we don't see it?' Flaky says.

'If you don't see it, proceed with the diversion exactly forty minutes from now, no matter what. Flaky you run down the beach towards the party screaming for help. Geordie, all you have to do is lie lifeless in the water.'

'Easy for you to say.'

'Oh, and Geordie, don't overplay your hand.'

He looks mortally wounded at my inference. 'And what does that mean?'

'It means—don't overact.'

He puffs his chest out. 'Me, overact! The very notion. My performance will be subtle but convincing.'

'Subtle, you don't know the meaning of the word,' scoffs Robbo. 'You're the worst hammy actor since Lord Hammy of Hammington strode the boards of the Old Vic.'

'Hey, Noddy, I'm the one who's going to be flailing about in the ocean in pitch darkness. If you want to take my place, be my guest.'

'Not on your Nelly. Dusk is feeding time for sharks. You won't get me in there.'

'Robbo, shut up. You're not helping,' I snap.

'Sharks?' Geordie whispers with eyes on stalks.

'Take no notice of him. They're only reef sharks. They won't bother you. Right, remember, you've nearly drowned, you've been rescued, which means you won't be able to say much.'

'The less you say the better,' Robbo adds.

'Geordie, you need to buy us some time. So don't suddenly jump to your feet after five minutes. No doubt every man and his dog will rush to your aid, but we'll still need ten to fifteen minutes to get inside and fill our backpacks. We'll see you both back at camp.'

'And tonight, we feast like kings!' Geordie says sporting a huge grin as he rubs his hands together.

'Yep, and a drink and a smoke,' Robbo adds as he pulls the ski hat over his head and down towards his neck. Only his eyes are visible through two improvised slits.

'Christ!' Flaky exclaims. 'You look like a rapist. Oh, Will, don't forget the dried seeds for Dorothy. Sunflower, caraway, whatever you can find.'

I stare at the ground and sigh. 'Yep, I'll get something for Dorothy.'

'Aye, that's right, don't worry about four humans starving to death. Let's feed the fucking bird!'

'She's our mascot.'

'She's our next meal if this caper goes tits up,' Geordie says aggressively.

'Come on, we're wasting time,' I say, weary of the bickering. 'Good luck everyone.' As Flaky and Geordie prowl south... bickering, Robbo and I set off north... in silence.

'It's bloody hot under this thing,' Robbo says complaining about the hat.

'You don't actually need to wear it yet. It's for when we get inside, you moron.' As we near Castaway Central we slink further into the shadows. I hold my hand up to signal 'halt'. I survey the building. The ground floor appears to be used as a storage area. The first floor looks like it is the main hang out; lounges, kitchen, and dining. I assume the second floor is where the bedrooms are.

'Can you see any sign of life?' I ask as I kneel and scan the extensive balconies which chaperone the giant building.

'I thought I caught sight of a figure in the main window. The big one in the middle.' Robbo says.

'First or second floor?'

'Third.'

I stare at him. 'There is no third floor, you dingbat. Do you mean second?'

'No, I mean first.'

I ignore the imbecile and rely on my memory. 'If Stu's description of the place is correct, that main window should be the large dining and kitchen area.'

'Stu, the security guard?'

'Yes, Stu, the security guard. I had a long chat with him the other day. Time to give Flaky and Geordie the signal.' I scamper back into the brush, clamber onto a rock and flick my torch on and off three times then head back to Robbo. 'We best hang back a bit until Bodgit and Scarper enact the first scene of their new melodrama—Lost At Sea.'

'I'm not sure it was a good idea to let Geordie play the drowning victim. You know what he's like once he has a captive audience. He's like Bonzo the Clown on crystal meth.'

'It's more plausible. Everyone on the island knows he's not a strong swimmer. And with the size of the big dolt, he'd be easily recognised on this mission even with a facemask covering his ugly mug.' I check my watch. 'Forty minutes gone. Any second now and we're on.'

We wait in silence for another ten minutes.

'They're taking their time,' Robbo drawls.

'What are they bloody playing at?' I say, becoming increasingly exasperated and despondent. 'It's a simple enough plan. They can't have stuffed it up before they've begun.'

Robbo raises one eyebrow at me. 'Are you joking? We're dealing with Geordie, here. Anything and everything is possible, no matter how outlandish.'

'Hmm... good point.' Another few minutes pass until a distinct shrill cry emanates from the shoreline. I can *just* make out a figure sprinting towards the party area.

'Right, keep your eyes on the building.' Five people appear on the balcony and hurry down the steps and onto the sand. I glance back at the beach. A snake of bodies races along heading east. The music abruptly stops. 'Okay, let's do it.' We both pull our bonnets down over our faces. We use a stairway at the back of the building to reach the first-floor entrance. I gently push open a swing door and poke my head inside. 'Coast is clear,' I whisper. I tiptoe inside. As I let go of the door a loud bang makes me jump.

'Christ! My fucking chin!' Robbo yells.

'Shush!' I hiss.

Robbo enters through the swing door rubbing his face. 'You dozy pillock! What did you do that for?'

'I thought you were directly behind me. Come on, stop your bitching.' I glance around to make sure there's no one else about. We're in a large open-plan kitchen. 'You go to the fridge and see what you can find, and I'll have a snoop around.' Robbo unhitches his backpack and creeps towards the fridge. Subdued lighting from downlights offers just enough glow to see clearly but also a modicum of cover.

The building is magnificent. Polished floorboards, ceiling fans, a giant plasma TV, a sound system, and more chairs and sofas than you could poke a shitty stick at, plus a sea view to die for. The kitchen and dining room are circular, with doors leading off to other corridors. A large sideboard contains spirits and mixers of every description. Newspapers, magazines, ashtrays, and cigarette packets are strewn across a giant wooden table in the middle of the room.

'How the other half live,' I murmur to myself. I take a peek outside where a large throng is gathered in a semi-circle halfway down the beach. I navigate a corridor, peering into bedrooms, bathrooms, and laundries. As I open one door I'm greeted with a familiar noise. I quietly shut the door again as my heartbeat explodes and I try to suppress an erection. I turn around and head back to Robbo. He's knelt next to the sideboard rummaging through a cupboard.

'Hey, Will, come here and take a look at this,' he says as he holds up a plastic bag.

'What is it?' I say peering through the shadows. He opens the bag, sniffs it, dabs a finger, and places it on his tongue.

He grins. 'Acapulco Gold, if I'm not very much mistaken.'

'Weed?'

'Yes. And this smells like a bloody good batch. There must be at least a kilo here. Bloody potheads,' he says with incredulity as though he's suddenly become part of the drug squad. He unzips his backpack and crams the stash into it.

'What the hell are you doing?'

'What does it look like?'

'Don't be bloody stupid. If a kilo of weed goes missing they'll know they've been done over. Take a little bit.' He reluctantly removes the bag, grabs a very generous handful, and pushes it into a small side pocket of the backpack. 'What did you get from the fridge?'

He stands and walks over to the table appearing distinctly disinterested in food and more interested in searching for paraphernalia for his weed haul.

'Eh, oh, a nice rack of lamb, some fillet steak and a pack of salmon fillets.'

'What else?'

'That's it.'

'You dipshit! We need non-perishables. Dried rice, peas, beans, lentils. Things which won't go off.'

'Yeah, yeah,' he murmurs. 'Ah, here we go, a box of Rizlas, thank you very much. And I may as well grab a few packets of smokes while I'm at it.' I ignore him and make my way to the kitchen pantry and load my backpack up with dried goods of every description until it is full to bursting. I open a packet of sultanas and stuff a handful into my mouth, taking a moment to savour the treat. As I pull at the zipper, there's another distinct bang.

'Did you hear that?'

'No, what?'

'A noise from downstairs.'

'What's downstairs?'

'It's a storage area, according to Stu.'

'Stu, the security guard?'

'Yes. Stu, the security guard.' I grab a twenty-pack of heavy-duty bin liners and slip it down the front of my pants. Another bang puts me on edge. 'There, did you hear it that time?'

'Yeah, I did. Shit, if someone's in the storage area they're going to notice us as we go back down the steps.'

'It's our only option. The stairs at the front leave us fully exposed. We'd be spotted for sure. Come on, let's get going.'

'What about the other rooms, have you checked them out?'

'Yes.'

'See anything interesting.'

'You could say that.'

'What do you mean?'

'A couple at it hammer and tong. I could have marched in there playing the bagpipes and they wouldn't have noticed me.'

He chuckles. 'What was the woman like... a bit of all right?'

'I couldn't see her face. But let's just say I believe she may be a gymnast.' As he saunters over to me, he grabs a full bottle of whisky from the sideboard. 'No! Bloody whisky's no good for us. We're already permanently dehydrated. Put it back.' He reluctantly replaces the bottle on the side. I have a thought. 'Actually, no, grab it. It may come in useful.'

'Surely, we can have a couple of snifters each to go with our meal tonight?'

I relent. 'Okay, I suppose so. But only a couple, mind.' We head back to the entrance. I hear footsteps coming up the stairs. 'Shit, we've got company. Hide!'

'Where?'

'I don't bloody know!' I frantically open doors and cupboards looking for a suitable hiding spot as Robbo spins around in a state of complete discombobulation. The padding footsteps approach. I pull at the door to a cupboard. A broom and mop are propped up at one end. It's narrow but deep. 'Quick, in here!' Robbo tries to squeeze into the cupboard full frontal.

'It's too tight,' he laments as his frame becomes stuck between the walls.

'Go in sideways, you tool,' I whisper.

'Oh, aye. Never thought of that.' He spins around and edges to the far end as I manage to close the door behind us at exactly the same moment a creak from the swing door sounds out. Indiscernible muted whispers are uttered, followed by the sound of cupboard doors opening and closing. It all goes quiet for a few seconds. The only thing I can hear is my ridiculously loud heartbeat. I half turn to Robbo.

'What are we doing here?' I ask wistfully, staring at the two holes in his ski mask.

'Hiding, aren't we?'

I sigh. 'No, I meant what are we doing on this island starring in this bloody TV show?'

'I've got to admit it wasn't one of your better ideas. I'm not sure why the others agreed to it.'

If I could actually lift my arms, I'd throttle the little git! 'It was you three who were for it! I was vehemently against the idea since it was first touted.'

'It's not how I remember it.' The door to our hiding place is thrown violently open. I scream, Robbo screams, and the two figures in front of me, who are wearing ski masks pulled down over their faces with improvised eye holes... also scream.

Chapter 19

Rumbled

Robbo collapses to the floor as I fall on top of him. The shady duo stumble backwards and land in a heap on top of one another. There's silence as we all try to regain our composure. Both men rise to their feet; one's tall, the other, average height. They tentatively edge towards us as they both lift their masks as I peel mine upwards. It's Brody Buchannan and Keith Patel.

'You cheating bastards!' Brody exclaims with a grin. 'You realise this is definitely against the rules and the terms of the contract we all signed?'

'Yes. And what's your excuse?' I reply as Robbo pushes me to my feet.

Keith steps forward, as he wipes sweat from his face. 'Bloody starvation. That's what. Plus, the fact the show's motto is survival at any cost. Well, this is survival.'

'My sentiments entirely,' I say staring at his eyepatch. I now realise I'm living in a parallel universe where the four celebrity chefs are in fact none other than the doppelgangers to the Shooting Tsars.

'Hello! Anyone there?' A familiar voice calls out from one of the corridors. We instinctively pull our hats down.

'Shit the bed!' Keith yelps.

'Quick, hide!' Brody says.

'Where?'

'In here,' he says as his palm thumps me in the chest, sending me sprawling backwards knocking Robbo to the cupboard floor again. Keith and Brody pile into the narrow broom cupboard and close the door.

'Hello?' comes the voice again as bare feet pad the kitchen floor.

'Come on, Stu, I'm not finished yet. Come back to bed,' a female voice implores.

'I thought I heard screams.'

'It will be from the party. Come on, I'm ready to go again.'

Stu chuckles. 'Good grief, woman! You're insatiable. I need a strong coffee to gird my loins after that session.' I hear a click followed by the rumbling sound of water on the boil.

'A few lines of coke should put some lead in your pencil,' the woman coos.

'Christ! This is like the holiday home of Pablo Escobar,' I murmur. Brody elbows me in the ribs. The heat in the broom cupboard from four nervous celebrities is intense. The smell isn't much better. It's like being in a sauna built for incontinent elves.

'I'll see you back in the bedroom,' the woman calls out.

'I'll be there in a jiffy,' Stu replies.

I lean towards Robbo. 'It's Stu,' I whisper.

'Stu, the security guard?'

'Yes. Stu, the security guard.' Water is poured into a cup followed by the clink of a teaspoon as it swishes around and around. Brody half turns to me and mutters, 'Can you get your dick out my arse cheeks!'

'It's not my dick. I only wish it were... I mean in size, not because it's wedged between the cleft of your buttocks. It's a roll of bin liners.'

'Oh, aye. I believe you... thousands wouldn't.' A wet fart is released from persons unknown from within the cupboard. The teaspoon stops swishing as I hold my breath. Silence follows for a good thirty seconds. It's no good, I need air. As I breathe in, my eyes begin to bleed, and I fear all my hair has just fallen out. Whoever dropped the fart has a serious intestinal problem and should seek urgent medical attention at their earliest convenience. Finally, footsteps leave the kitchen and pit-a-pat along the floorboards until they can no longer be heard. Someone inside the cupboard sniggers, as a distant bang signifies a door shutting. Keith throws open our door and we all pile out, gasping and wheezing as we rip our hats off.

'Who dropped one?' I hiss. I'm met with three furious denials. Someone is lying. 'Christ, death by flatus inhalation! What a way to go. Whoever it was, you need expert help!'

'Never mind about that,' Brody says. 'Where's all the good gear?'

'Fridge is over there,' Robbo says pointing across the kitchen. 'There's a humongous bag of weed in the dining room. It's in the sideboard cupboard. There's booze on top, and ciggies and ciggy papers on the table.'

'Nice one, Robbo,' Brody says.

'Forget about the booze and drugs, where's the dried food kept?' Keith asks, wearily.

'In the walk-in pantry next to the fridge,' I inform him.

'Cheers,' Brody and Keith say in unison as they pull their masks down and head off in different directions.

'We should do this more often,' I call out. I grab Robbo and pull him through the swing door. We shuffle quietly down the steps and survey the scene on the beach. The crowd is dispersing. I notice a door to the underground storage area and try the handle. It gives. We both tiptoe in.

'It's as black as pitch,' Robbo says. I can just make out a white chest freezer at the far end of the cavernous room. I tentatively stalk my way towards it and lift the lid. The light inside flicks on and illuminates the room with ghostly light. There are pallets of dried goods stacked neatly against the side wall.

'Nothing for us here,' I say. 'We've got all we can carry, anyway.' I turn my torch on as we make our way back to the door. Stacked up in one corner is a pile of sporting equipment. I creep over for a closer inspection. There are tennis rackets, bar football, soccer balls, baseball bats, and something very interesting—a pile of badminton netting.

'Come on, Will. Let's get going. We've ridden our luck for too long. We don't want to get busted right at the death.

'Any room left in your backpack?'

'Nah, chocka. Why?'

'The badminton netting,' I reply.

'Not my cup of tea, really.'

'What isn't?'

'Badminton. I've never been good at racket sports.'

Christ! Give me strength. I grab the netting, roll it into a tight ball and stick it under my T-shirt. 'Right, let's go.'

>>>> <<<<

I nervously check my watch again as Robbo throws wood onto the fire.

'Four hours they've been gone,' I say as I nervously rub the back of my neck. Robbo clambers into his hammock and rolls a joint—his sixth since we arrived back. 'Take it easy with that shit,' I snap at him. 'You're going to smoke the entire stash before morning at this rate.'

'Calm the farm, brother. I'm making shandies. Two thirds tobacco, one third weed. Once I've smoked this, I reckon we get some food on the go. I'm getting the munchies.'

'I told you, we're not eating until they get back. We're a team.' He throws me a cigarette. I stick it in my mouth, light it and suck in a deep lungful of smoke. A brief calm floods over me, but not for long. 'You don't think something actually *did* happen to Geordie, do you?'

'Such as?'

'Maybe he was attacked by a shark?' He doesn't have time to answer as two squabbling voices can be heard from the beach track.

'That's them now. Moaning in tandem. They're like an old married couple.' Flaky appears first, red in the face followed by Geordie. He's wearing a severe scowl. 'Here they are,' Robbo exclaims. 'Bill and Ben, the flowerpot men.'

'You can shut your cakehole,' Geordie barks. 'I've just spent the best part of four hours in the bloody medical tent being prodded and poked at by the doctor and paramedics. I had tubes down my throat, tubes in my arm, they even wanted to put a tube down my bloody spam javelin. I drew the line at that. And they made me drink something to throw up the seawater. It was disgusting.'

'Well, it serves you right. Will and Robbo warned you not to overact, but you paid no heed.'

'This sounds interesting,' Robbo says with a mischievous cackle as he sits up. 'Pray, continue my good man.' Geordie spots the joint hanging from Robbo's mouth and snatches it from him. 'Oi!'

'Button it, Biffo. I need this more than you do. The entire experience was hellish.' Flaky goes to the water bucket, fills a bottle, and takes a hearty swig.

Well?' I quiz him. He looks at me and shakes his head.

'It all started off superbly. We made it into the water without being seen. We bobbed about for a few minutes until I spotted the signal. I ran from the water screaming for help. It wasn't long before the whole production team came charging up the beach.'

'It wasn't the whole production team!' Geordie grizzles.

'It was a good portion of them. I told Felix and Jerry I'd been swimming with Geordie, and we got caught in a current which dragged us along the shoreline. When I managed to get ashore, I couldn't see Geordie anywhere. Dozens of people then rushed into the water, and someone spotted him floating a few feet from the beach and dragged him out.'

'All's good so far,' I say.

'Yes... that's when it all changed. Anyway, they drop him on the sand and the paramedic, the young woman with the ponytail, starts giving him mouth to mouth resuscitation. Instead of coming to, the big oaf keeps pretending to be unconscious. And then... oh, God, it was so embarrassing,' he says as he takes another slug of water.

'Go on,' Robbo encourages, sporting a huge beam.

'He got an erection.'

'It was not an erection! There was a bit of movement going on downstairs, I'll grant you but that's all.'

'I was standing right above you! I know what an erection looks like when I see one. Anyway, after five minutes of the woman performing CPR, the other paramedic goes to take over.'

'The man?' I ask.

'Yes. All of a sudden Geordie's on his feet. He was like Lazarus on Dexedrine. I threw him a look to indicate we needed to drag it out longer. The moron begins staggering around clutching at his heart, reciting the lyrics to Nightswimming by R.E.M. As the doctor tried to inject him with a sedative, Geordie punched him in the face.'

'I didnae punch him. I was trying to knock his hand away and, in the kerfuffle, I caught him a glancing blow on the chin.'

'A glancing blow! He was out cold! It was complete pandemonium.'

'Anyway, never mind about all that now. Were you two successful?' Geordie says as he scans the camp looking for goodies.

'Mission accomplished. It ran like clockwork. Apart from bumping into Brody and Keith from the chefs. Apparently, great minds think alike. Oh, and we nearly got rumbled by Stu.'

'Stu, the security guard?'

'Yes, Stu the... why does everyone ask that? How many other bloody Stu's do we know on this island?' I shout, exasperated.

'Keep your hair on, Captain Grumpy. I was only asking. Where's the food?'

'It's all triple wrapped in bin liners and safely hidden in Tom, Dick, and Harry. On the menu tonight we have three fillet steaks topped with blue cheese for the carnivores and a fat juicy salmon steak for the pescatarian. The side dishes are boiled potatoes, peas, and carrots. For dessert we have raspberry ripple ice cream, which will need to be eaten tonight and as a nightcap, a wee dram of single malt.'

'Scottish?'

'Yes, Scottish whisky.'

He rubs his hands together with glee. 'Oh, yes. Long may yer lum reek.'

'Anybody care to translate the gibberish?' Flaky enquires.

'Something about good luck and good fortune, I think,' Robbo replies.

'You Sassenachs. I don't know how I put up with you.' Dorothy flutters down from her perch and lands on Flaky's shoulder.

'Did you get Dorothy some seeds?' Flaky asks, perturbed.

'Yes. Sesame, caraway and sunflower... just as you asked,' I reply.

'Did you hear that, Dorothy,' he says as he kisses the damned bird on the beak. 'You can feast with us tonight.'

'That pigeon is already obese. If you feed it anymore, it won't be able to take off,' Geordie says, sneering at the bird.

'It's ninety percent plumage.'

'It's ninety percent fat.'

'Ignore the big bad ogre, Dorothy,' Flaky says in a sickening baby voice which makes the rest of us gag. I throw the rolled-up badminton net at Geordie who catches it one-handed then scratches his head.

'What's this?' he says evidently bemused.

'Badminton net,' Robbo responds as he puts a pan of water on the coals.

'Badminton!' he huffs. 'Like we have the time or energy to play games.'

'My God! You two are as dumb as dogshit! With a bit of ingenuity, we can turn it into a fishing net.'

'If you're looking for ingenuity from those two, you'll draw a blank,' Flaky adds.

Twenty-four hours ago, I was a pariah, then I was forgiven for my sins. My successful food plan has put me in everyone's good books. I've dodged a bullet... but for how long?

Chapter 20

Fatal Distraction

It's enlightening to observe everyone's daily routine, especially my own. I have been keeping notes in my journal on everyone.

I wake at dawn every day, like clockwork. First up, I split a coconut and drink the water then hoist my backpack on and head to the beach. After beachcombing for an hour, I make my way back to camp. It's at this point I invariably pass Marmaduke Smythe out for his morning walk. We stop for a quick natter then both go our separate ways. It's always between 7 and 7:30 am.

I've never been one for a predictable routine but now I see the benefits. My energy levels are high in the morning so that's when I get all my jobs done. By early afternoon, when the heat is intense and the humidity akin to a heavy wet blanket, I lie in my hammock and snooze. By late afternoon, as the temperature ebbs, I come alive again. After a refreshing dip in the ocean, I'm ready for some hunting and scavenging. We eat dinner, or supper, around 7 pm. I then head out on my last walk of the day and usually catch up with Chloe for an hour of adult chat... and things... or should I say... about things. After that, it's back to camp and bed. It's strange, after all these years, I've discovered having a daily habit is actually beneficial. I can get way more done than if I left it to chance and whimsy. When I return home, I intend to continue with my new custom.

Today, a team is going home. An elimination challenge, between the Rock Stars and the Celebrity Chefs, commences in three hours. It's two days since our night raid on Castaway Central and we are all in better spirits due to a drastic increase in our calorie intake. Even if we fail to catch any fish, we still get a nourishing meal of rice, peas, beans, and lentils at the end of the day. I'm assuming the Chefs are also suitably rejuvenated.

I stumble from my hammock and have a good stretch before gulping down two cups of coconut water. I retrieve the bottle of whisky from our subterranean larder and return to camp, making sure the camera isn't active. Robbo stirs and lifts his head as he squints at the amber fluid.

'Bit early for the hard stuff, isn't it?'

'It's not for me.'

'Oh, aye. That's what they all say. Classic warning signs of a rampant alcoholic. Not that I give a shit.' He yawns and stretches. 'This might be our last morning on the island. What do you think our chances are of beating the Chefs?'

'Chances? Never leave life to chance. Life is about fixing the game in your favour.' I slip the whiskey into my backpack, check my watch, and set off for the trail. 'I'll be back in about half an hour. Get the others up. We need to be on the ball this morning.'

As I arrive at the beach, I survey my surroundings. In the distance is the wobbling figure of Marmaduke heading my way. He's still some way off and I don't think he's spotted me, not that it really matters. I know he enjoys walking right on the edge of the water. I pull the whisky out, dig a hole in the wet sand and force the bottle into it at an acute angle so it can easily be spotted. I retreat to a hiding spot in the jungle. As Marmaduke nears, I experience a twang of guilt. He cuts a rather hapless, lonely figure. His career, if not over, is definitely in decline and my little plan, if it plays out, will not help his comeback one little bit. But the die is cast... it's either us or them who go home today, and I need to give us an advantage.

As he nears the bottle, I become nervous. *Come on, come on, that's right, keep looking down.* Damn it! He's walked right past the bottle. Maybe he'll spot it on the way back? I should have left it in plain sight instead of half-burying it. No, wait! He's stopped.

Almost as an afterthought, he turns. His face is creased, confused. He totters back a few steps and squats. His eyebrows arch as a smile melts across his face. He nervously scans the beach in all directions before pulling the bottle from the wet sand. As a wave languidly washes up the beach, he rinses his prized possession in the water then unscrews the cap. There's a pause in proceedings; I assume he's wrestling with his demons.

What's stronger—logic and reasoning or addiction? The top of the bottle touches his lips as he takes a healthy gulp of whisky. He re-screws the cap back onto the bottle. I think he's gone to heaven and back. He drops the bottle into his bag, turns on his heels and sets off back towards his camp. My mission is accomplished, albeit with a heavy slug of remorse.

⤜⤜⤜ ⤛⤛⤛

We are in the headmaster's office, not literally but figuratively. We are lined up near the challenge zones as Jerry tries to throw his weight around. It transpires Castaway Central had a break in two nights ago. I'm appalled and outraged to think we have cheats on the island. What is the world coming to?

Jerry is very coy about exactly what was stolen. The culprits have two options. One—they own up and will be expelled from the show, immediately, or two—Jerry *will* find out who the thieves are, and they will be expelled from the show, immediately. As far as incentives go, there's not much on offer. His mood is dark, and it's not helped by the fact the Celebrity Chefs are missing in action.

'Would anyone like to step forward and own up?' he barks as he parades down the line up of three teams, holding his trusty cane behind his back like a Sergeant Major. He quickly strides past the Weathergirls and the Entrepreneurs but slows to a snail's pace as he confronts our team, eyeballing us intently. 'I see, it's like that, is it?'

'We can't own up to something we haven't done,' Geordie says.

'Jerry, if I could say something?' Piers Conrad breaks rank and moves forward.

'Yes, what is it, Piers?' Jerry snaps.

'I'd say it's perfectly obvious who the culprits are.' He sneers at me.

'Really? Please elaborate.'

'The best way to break into Castaway Central without being noticed would be to cause a diversion.' Jerry stops dead in his tracks, raises one eyebrow and glares at the four of us furiously.

'Hmm... quite.'

'A diversion such as... someone drowning, perhaps.' There's an unwelcome silence as I'm transported back to the real headmaster's office of thirty years ago. I'll no longer be bullied and browbeaten by men like these... those days are long gone. I'll have a voice.

I speak up. 'Alternatively, if an opportunist witnessed a near drowning episode, it would provide them with the perfect cover for them to stage the break in without the finger of suspicion being pointed their way.'

Jerry taps the top of his cane against his pursed lips. 'Possibly,' he replies cautiously, now fixing his attention back onto Piers and the other entrepreneurs.

'You have over two hundred crew stationed here,' Geordie begins. 'It could have been any one of them. Why would you assume it would be one of the contestants?'

'Because of the things which were taken, that's why,' Jerry snarls.

'Which were?' Robbo asks.

'Things...' is his cryptic reply. He's distracted as he pulls his walkie-talkie from his lapel. 'Where are those damn Chefs! Come in Security Team 1— over.' The radio crackles into life as Stu, the security guard, returns fire.

'Security Team 1—over.'

'Are you at the Rock Stars camp yet?'

'Yes, Jerry. I've given it a thorough search. It's clean.'

'Come in Security Team 2—over.'

'Security Team 2—over.'

'Have you reached the Chefs camp yet?'

'About two minutes away Jerry—over.'

'Have you seen any of them? Over.'

'Yes, Marmaduke Smythe was heading to the games zone. He should be there any minute. He was in a terrible state. There seems to have been an incident back at the camp. Over.'

'What sort of incident? Over.'

'He was hard to understand. Screaming and slurring his words. But he said there's been...' A pregnant pause follows.

'Yes... what? Been a what?'

'Ahem, a murder. Unless Marmaduke suffers from a cognitive impairment, I'd say he was roaring drunk. Over.' The conversation is brought to an abrupt end as a scream in the distance makes everyone spin around.

'Shit the bed,' Robbo murmurs in disbelief. Marmaduke is running towards the group screaming and shouting incoherently as he staggers and stumbles from side to side. Most disconcertingly of all, he's completely stark bollock naked, well, apart from the near empty whisky bottle he's clutching.

'Get me off this island at once!' he screams in Jerry's face. 'I won't stay a moment longer. There's been a murder I tell you, a murder!'

'Marmaduke, calm down,' Jerry pleads as he grabs a towel and hands it to him to cover his modesty. Marmaduke tosses the towel into the air with contempt, knocks back the last of the whisky then turns tail and sprints towards the sea, screeching.

'Murder! Murder! Murder!' Jerry nods to some of the crew who chase after him. There's stunned silence.

'The things which were stolen the other night... it didn't include a bottle of whisky, did it?' I politely enquire. Jerry takes a moment to compose himself. He coughs, embarrassed.

'I owe you all an apology,' he whispers to us.

'Apology accepted. Although, next time get your facts right before you go besmirching people's characters,' Geordie says with a hurt expression worthy of an Oscar.

'Is the elimination challenge between the Rock Stars and the Chefs still going ahead?' I ask in my most innocent voice.

'Ahem... no. Under the circumstances, you shall pass through to the next round by default,' Jerry replies as he removes his cravat and uses it to wipe his sweaty balding head.

⇶⇶ ⇷⇷

Robbo's nobbled the camera again as I prepare lunch. Rice, peas, lentils, and sweetcorn, laced with chilli flakes, a good dash of our homemade sea salt and a beef stock cube which I've told Flaky is vegetable based. The air thuds with a recurring sonic boom, causing a pressure displacement as Geordie enters camp.

'Did you find out what happened?' I ask.

'Aye, storm in a teacup. Marmaduke got shit-faced on the whisky, runs into camp, and starts to throw everything on the fire. Keith, Brody and Xavier tried to restrain him, and Xavier got a knife in the arse cheek and to his upper arm.'

'How?'

'Brody was peeling a walnut at the time.' Geordie says it in such a matter-of-the-fact way I'm momentarily blindsided.

'Peeling a walnut?' Robbo quizzes. He's as perplexed as I am.

'Aye. That's what he said.'

'How the hell do you peel a walnut?'

'With a very sharp knife I assume—hence the deep lacerations. You know what celeb chefs are like. They're all highly strung. What's for lunch?'

'A savoury rice dish,' I say as I give the pan a stir.

'Nice. The chopper is about to take off now. In a few hours' time, they'll all be in a luxury 5-star hotel in Dubai for the night... well, apart from Xavier... I think he'll need hospital treatment. Oh, and they put Marmaduke under heavy sedation. They classified him as a possible troublemaker on the chopper. Xavier was accusing Brody of deliberate grievous bodily harm. Said he was going to sue him for every penny he's got.'

'And how were Brody and Keth... I mean Keith?'

'Brody—laissez-faire. Keith—world-weary, tired, exasperated. Oh, by the way, I had a word with Brody. The Tuscany holiday is still on. Next summer, two weeks in his villa. He also said to bring our wives and kids along. *We'll have a ball.'*

Chapter 21

Back In Yorkshire—Part 2

The women are sitting in their chairs, excited, scared, enthralled.

'I've seen the trailers for tonight's show,' Julie begins. 'Something bad has happened.'

'I haven't seen them,' Jackie says. 'What do you mean, something bad has happened?'

Julie takes a gulp of white wine and places her glass on the table. 'It shows our boys, the Rock Stars, then the Celebrity chefs... and then...'

'Then what?' Fiona asks.

'Then a voiceover says, the first elimination challenge is thrown into chaos. You won't believe what you are about to see... and that sort of nonsense, you know with the deep, slow, rasping voice.'

'Not the deep voiceover. I can't bear it,' Jackie says.

'If something terrible had happened, I'm sure someone from the show would have been in touch with us by now,' Gillian comments.

'Shut up, it's starting!' Fiona exclaims as I Will Survive blares out from the speakers. Felix Cain's blemish-free face fills the screen. He's in a sombre mood.

"Hello, Felix Cain here. Today was supposed to be the first elimination challenge between the Rock Stars and the Celebrity Chefs. However, the elimination challenge never took place because of the scenes you are about to witness. Scenes which will shock you to your very core. Our camp cameras recorded events, live, as they unfolded. And a warning; some viewers may find the following footage distressing and disturbing. They contain images of nudity and violence."

'Oh, my God!' Julie cries. 'I've got a bad feeling about this. There's going to be a big bust-up, I can feel it in my water. It's bound to be our lot.'

'We should never have voted for them to take part in the damned show. It's all our fault,' Fiona moans sporting a grave expression.

'If you remember rightly, Will was always dead-set against the proposition. He said it would end in tears. And for the record, I abstained from the vote,' Gillian says.

'Oh, aren't you Miss Goody Two-shoes!' Fiona replies snapping at her. Gillian stiffens, taken aback at Fiona's loaded attack.

'Girls, let's just calm down. We don't know what's happened yet. We can save the recriminations until after the show when we've got all the facts,' Jackie advises, playing peacemaker.

The screen splits into two; on the left—the Rock Stars camp. On the right; the Chefs. The scenes from both camps are similar and show nothing untoward. People mooch around going about their daily routine. Firewood is thrown on the fire; water is boiled, and pans and dishes are washed. The contestants from both teams wander in and out of shot.

'There's not much happening,' Julie says. 'It's all pretty boring, really.'

'They're building it up,' Jackie replies. 'With the elimination challenge cancelled they need to find thirty minutes of something to fill the gap.'

'Actually, it's odd,' Gillian says, eyes narrowing as she peers intently at the TV.

'What is?' Jackie asks.

'The Chefs. I can only see three of them.'

'Oh, yes you're right. Who's missing?'

'Well, Brody's sitting on a log holding something. Xavier Pompadour is swinging in his hammock and Keith Patel is writing in his journal,' Fiona adds.

'It's Marmaduke Smythe. He's not there,' Julie says. Felix returns to the screen.

"You're probably wondering what all the fuss is about? Two teams going about their daily chores in relative calm. Join me after the break when what happens next will leave you stunned... and horrified."

'They do this on purpose, so you don't change channels. It bloody pisses me off!' Julie complains. The women refill their glasses and nibble on cheese and biscuits nervously as they await the return of the drama.

"Welcome back as we take you to the camps of the Rock Stars and the Chefs. A seemingly normal, run-of-the-mill morning on I Will Survive."

'Get on with it, you puffed up windbag!' Jackie shouts at the screen.

'Ooh, look, they've got a clock on the top right of the screen now,' Gillian notes. '9:47 am, it says.'

'Christ, give me strength,' Julie whines. 'Now we're having a bloody countdown to the action.'

Another few minutes elapse until the kerfuffle begins. It happens so fast it's over in a flash.

'Was that it?' Jackie cries.

'I don't understand... what happened? I was too busy watching our boys to notice the Chefs,' Gillian says.

'I'm not sure myself. There was a scuffle in the Chef's camp, but I missed most of it,' Fiona adds. Felix returns.

"Missed the action? Don't worry. We will replay the shocking events in slow motion with digital enhancements to improve the quality. Watch carefully."

The split screen disappears as the Chefs camp takes centre stage. Nothing much has changed as Brody sits on a log, Xavier slumps in his hammock and Keith scribbles in his journal. Felix narrates the ensuing action.

"Take a look at the clock on the screen—9:47 am. Another minute elapses as the loudspeaker summons the Rock Stars and the Chefs to the games zone in fifteen minutes for the elimination challenge. At 9:49 am Marmaduke Smythe appears for the first time on the bottom right of your screen. He staggers into camp clutching a near-empty whisky bottle clearly under the influence."

'Where the hell did he get a bottle of whisky from?' Fiona cries.

'Shush!' Julie hisses.

"Marmaduke tosses the whisky bottle onto his hammock and proceeds to run around camp collecting his colleagues' possessions and throwing them onto the fire. Xavier is the first to spot his teammate's erratic behaviour and leaps from his hammock just as Marmaduke snatches Keith's journal and flings it onto the inferno. It's at this point that Keith Patel, and Brody Buchannan—who is busily peeling something, realise there's trouble in the camp."

The camera zooms in on the knife in Brody's hand and a small round object in his other.

'What's he peeling?' Gillian asks.

'I'm not sure?' Jackie begins. 'It looks like a walnut.'

'Don't be ridiculous! Whoever heard of anyone peeling a walnut,' Fiona says with a cackle of laughter.

"As Xavier grabs Marmaduke in a bear hug, Brody leaps to his feet and attempts to rugby tackle Marmaduke to the ground at exactly the same time as Xavier spins him around. As you can see when we zoom in, Brody is still clutching his knife. The knife enters the left buttock cheek of Xavier Pompadour causing him to scream in agony and release Marmaduke. As Keith joins the fray Brody attempts a headlock on Marmaduke but he manages to wriggle free and push Brody away. Brody stumbles backwards and stabs Xavier in the bicep severing the median nerve and the brachial artery. At this moment, Keith takes charge of the situation as he realises urgent attention to Xavier is more important than subduing Marmaduke. As Keith rushes for the first aid kit, Brody applies pressure to the deep wound with his palm, as he's splattered with blood. If they cannot apply a tourniquet quickly enough, Xavier could bleed out. Meanwhile,

Marmaduke has disrobed and thrown his clothes onto the fire while performing an Irish jig and singing "Congratulations" by Cliff Richard.

We apologise for this unbecoming scene. Nude, drunk, disorientated, completely stark staring bonkers, and singing a terrible song, Marmaduke notices his blood-soaked colleagues for the first time and screams, murder! murder! murder! three times before staggering from the camp after retrieving his whisky bottle from the hammock. Keith quickly applies a tourniquet to stem the blood loss. A moment later one of our security guards arrives at the camp and radios for the paramedics. Join me after the break as the aftermath of the saga unfolds."

The women sit in stupefied silence for a while.

'I'm not sure what to say,' Fiona mumbles.

'Do you know what the strangest part was?' Julie questions.

'What?' Gillian replies.

'I think Jackie was right; he was peeling a walnut.'

⋙ ⋘

As the show returns, the cameras focus on the medical helicopter as it descends to the beach. Two paramedics from the show carry a stretcher bearing Xavier Pompadour. He gives a weak smile and a thumbs-up to the cameras as he's lifted into the chopper. In the background is another stretcher being carried but it is unclear who it bears.

'Who the hell's in the other stretcher?' Julie says.

'I'm not sure. They didn't say,' Jackie replies.

'There's Brody and Keith Patel in the background so it must be Marmaduke Smythe. They've probably sedated him. He was off his rocker. I don't think we'll see him on our TV screens again,' Fiona murmurs. The show meanders on for another twenty minutes with filler material to make up for the cancelled challenge. As it reaches its anti-climax Felix holds court as he explains the next elimination challenge in two days' time. The Rock Stars, the Weathergirls and the Entrepreneurs are lined up next to each other.

"After almost four weeks and twelve challenges we are now entering the finale. Just four days are left, and two more challenges will determine who is the inaugural winner of Celebrity I Will Survive. The next challenge will be the toughest yet—The Skull Mountain Death Run—the last of the leaderboard challenges. One team *will* be going home."

The camera pans away to the dormant volcano in the background, which looks nothing like a skull. Felix is energised as he explains the rules.

"It will be a staggered start. Each team will begin their challenge fifteen minutes apart. It's a six-mile hike to the top of the mountain where you will find a treasure chest marked with your team colours. The chest holds a key. You must retrieve the key, make your way back down the mountain and place the key in the clock to stop the timer."

The camera zooms in on three brightly coloured giant clocks mounted on poles in the sand.

"The fastest team will earn thirty points on the leaderboard. The second team, fifteen points. The team who comes last—nothing."

'Oh, well, that's our boys out,' Julie says with a sigh. The vision homes in on the Rock Stars.

'They're actually looking very rugged and handsome,' Fiona says.

'Yes, they look like real men for a change,' Jackie comments.

'I think Will's beard really suits him,' Gillian adds. Jackie and Fiona exchange glances.

"Rock Stars, I can't over emphasise the enormity of the challenge you're up against. You are thirty points adrift of the Entrepreneurs who are in second place. To make it to the final not only must you win the race, but the Entrepreneurs would need to finish last. Even *then* it would only bring you level with them on points, which would mean a sudden death shootout."

The boys nod thoughtfully as the camera pans to a sneering Piers Conrad.

'Oh, look at the smarmy get!' Julie cries. 'He makes my skin crawl.'

'What are the odds girls?' Jackie says as she refills everyone's champagne glasses.

'Snowball and hell come to mind,' Fiona says laughing.

'About as much chance as a one-legged man in an arse kicking contest,' Julie says.

'I think you're all being a little unfair on the boys,' Gillian declares.

'Face facts,' Jackie begins, 'those Weathergirls are super fit, they haven't got an ounce of fat on them... bitches. There's no way our lot are going to be faster than them.'

Felix continues as he turns to the Weathergirls.

"Ladies, you are already into the final. Even if you come last, you can't be overhauled on the leaderboard."

The camera focuses on the Entrepreneurs.

"Gentlemen, your destiny is in your hands. The challenge is yours to lose. The weather is forecast for eighty percent humidity with the temperature in the mid-thirties. Teams, I suggest you retire to your camps, rest, eat, and rehydrate. The Skull Mountain challenge will begin at 9:15 am in two days' time. Good luck everyone!"

Chapter 22

Skull Mountain

Robbo's suffering from constipation again.

'Have you taken the laxatives you got from the doctor?' Flaky asks in a head-masterly fashion.

'Taken the whole packet in three days. Nothing.'

'Do you mind not speaking about constipation while I'm eating,' Geordie yells as he shovels rice into his mouth. He throws Robbo and Flaky a disgusted look. They both ignore him.

'You need to get it sorted and quickly. Are you in any pain?' Flaky enquires.

'No. Not really. I just feel bloated.'

'When was the last time you passed a motion?'

'About four days ago,'

'For God's sake,' Geordie mumbles through a mouthful of rice.

'And what was the consistency?'

'It was like shitting a brick.'

'I'm warning you two!'

'Hmm...' Flaky ponders. 'Will, can you look up constipation in your survival handbook?' I grab the manual and scan the index. 'It can be deadly if not treated,' Flaky adds.

'Deadly!' Robbo cries, alarmed. 'I've never heard of anyone dying of constipation. You're overreacting.' I flick to the appropriate page.

'Well, what does it say?' Flaky asks.

'Erm... let me see. Eat plenty of roughage, keep your hydration levels high, blah, blah, blah. Oh, hang on. It says here that severe cases of faecal impaction can lead to serious illness or even death if not treated in a timely manner.'

'Told you so,' Flaky says triumphantly. 'Any quick solutions to the problem?'

'Hang on... yes. Administer an enema.'

'Right, that's it!' Geordie explodes as he throws his remaining rice onto the ground. Dorothy swoops down and pecks at the offering. 'Thank you very much for putting me off my food.'

'There's no way I'm having an enema,' Robbo wails. 'Over my dead body.'

'If you refuse an enema, then it may *be* over your dead body. Stop being so bloody squeamish. It's a medical problem with a viable solution.'

'It says here to heat some water until it's warm to tepid. Put it in a drinks bottle, attach a rubber tube to the top, lie on the ground, insert the tube into the anus then squeeze the bottle. Hold it in for as long as possible. Repeat until the impaction softens and a stool can be passed.'

'Give me strength,' Geordie grumbles. Flaky is already filling a drinks bottle with water from a pan.

'Lie face down in your hammock and drop your pants,' Flaky orders.

'Hang on a minute, aren't we all being a little hasty?' Robbo pleads. 'And we don't have a rubber tube, anyway.'

'We'll improvise.'

'How?'

'I'll stick the top of the bottle up your anus.'

'Like hell, you will!'

'Don't argue! Just do as I say!' Flaky yells.

'He's right, Robbo. Better out than in. The longer you leave it, the worse it's going to become. Like a logjam,' I encourage.

'It's funny how none of the rest of us has suffered from it,' Geordie declares.

'Luck of the draw, I guess,' Robbo states forlornly as he clambers reluctantly into his hammock.

'Luck, my sweet arse,' Geordie replies.'

'What do you mean?' Robbo asks.

'I'll tell you what I mean; you're not active enough. You spend half your time swinging in that bloody cot. Even when you are up and about you move at the speed of a glacier. You've no vim and vigour. You've always been the same.' Flaky screws the top on the bottle and makes his way over to Robbo.

'Right, on your front, pants down,' he demands.

'Strewth, this is the most undignified thing I've ever gone through,' he murmurs as he rolls onto his stomach and pulls his shorts down.

'Stop your moaning,' Flaky says. 'If you could spread your buttocks... let the dog, see the rabbit.'

'Christ,' Geordie mutters. 'I'll give you one thing, Flaky; you must have an iron clad constitution. There's no way I could stare at Robbo's rusty bullet hole let alone go anywhere near it.'

'Okay, brace yourself, Robbo.' Flaky forcefully rams the bottle between the spreadeagled cheeks. Robbo emits a painful cry.

'Hells bells! Could you have not used some lubrication?'

'Spoken like a true virgin,' Geordie sniggers.

'It's no good,' Flaky says as he removes the bottle. 'The water's not going up, it's leaking out.'

'Hi, lads... security,' Stu's voice echoes out as he slopes into camp. He stares at the scene in front of him, bewildered, mouth open, stunned into silence.

'Oh, hi Stu,' Flaky replies nonchalantly as he glances over his shoulder. 'Hold tight, Robbo. I need to get this bottle a lot deeper into your anus if you want to experience some relief.'

'Are you enjoying this?' Robbo mumbles into the canvas hammock. Stu edges backwards, eyes on stalks.

'I think I may have to push and pull it out a few times. Geordie, Will, can you please fill some more bottles? We need to get a lot more into him. It needs to be a team effort.' Stu looks like he could pass out at any moment.

'Did you want us for something, Stu?' I ask.

'What? No... no, it can wait. It's not important!' Robbo's scream reverberates around the campsite, startling the sleeping birdlife. Stu turns on his heels and scampers off through the bushes.

⋙ ⋘

Night is drawing in as I laze on my hammock. I'm drowsy from the crackle of the fire and smoke. The boys are chatting for a change instead of bickering. The cooing of Dorothy soothes me as I rest my eyes. Flaky is preparing our meal.

'I guess this may be our last supper, so to speak,' Flaky says softly.

'Aye, I suppose you're right. We've tried our best but failed. I don't mind losing to the Weathergirls but to be beaten by the Entrepreneurs is another thing,' Geordie comments.

'We haven't just failed... we've failed miserably,' Robbo adds mournfully.

'What do you mean?' Geordie enquires.

'We're only here by default. If Brody Buchannan hadn't gone on a knife rampage and Marmaduke Smythe hadn't got hammered, we might have been kicked out two days ago.'

'Aye, I suppose you're right. Although, who's to say we wouldn't have beaten the chefs in the elimination round.'

'In a way, I'm going to miss this place,' Flaky reflects. 'I know we've had our difficulties and disagreements along the way.'

'The master of understatement,' Geordie scoffs. Flaky ignores him and continues.

'But we have come through it. I think it has made us all better people overall. Spiritually, I've grown, I'm stronger now. I must confess, my faith was sorely tested, but it just goes to show the tenacity and endurance of the human spirit.'

'Any last-minute master plans?' Robbo asks me. I reluctantly turn my head and gaze at him as he puffs away on a massive reefer.

'No. There's no way out of this one. I'm gone. Done and dusted. The tank is empty.'

'Any regrets?' Geordie asks.

'A few, but one especially.'

'Don't tell me... the Entrepreneurs?'

'No, not them as a team. The other three are decent enough guys. But... Piers Conrad, he's my biggest regret. I wanted to wipe the oily smile off his face.'

'Aye, the man's a walking arsehole.'

We sit in silence as we finish our supper. Flaky gathers the pots together and scrapes out a few remnants of rice onto the ground.

'Here you go, Dorothy,' he says. The bird flutters down from its perch and feeds on the offering. 'I'm going to miss her,' he says with a sad expression.

'Take her with you,' Robbo suggests.

Flaky looks at him indignantly. 'Don't be bloody stupid. What are Customs going to say when I pull a pigeon, native to the tropics, from my backpack?'

'Tell them it's a carrier pigeon which got lost.'

'Buffoon.'

I climb into my hammock and close my eyes as sleep washes over me.

My vivid dream ends as I slip back into reality. I stare up at the gently swaying canopy. It's early morning. The boys are still asleep. Fragments of my night-time reverie tumble back into my mind. I go over and over them, putting together the pieces like a cerebral jigsaw puzzle. After twenty minutes of deep thought, I leap from my hammock.

'Lads, wake up!' I shout excitedly, energised. They all groggily lift their heads and stare at me.

'Fuck me drunk!' Geordie exclaims. 'What time is it? Have you shit the bed?'

Robbo groans. 'Don't tell me; you've come up with a cunning master plan?'

'Robbo, my little sheep worrier, this is *the* most cunningly cunning of all master plans since Count Cunny Cunningham of Canny Castle invented the drawbridge.'

'Here we go,' Flaky yawns with a definite lack of enthusiasm. 'Let's hear it.'

➳➳➳ ⥽⥽⥽

It's nudged past 9 am as I meander over to the start of the Skull Mountain challenge. The two other teams are already there, mulling around. The crew is busy tending to their equipment as Jerry offers advice to them. Felix is chatting with the Weathergirls. The Entrepreneurs are huddled in a circle talking eagerly in low voices. Piers glances over his shoulder as he spies me and sneers. Jerry breaks off from directing the crew and saunters over in his grey safari suit topped with a scarlet polka dot cravat.

'Ah, Will, you're cutting it fine, aren't you?'

'You said 9:15. Plenty of time.'

'Where are the others?'

'Still asleep back at camp.'

His brow furrows. 'Is this some sort of joke?' he cries drawing attention from all around.

'No. No joke. They're conserving their energy for the final leg.' A small crowd has now gathered around us.

'Are you telling me you aim to run to the top of Skull Mountain, retrieve the key, and run all the way back down again, by yourself?' *There won't be much running!*

'Yes.' There're muted chuckles from the Entrepreneurs and worried frowns from the Weathergirls.

'But it's madness! Do you understand the full enormity of the challenge at hand?'

'Yes. Get to the summit, grab the key, come back down, and stop the clock. Have I missed anything?' Piers edges forward bearing a smarmy all-knowing smile.

'Pathetic! Typical of your type. You know you can't win so you throw the towel in. Pick up your bat and ball and sulk off home.' If he says, "my type" one more time, I swear I'm going to swing for the piss stain.

'We haven't thrown the towel in. We'll win. And your lot certainly won't beat the girls, which means we'll be on equal points.'

'And a shoot-out challenge,' Chloe adds smiling sweetly. I fix Piers with a steely glare. He chuckles for a moment until he recognises I'm being serious. He turns to Jerry.

'Jerry, I smell a rat. Can you please go over the rules again so there can be no misunderstandings? I don't want his shower going through by default again.'

Jerry puffs his chest out and stands tall. 'Certainly. It's quite simple. Retrieve the key from the treasure chest on top of Skull Mountain, place it in the clock to stop the timer and once all the teams have completed the challenge, Felix and I will calculate the times it took each team to complete the task.

It's a staggered start because of the narrowness of the track. We didn't want twelve challengers all jostling and barging their way past one another in case it led to injury or foul play. As the Rock Stars are bottom of the leaderboard, they set off first. After fifteen minutes, the Entrepreneurs set off followed fifteen minutes later by the Weathergirls. And those are the rules. There's nothing to stop one individual trying to cover the course by themselves if they're foolhardy enough to try it.'

Piers smiles. 'Good. So, I was right. They have thrown the towel in.'

I adjust the straps on my backpack and click the front strap together as Jerry gives us all one last sermon.

'Listen up guys and girls. Because of the difficult and dangerous terrain, we will be using drones to capture most of the footage. We have two paramedics who will set off after the Weathergirls have departed. If you sustain an injury, stay put and help won't be too far away. It's another warm and humid day so I hope you've all brought plenty of water with you. Two minutes, Will, and you're set to go.'

'Good luck, loser, you're going to need it,' Piers says followed by a hollow laugh. Chloe wanders over to me.

'Will, this is going to be gruelling. Don't push yourself too hard... I don't want anything to happen to you. You've got nothing to be ashamed of in getting eliminated. You've had a terrible run of luck and I suppose what happened between us didn't help team morale, either.' She takes my hand and gives it a squeeze.

'Don't worry about me. I'll be fine. What's your plan of attack?'

'We set off as a team and once we've covered about a mile, I'm going to stop and conserve my energy. I'm the fastest over a short distance so I'll do the last leg back to the finishing line. The others will continue up the mountain. Every couple of miles, one will stop. Lucy has done marathons in the past, so she'll be the one to head to the summit. On her way back down, she'll hand the key on. It's kind of like a relay, with the key as the baton.'

'Sounds like a smart plan.'

'There's no other way to do it.'

'Hmm...' She leans in to give me a kiss, but I pull away. Her wounded frown tears at my heart. 'Cameras everywhere,' I offer weakly.

She blinks. 'Of course. Well, good luck and be careful.'

'Yes, and same to you.'

'Will, if you'd like to make your way to the starting line,' Jerry says. 'On the firing of the pistol, you can begin the Skull Mountain Death Run.' Felix is already in front of a camera crew explaining the challenge to the viewers back home. As the pistol cracks, I set off at a gentle jog along the sandy track to the sound of Gloria singing her song again.

Chapter 23

A Tough Ask

As soon as I round the first bend, and check I'm out of sight, I slow to a steady walk; there's no point overdoing things. I may have been a bit too cocky with everyone. There's no guarantee the plan will work. There is a myriad of possibilities which could unravel the strategy. I could end up looking like a right idiot. But the fact is, if we'd tackled the challenge the same ways as the others, we'd have finished second at best, and would be eliminated. I jog on for another ten minutes fighting my turmoil and the possible consequences of losing.

The whip-like snap of the starting gun ends my negative thoughts. I pull a bottle of water out and take a thirsty gulp as a drone circles high overhead. I've already risen some distance up the hill and can see the throng of competitors and crew below. I stare up at Skull Mountain. I'm not sure it can really be called a mountain. It's an ancient dormant volcano. An image of Inglegor Pike, in the Dales, flashes across my mind. Melancholia visits me again like a stray dog searching for a home. *Come on, Will. One last push. It will soon be over—for better or for worse.*

I check my watch. I've been going for nearly thirty minutes and the first challenger is approaching at a steady click behind me. It's Cliff Zimmerman, another marathon runner. As he passes by, sweating profusely he offers me good luck. It's not long before Jasper Ogilvy from the Entrepreneurs bears down on me. I sit down on a boulder and take a swig of water as he nears. He's panting hard as he reaches me. I hold out the bottle for him.

'No thanks,' he says as he stops and takes his pack off. 'You'll need it for yourself.' He leans against the rock and pulls water from his bag. 'Christ, this is gruelling.'

'Can I ask you a question?' I say as he glugs his water down.

'Sure. Fire away?'

'What do you think of Piers?'

A wry smile spreads across his face. 'Is this a fishing trip?'

'No. You're a successful entrepreneur, I just wondered what people from your background thought of him.'

'You want the truth?'

'Yes.'

'I despise the man, as do the other two, Cliff and Dick.'

'Why?'

He puts his bottle away and hoists his backpack over his shoulders. 'He's arrogant, conceited, bigoted, and sexist. But what really riles me is his belief his wealth somehow makes his opinions more valid. He assumes the more wealth you have, the more important your view must be. He thinks money equals respect. It doesn't. Respect equals respect. Why do you ask?'

'What's the old quote; know thy enemy and know yourself.'

'Hmm... a quote attributed to Sun Tzu. I understand you two don't get along, but you want to watch out for Piers Conrad. He's a ruthless bugger and vindictive. I wouldn't push him too far.'

'I'm a big boy. I can look after myself.' He sets off up the hill, then stops and turns to me.

'The wise warrior avoids the battle... that's another Sun Tzu quote.'

＊＊＊

As I navigate a steep, rocky outcrop, I stop to admire the views. The ocean shimmers aqua blue under a ruthless sun. Birds ride thermals; palms sway, dreamily in a balmy, lethargic breeze. The smell of wild garlic and aromatic herbs reminds me of my visits to Greece. I'm going to need a holiday after this. A voice from behind startles me.

'Well, well, well... it's the loafer, the quitter, the loser. What an unpleasant surprise.'

'Piers Condom, funny seeing you here. You look hot, bloated and sweaty, although to be fair, it is your normal disposition.'

He puffs and pants his way towards me. 'Have you no shame, man? There's not an ounce of self-worth or honour in you. Imagine how your family and friends will feel when they see this back home. The ignominy and disappointment they'll have to endure. You know what they say?'

'No, but I'm sure you're going to enlighten me.'

'When the going gets tough the tough get going and the weak go home.'

'Do you act stupid, or does it come naturally? I told you, we're not going home... not today, anyway.'

He drops to his haunches as he draws deep breaths. 'Stop speaking like a bloody fool, Will. You're clearly delusional. Cliff and Jasper have already passed you and two of the Weathergirls are only five minutes behind. You're finished, accept it. I suppose your only redeeming feature is you volunteered to take part in the challenge at all, unlike your feckless friends... if you can call them friends.' He stands and places his hands on his waist as he stares at me.

I jab my finger towards him. 'At least I have some friends. And for your information, they'd go to the ends of the earth for me, and I for them.'

'But not up Skull Mountain for you, it appears.'

'Like I said. They'll be doing the last leg.'

'Of course, they will. It's disappointing but to be expected, I suppose. A complete lack of moral fibre. The apple doesn't fall far from the tree. Your type come from a lengthy line of failures. As I said before, it's built into your genes.'

He's said it again! I raise my fist to him. 'I'm not a violent man, but I could make an exception in your case. You need to be careful what you say. You're standing on the edge of a hundred-foot drop.'

He glances nervously over his shoulder. 'You wouldn't have the balls,' he says, without much certainty.

'Wouldn't I? There's no one around, no cameras at the moment. It's perfectly plausible a slightly rotund, middle-aged man on a strength sapping challenge could lose his footing and plummet to his death.'

A flicker of fear dashes across his face. He stares up at the sky and smiles. 'Unfortunately, for you, we are on camera.' I peer up at the drone as it zooms down from high above. He moves away from the edge and sits on a boulder. 'What is it you lot do?'

'You know what we do. We're musicians, songwriters.'

'Yes, but what do you really do? I'll tell you the answer, shall I? You *do* nothing, you *change* nothing.'

'Not true.'

'Do you still harbour fanciful notions music can change the world? Because if you do, you're a lot dumber than you first appear.'

'No. I realised a long time ago it can't change the world. It can't change governments or start a revolution. But it can change individuals. As all art forms can.'

He snorts derisively. 'Poppycock! Wishy-washy, neo-liberal, hippy hogwash.'

'Art may be closed off to a mind like yours. A mind that is cold, hardened and only sees value in something if it has a price tag. But to most of humanity art offers them a glimpse into a different world. A world of wonder and beauty. A place where they can find solace, or happiness, even if only for a few minutes each day. Without art all that's left is the daily grind, monotony, monolithic corporations and capitalist or communist doctrines, insatiable soul vampires. I feel sorry for you. I'd hate to live in your world. It would be an endless road of beige.'

'Ha! No need to feel sorry for me. I could buy and sell you a hundred times over.'

'No, you couldn't. I'm not for sale.'

He takes a grubby handkerchief from his pocket and mops his brow. 'Fool. Everyone is for sale. It's simply a matter of finding their price.'

'Do you ever think about death, Piers?'

'What sort of damn fool question is that?'

'I'll rephrase it. Do you ever ponder your own mortality?'

'Not particularly. I'm not one for navel gazing or introspection.'

'Okay, well here's a little story. There was once a wealthy man, so wealthy he couldn't possibly hope to spend all his money before he died. Then one day he did die. He had no wife, no children, no friends. After a few weeks, most people had forgotten he had ever existed.'

He slowly claps his hands. 'Bravo! What a riveting tale. Here's another little fable. There was once a musician, not very wealthy, he died, and everyone forgot about him.'

I throw my pack on. 'Except they didn't forget about him, did they? Same as the world hasn't forgotten about Elvis, or Lennon, or Beethoven, Mozart, Buddy Holly. The artist has a legacy which will live on for as long as humanity exists. The businessman has death duties. I'll see you later.' I turn to tackle a steep incline.

'The next time I see you will be at your elimination farewell. Enjoy your walk! I'll be putting my feet up for the next hour or so.'

⟶≫⟩ ⟨≪⟵

I am the last contestant to reach the summit. Three coloured treasure chests sit idly on the ground. Two have their lids in the upright position. I gaze down upon the rocky path I've climbed and watch streaks of blue, and green as the challengers descend the mountain. Some saunter, as their part of the relay is over. Others jog on at a steady pace. I amble over to the chest, remove my backpack, and carefully place it on the ground. I pull at the lid, but it's locked with a combination padlock. *Shit, we've been nobbled again!* But as I glance at the two other chests lined up alongside, I notice they all have padlocks attached to them, only theirs are open. The lid has some writing on it covered with a bit of dry dirt. I brush it aside. Great! There are two riddles scrawled into the wood.

Riddle Me This (come on, you didn't think it would be straightforward, did you?)Solve the riddles to unlock the padlock and open the chest but don't waste time. Find your key by thinking outside the box.

One: 16, 06, 68, 88, ?, 98. What does "?" equal?

Two: "Two years ago, I was three times as old as my younger brother. In three years I will be twice as old. How old am I now?"

Shiver me timbers and strike a light! I need this like a hole in the head. Fatigued and dispirited, I slump down and lean up against the box. I don't have the mental capacity to tackle a riddle. I peek inside my backpack... all is good. Thirstily, I gulp down more water and throw a handful of sultanas into my mouth. Within a few minutes I revive as the sugar galvanises my thought processes. There are two options; fiddle about with the combinations in the hope I stumble upon the correct numbers or try to solve the damn riddles. I study the conundrums again. The first one is not a mathematical equation, it's about lateral thinking. I'll come back to that one later.

'Two years ago, I was three times as old as my younger brother. In three years I will be twice as old. How old am I now?' I pick up a stick and scratch the number "3" into the ground then set to work. After a minute of calculations, I realise my first attempt is wrong. But it's a promising start. Number "4" falls at the first hurdle unless I start getting into fractions, so I move onto number "5". I waste another ten minutes on the stupid bloody puzzle. I think I may have it! The elder brother is 17!

Right, back to the first clue. *Come on... don't look at the value of the numbers, study the sequence.* Eureka! Spin the numbers upside down and they read; 91, 90, 89, 88, ?, 86. The missing number is 87 which means the padlock's combination is 8717. My trembling fingers turn the dials, and the lock clicks open. I throw the lid up and stare at a casket full of red plastic balls.

'Oh, come on, give me a break.' I fumble around frantically as time ticks by. I upend the chest sending an avalanche of balls bouncing across the rocky summit. I hope someone's going to clean this mess up. The key is not there. I'm becoming desperate. I can already see the giant, gloating sneer on Piers Conrad's repulsive mug. I slam the lid shut and read the riddle again.

Solve the riddles to unlock the padlock and open the chest but don't waste time. Find your key by thinking outside the box.

'You bloody smartarses!' I yell as I leap to my feet and walk around the box. Taped to the back of the chest is the key. What a waste of time! Well, they did warn me. I pull a piece of twine from my pocket, thread it through the eyelet of the key and tie a secure knot. Carefully unzipping my backpack, I lift Dorothy out, holding her steadily with both hands. She coos gently as I plant a tender kiss on her head.

'There, there, Dorothy. You'll soon be back home,' I whisper as I place her firmly under my arm. I extract her left leg, place the key alongside it and use the remaining twine to wrap around her leg and the key five or six times before securing it with two half-hitches. Luckily, the key is only a few inches long. Whirring distracts me as I spin around. The sight gives me a start. It's a bloody drone, about six feet off the ground slowly edging towards us. The thing gives me the creeps; it's like an alien spaceship. I hold Dorothy up in dramatic fashion and throw her into the air. She lists badly to the left for a moment, flapping erratically before righting herself and accelerating away. Unfortunately, the drone flies after her. Both disappear into the distance. At least she's heading in the right direction.

I take a good swig of water and throw my pack on. As I near the edge of the summit, my heart sinks. Dorothy whizzes past me about twelve feet up. Close behind her is the drone. The bird obviously thinks the drone is a predator. She throws a number of sharp turns left and right, does a 180 and heads back towards me. The drone is left bamboozled and hovers as it spins around in a circle trying to locate the bird. Dorothy swoops down towards me, and I have to take evasive action. Her wings ruffle my hair. I'm not sure if it was an affectionate flyover or whether she's bloody pissed off with me.

Either way, she's speeding home and will be back at camp before any of the challengers are even halfway down the mountain.

Chapter 24

Meltdown

I make steady progress down the rock-strewn track thanks to gravity and the rapidly falling temperature. I gaze out at the horizon; dark grey, ominous clouds are forming high in the stratosphere. Bad weather is brewing.

I'm pleasantly surprised as I walk into camp. The fire is full of embers. Geordie is attending to a pan of food. Flaky is basket weaving and Robbo is stitching up holes in the badminton fishing net. Geordie springs from his haunches as he spots me.

'Aha! The wandering minstrel returns. What a bloody master plan, Billy Boy! Here you go, get this into you,' he says as he hands me a pan of rice, lentils, and beans, then slaps me on the back. 'No doubt we'll be summoned to the games zone in the next hour or two. We've all eaten and had a good snooze already. Refreshed and ready to go. Make sure you get a good litre of water into you after your food then get your head down for an hour's kip. You need to recharge your batteries.' I tuck into the food with abandonment, only stopping occasionally to slurp on tepid, but blessed water. Halfway through I finally find the energy to question them.

'How did it all go?'

'It ran like clockwork,' Flaky replies. 'Dorothy fluttered up to her perch. I placed some sultanas and a small bowl of fresh water on the ground, and she came for a feed. I gave her a few minutes to recuperate from her ordeal, removed the key and gave it to Geordie.'

'I sauntered along the track until I reached the beach where I handed it to Robbo,' Geordie continues. I glance at Robbo.

'All cool. Half walked, half jogged, until I reached the games zone. Put the key in the clock and stopped it. Did a few words with Felix with the cameras rolling, then headed back here,' he says without a care in the world.

'Did you spot any of the other teams?'

'Not sure. As I was ushered away from the zone, I did notice one figure way up the beach, but I couldn't really tell who it was.'

'Male or female?'

'At a guess, I'd say female.'

'Yes!' I shout spluttering rice and lentils everywhere. 'It could have been Chloe! She said she was going to do the last leg.'

'Let's not get overexcited, Will,' Flaky begins. 'We don't really know who has won until it's announced.'

'Aye, he's right, Bill. And we've been set up to fail before. Let's play it cool.'

'Yes, you're right.' I finish the meal, knock down the water then retire to my hammock. As I drift into a coma, all I can hear is the crackle of the campfire, the murmur of the ocean and Dorothy's gentle cooing. It's perfect.

⤜⤜⤜ ⤛⤛⤛

The song, the song, the bloody, song! It wakes me again. It's a recurring nightmare. I've got nothing against Gloria, but you can become cheesed off with anything if you're subjected to it enough times, well... apart from Guinness and sex, although not at the same time.

We are gathered at the games zone awaiting the results as the production team sort out some technical issues. All three groups are huddled together. I've told the boys to wear their best poker faces until the winner is announced. I want to savour this moment... the look on Piers Conrad's face. I glance over at him, and he grins back as he gives me a tiny backward wave, indicating it's time for me to leave. What is it they say; revenge is a dish best served cold.

We line up in our respective teams as the cameras begin to record and Felix goes through his spiel like a hyperventilating goose. A camera crew moves in for close ups of the contestants.

'This was an elimination challenge,' Felix says in a grave tone, like a judge handing out a death sentence. 'The Weathergirls were already safe with an unassailable lead,' he says strolling up and down the line of women. 'This challenge was always going to be a contest between the Rock Stars and the Entrepreneurs.

For the Rock Stars to remain in the game they had to win the Skull Mountain challenge and the Entrepreneurs would need to finish last. And even then,' he shouts with a dramatic flourish of the arm, as though he's the lead part in a Shakespearean tragedy, 'it wouldn't have guaranteed them a place in the final. It would have placed them on equal points with the Entrepreneurs—meaning an elimination shootout between the two teams. As you can see, the enormity of the task for the Red team was huge.'

'This sounds promising,' I whisper to the others.

'It means nothing. He's merely creating drama. It's his job,' Flaky replies, ever the optimist. Felix walks past me and stops dramatically.

'But enough of the talk!' he declares. For once I agree with him. 'Time to announce the winner of the Skull Mountain challenge.' There's another convoluted delay as Jerry rearranges some of the camera crew so Skull Mountain is captured behind us. He explains it will add to the tension. I'm calm, relaxed, and more importantly, I'm feeling refreshed and energised.

'I will read the results out in reverse order,' Felix declares as he opens an envelope and pulls a piece of parchment from it. 'In third place with a time of 5 hours, twenty five minutes and thirteen seconds... the green team, the Entrepreneurs,' he says in a low growl heavy with shock and awe. The camera crew do another close up of us all. I shoot a quick glance over at the green team. They appear puzzled as if they forgot where they placed their car keys.

'Look at their mugs,' Robbo chuckles. 'Pure gold.'

'In second place,' Felix shouts so loud it gives me a start. 'In second place,' he yells again, 'with a time of 5 hours, 2 minutes, and five seconds, are...' He pauses. I'm guessing this is where an ad break kicks in back home. 'The Weathergirls!' There are gasps of disbelief from the other two teams. I peer over at Chloe as she smiles and gives me the thumbs up. I nod my appreciation. There's not much smiling going on with the Entrepreneurs, though. They look completely blindsided. Piers rushes over to Jerry who yells "Cut!" We flop down on the sand.

'What the hell is going on?' Piers screeches at him, red in the face. 'It's impossible! There must have been some mistake; they must have cheated. I know for a fact Will Harding was the last one to the top of the bloody mountain and he certainly didn't pass any of our team on the way back down.'

'Piers, calm down,' Jerry says, patiently.

'Don't tell me to bloody calm down. I demand a retrial!'

'Christ,' Robbo mutters. 'I think he's about to have kittens.'

'If he carries on like this for much longer, he'll pop a roid,' Geordie adds with a cackle.

'I think he popped his roid a moment ago,' Flaky says. Piers stomps over to us, fists clenched.

'You bunch of dishevelled, delinquent, cheats!' he screams at us. He's met with emotionless stares. Our demeanour only seems to infuriate him further. 'There's no way you won the race fairly! You dishonourable, reprobates. I'll sue you! I'll sue all of you!' he bellows as he swings around jabbing his finger at Jerry, Felix, the camera crew and even the Weathergirls who are completely innocent in the whole saga. He stomps off back to Jerry. 'I demand an inquest!'

'I think the guy has delusions of being a high court judge,' Robbo says.

'Piers, please calm down and I'll explain everything,' Jerry says as he places his hand on Piers' shoulder. Piers roughly knocks it away.

'This is a setup! There must have been a malfunction with the clocks. I thought we were friends, Jerry? We go back a long way.' The man's raving like a lunatic. I notice one of the camera guys is still filming. He wears a sly smile. It would make extraordinary footage for the viewers, but I guess it will never be seen. Nevertheless, if it were ever to get out into the public domain, it's the sort of thing which would paint someone in an awfully bad light. Jerry purses his lips until the human volcano stops spewing his shit into the air.

'Good, let me explain,' Jerry says. 'We have studied all the footage and there was no cheating. There is nothing wrong with the clocks either. We tripled checked everything.'

'Then how do you explain...'

'They used a pigeon.'

'A pigeon?'

'Yes. You know, a bird.'

'I know what a damned bloody pigeon is!' he explodes again.

Robbo giggles. 'Oh, this is classic,' he says. 'I haven't enjoyed myself so much since Geordie dressed up as Santa and traumatised the children.'

'Will carried a pigeon to the top of Skull Mountain in his backpack. He attached the key to it, and it flew back to their camp. Flaky removed the key and passed it to Geordie who walked onto the beach and handed it to Robbo, who casually jogged to the finishing line and stopped the clock. That's how they won. Very ingenious if you ask me.'

'That's not in the bloody rules! This was a team challenge. You can't allow this result to stand. Employing an animal to aid and abet is completely out of order!'

'I'm afraid it's not, Piers. We were very clear about the rules of the challenge. Remember the motto of the show; survival at any cost!'

'You can shove your motto up your sweaty arse!' His teammates, Cliff and Jasper approach and try to calm him down.

'Piers, face facts. We were beaten fair and square. Don't upset yourself. We can still win the shoot-out,' Cliff says as he places an arm around him. Piers swings around and throws an uppercut which sends Cliff reeling. The next five minutes is great fun as an all-in melee between the green team, Felix, Jerry, and the security guards, ensues. It's more of a scrum than a real fight.

There's a lot of pushing and shoving and rolling around in the sand, but it's great entertainment, far better than the show.

'This will be good for the ratings,' Flaky comments.

'Aye. Best comedy I've seen in years,' Geordie adds. When the dust settles, Jerry calls for a thirty-minute break for everyone to cool down. I'm not sure what he's talking about? We're as cool as cucumbers in an ice bath.

Chapter 25

Shoot Out

The challenge is daunting because of the mud. In front of us is an assault course. There are ladders to climb, flying foxes to swing from, a wooden wall to scale, netting to crawl under, a maze to navigate but before we get to those, we need to traverse a pool of mud.

Strategically placed somewhere in the sea of mud are four bags, each containing a coconut. They're fond of their coconuts on this show, I'll give them that. One person from each team sets off on the sound of the starter pistol. They have to locate a bag, with coconut inside then traipse it around the assault course. When they get to the end of the course, they sound a Klaxon, and the next team member sets off.

It appears the Entrepreneurs have had a bit of a "love-in" and are now all chummy again, on the surface. Piers can't help himself though. He keeps throwing verbal abuse our way. My dish of revenge is getting colder by the second. We should be in with a good chance of winning, but then again, who really knows? Cliff, Jasper and Dick Honeyman are all super fit. Their weakest link is Piers. Anything could happen and I don't like to leave things to chance.

'Any ideas how to tackle this?' I say as the production team set up the cameras, sound equipment and position the boom crane.

'What's the biggest challenge?' Flaky asks.

'The mud,' replies Geordie. 'We'll be caked in the stuff before we even attempt the course. It will make things slippery.'

'Finding those bloody bags won't be easy. We could lose a lot of time there,' Robbo says. The mud bath is about six metres square.

'Hmm... you're right. Anyone got any brainwaves?' There's silence for a moment.

'Yes, I have,' Geordie says rubbing at his bushy beard.

'There's a first time for everything,' Robbo drawls.

'I suggest the first person finds all the bags and dumps them in a corner. It will take longer, and we'll drop behind. But isn't it better for one person to search for the bags, knowing the ground they've already covered instead of doing it individually?' I actually think he's on to something.

'Not a bad idea, Einstein. It needs to be done in a logical manner,' Robbo says. 'A pattern. Either up and down or side to side. Make one pass from A to B, then repeat, a few feet further down.'

'Sounds like a plan. Whatever time we do lose, we'll hopefully make it back on the following runs, a bit like the nuts in the underwater cage challenge,' I say. 'Okay, is everyone agreed?' They all nod. I hold my arm out in front of me as they all pile their hands on top. 'All for one...'

'And one for all!' we cheer.

We agree on the starting line-up. Geordie will go first. With his long arms and legs, he'll cover the mud bath a lot quicker than anyone else. I'll go second. Even though I'm feeling fresh, once I've tackled a few obstacles I think my energy will wane. Robbo is third and Flaky will bring up the rear. We wait at the starting line as Felix builds the whole thing up into a monumental event for the cameras. You'd think it was the morning of the Normandy landings.

'You're going down, Harding,' Piers calls out. 'You're going down,' he reiterates with a low growl.

I nod at him. 'Good luck,' I reply nonchalantly.

The crack of the pistol reverberates across the island as Geordie and Cliff run into the mud bath. I'm surprised at how deep it is. I was expecting it to be about a foot deep but it's more like three feet. As they each hit the mud their pace is reduced to nothing more than a slow trudge as they battle the thick slurry. Geordie starts trawling at the nearest edge working from side to side. He bends double and sticks his hand into the gloop. Cliff has chosen a different tactic. He's aimlessly thrashing about all over the place. I think we may have hit upon a winning formula... at least for retrieving the coconuts. After a few minutes, Geordie finds a bag and pulls it up at the same time as Cliff also finds a bag. Geordie tosses the sack into the far corner nearest the first obstacle—the wooden wall with a rope dangling from it. Cliff trips and slips his way to the perimeter of the mud bath and steps out. A few precious seconds elapse before Geordie rips another bag from the filth and lobs it into the corner.

'I think it's working,' I murmur.

'Early days,' Flaky replies. Cliff throws his bag over the wall, grabs the rope, and pulls himself laboriously up the wooden structure. He's dripping in mud which must add some considerable weight.

'Crikey, that looks tough,' Robbo says.

'It will be easier for us. We'll only have mud up to our thighs,' I say.

'Any tips for getting over it?'

'What's strongest; your arms or legs?' Flaky asks.

'Legs.'

'Grab the rope, lean back then climb the wall using your feet, pushing back, creating tension. If you were strong in your arms, then you'd just haul yourself up using your feet as resting anchors on the rope.' Cliff is soon climbing a wooden ladder attached to the side of a tower which must be twenty feet high. Geordie has traversed about two thirds of the mud as Felix goes into excited overdrive about the two teams' different tactics. Another bag is pulled from the mire and flung with the others. We shout our encouragement. Cliff shoots up the ladder, grasping the bag in his teeth.

I call out to Geordie. 'Hey, Geordie!' he gives me a half-sideways glance. 'When you're climbing the tower, hold the bag in your teeth!' He nods and gives me a thumbs up. As Cliff attaches the safety rope to the flying fox, doubts about the plan trouble me. Cliff only has two more obstacles to navigate before he reaches the finishing line; the single zig-zag planks and the maze.

'I remember watching a show about mazes,' Robbo says.

'Really? You amaze me,' I say with a grin.

He ignores me. 'All you need to do is keep going left. Eventually, it will lead you out.'

'Are you sure?' Flaky asks, unconvinced.

'That's what the experts said.' Cliff zooms down the zip wire and crashes into a pile of hay. When he emerges, he looks like the straw man from the Wizard of Oz. Geordie locates the last of the bags and strides his way towards the wooden wall.

⟫⟫ ⟪⟪

I'm standing on the dais with Geordie. We're both caked in rapidly drying mud, watching on, as Robbo scales the ladder to the zip line. He's well ahead of Dick Honeyman who has only just jumped from the wooden wall and is now crawling beneath netting in another slurry of mud. Robbo comes to a halt.

'What's wrong with him?' Geordie says as he paws nervously at his scraggly hair. Robbo is halfway up the ladder grimacing.

'Robbo, what's the matter?' I yell out.

'Bloody cramp in my calf,' he replies.

'Hell, that's all we need,' I murmur.

'Do a calf-stretch!' Geordie bellows.

'Pretty hard to do when you're fifteen feet off the ground standing on a bloody ladder!'

'Stop your whining and get to the top, then you can stretch.'

'What a great idea. Why didn't I think of that,' Robbo shouts down as he painfully ascends rung by rung at the pace of a sloth on elephant tranquillisers.

'Christ, he's going to blow our lead,' Geordie growls.

'You can't blame him for getting cramp.'

'Can't I.'

'It could have happened to any of us.' By the time Robbo hits the straw at the bottom of the flying fox and hobbles into the maze, Dick is right behind him.

'Come on Robbo, you've got Dick up your arse!' Geordie shouts.

'It's just the way I walk,' Robbo retorts with a grin. It doesn't take long for Dick to set off the horn and unleash my pot-bellied nemesis—Piers. Finally, Robbo limps out of the maze.

'Come on, Noddy! Shift your saggy arse!' Geordie encourages. Piers locates his bag, lifts it aloft and emits a high-pitched scream. By the time Robbo slams his palm onto the horn, Piers has already scaled the wall and is now shuffling along under the cargo net like a giant slug. Flaky sets off way too fast and as he enters the mud bath falls flat on his face.

'Jeez, are we blessed,' Geordie murmurs. It's not looking good, and I'm glad I kept my gob shut in regard to Piers. There's nothing worse than being made to eat your own words. By the time Flaky has scraped mud from his eyes, Piers emerges from the netting and rushes towards the ladders, whooping and laughing like a man demented.

'We're going home,' Geordie states without emotion.

'Hmm... possibly. At least we gave it our all.'

'If it hadn't been for Peg-leg and Laughing Gravy, we'd have won this,' he adds as he throws a withering glance towards Robbo, who is scowling as he stretches his calf muscle. Flaky bends down and pulls at the bag in the corner. It offers some resistance, and as he pulls harder, it suddenly gives sending him crashing back into the mud.

'Hell's bells, give me strength,' I gasp.

'Is he taking the piss? This is bloody painful to watch. It's supposed to be an elimination shoot-out not a night of slapstick at the local circus. Whose bright idea was it to send him last?' It's handed more valuable seconds to Piers who is halfway up the tower.

'Flaky, it's now or never, mate!' I yell. He gives me the thumbs up as he pulls himself from the sludge, coughs crap through his nose, and mouth, and plods his way towards the wall. Piers stops for a breather as he reaches the top of the tower. Flaky tackles the first obstacle in a jiffy and is soon shuffling along at a cracking pace under the netting. 'This could be tight. Piers is slowing down and Flaky looks like he's just done an ounce of whiz.'

As Flaky swoops down the flying fox, Piers is already leaping from the last of the planks and heading towards the maze. He has a big fat smile on his face... bastard. I think it's over, bar the shouting. Flaky deftly detaches himself from the zip wire and scoots across the zigzag of planks in no time. Piers appears disorientated as he rushes aimlessly around the maze. There's still a chance.

'Flaky,' Robbo calls, 'remember what I said. It worked for me, Will and Geordie.' Flaky halts, peers at Robbo... then nods. He enters the maze and holds his left hand out towards the wall. He sets off at a steady jog, turning left, left, and left. The huge grin which spills across the chubby mush of Piers, indicates he may have spotted the exit. Flaky is still bobbing about back and forth. To the untrained eye, it appears he's going around in circles. Piers emerges from the maze and walks casually towards the Klaxon. His smugness could blot out the sun.

'As I said before, your type come from a long line of losers,' he says with a gigantic sneer. I freeze, not wanting to give anything away. Flaky sprints from the exit of the maze and rushes towards the siren. Before Piers can realise the danger, it's too late. Flaky overtakes him and slaps his hand down, hard, on the horn.

⋙ ⋘

All we want to do is rush into the ocean and clean the muck from our aching bodies, but Jerry has different ideas. He insists it will make for compelling viewing if we all line up, encased in mud as the final shots of the day are taken. I'm beginning to feel like I'm being abused. Felix wraps up his soliloquy and shakes hands with the Entrepreneurs. They make their way over to us, well, three of them do and walk down our line shaking hands and slapping our shoulders.

'Well, done boys,' Cliff says. 'Worthy competitors and worthy winners,' he offers graciously.'

'Aye, well done to you, too,' Geordie replies. Piers stands off to the side a few feet away, seething. If he were a volcano, I'd say he's about to erupt. Jerry doesn't miss the drama and instructs two of the camera crew to focus on me and Piers. We glare at each other. As the other three walk off, Piers joins them. The time has arrived to remove my dish from the fridge.

'Oi, Piers!' I call out. He halts and spins on his heels. Our eyes lock onto each other again.

'What?' he hisses with contempt.

I put on my best arrogant, superior, grin. 'Pip, pip... old chap.' He lopes towards me until his nose is nearly touching mine.

'When I came on this show, you were nothing but a minor irritant, a pimple. You have just made the biggest mistake of your life.'

'Really? Why's that?'

'Because I am now your enemy.'

'Join the queue. Friends may come and go but enemies accumulate. Now jog along, there's a good chap. I've had enough of your type.'

'I'll bring you down Harding... mark my words,' he growls then storms off. I turn to Geordie.

'He's one of those guys who has always got to have the last word. Right, I'll see you lot back at camp.'

'Why, where are you going?'

'I need to have a little chat with one of the cameramen.'

Chapter 26

Back In Yorkshire—Part 3

Fiona bustles through the door with a tray of champagne, glasses, and nibbles.

'Just in time, Fi,' Jackie says. 'Hey, guess what? It's a special edition tonight. They've added an extra hour.'

'Oh, I wonder why?' Fiona says.

'Because of the elimination, I suppose. You know how they like to milk those situations.'

Fiona laughs. 'We all know who's going to be eliminated tonight,' she replies raising her eyebrows.

'You never know,' Gillian counters. 'You said that the other night when they were supposed to be facing the Celebrity Chefs. I'm not sure why, but I think they're still in with a chance.'

'So, it's true?' Julie enquires.

Gillian is puzzled. 'What?'

'You believe in miracles.' All the women laugh as Fiona pops the cork and fills the glasses.

The opening scene shows the Weathergirl's camp before the race begins. It's a hive of activity. They perform stretches, massage each other's calves and hamstrings, drink water, and offer each other words of encouragement. Felix Cain's commentary is complimentary. The next scene is of the Entrepreneurs as they limber up and discuss tactics. A timer on the screen shows there are twenty minutes to go until the Skull Mountain challenge. The camera finally cuts to the Rock Stars encampment. Four hammocks gently swing back and forth. A slender thread of smoke snakes idly from the embers of the fire. All is quiet.

'My God!' Jackie exclaims. 'It's sleepy hollow. What are they playing at?'

'I don't like the look of this. I know they've got no chance of winning—those Weathergirls are like whippets—but I hope they're going to compete,' Julie adds. Gloria sings followed by Jerry's voice requesting all teams to rendezvous at the starting line. The Weathergirls excitedly decamp, chattering nervously. The Entrepreneurs all shake hands and wish each other good luck as they slap each other on the back. At the Rock Stars camp, after a minute of nothing, Will Harding eventually flops out of his hammock and yawns. He very carefully hoists his backpack onto his shoulders.

'I'll see you tossers later,' he remarks as he heads off. There are a few muted grunts but nothing which could be described as discernible language—not in the modern sense.

'Good grief. The four cavemen! Why aren't the others going?' Fiona says. 'They can't expect Will to run up the mountain and back down again in the heat and hope to win.'

Jackie huffs and stands up to refill her champagne glass.

'They've given up, that's what! They're a bloody embarrassment. It's okay to lose, there's no shame in it, but to lose without even trying, well...'

'Maybe they have a plan?' Gillian notes.

'A plan? That lot don't even know how to spell it,' Julie splutters.

'You don't give them enough credit.'

'I think I give them too much credit!'

Felix finishes his explanations of the rules, and the firing pistol marks the start of the race. Will sets off at a steady jog. A drone follows him, high above. As he rounds the first corner, he stops and pulls out a water bottle.

'Well, that didn't take him long,' Fiona says, disapprovingly, as the ads break kicks in.

'He looks rugged and handsome with his short beard,' Gillian comments.

'Yes... yes, he does,' Fiona concurs, privately seething at the remark as she glares at Gillian. 'Hey, do you realise if they're eliminated today, they'll be back home in three days? Then I'll have *my* husband all to myself.'

'No. they'll be home in 24 hours. This footage was shot two days ago,' Gillian corrects.

'Oh, my! Yes, you're right. I'm kind of hoping they get eliminated. I've missed him. How has everyone else got on without their lesser halves?'

Jacki laughs. 'The first week was absolute bliss. I could stretch out in bed. No snoring, no farting. No pots and glasses getting broken. He's such a clumsy oaf sometimes. Mind you, he is a big man. But by the first weekend, I was bored. There was no one to talk to. I don't mean deep meaningful conversations, it's rare you get that with Geordie, but just the ordinary mundane stuff about your day. It's funny how the trivial things actually mean quite a lot.'

'Yes, I agree. Me and Flaky run together on the weekend and it's felt really strange without him.'

'And what about you, Julie, what have you missed the most about Robbo?' Fiona asks.

'I never thought I'd hear myself say this, but... the sex.' There are howls of laughter from the others. 'It's true. Believe me, Robbo is not the greatest lover; his idea of foreplay is to ask me if I'm awake. But nevertheless, I'm hanging out for it.'

'What's Flaky like in the sack?' Jackie says.

Gillian blushes as she pauses to gather her thoughts. 'Oh, he's considerate enough.'

'I can feel a "but" coming next,' Jackie says.

'Well... he can be a little conservative at times, one-dimensional.'

'You mean boring?'

She giggles. 'Don't be cruel. I once suggested we make love in the car.'

'And?'

'He wasn't keen on the idea; it had just been valeted. What's Geordie like?'

'Oh, he's a right randy get. If I suggested having sex on the cheese counter at Safeway, he'd be up there like a rat up a drainpipe.' The adverts finish and the show resumes. A drone follows a line of challengers up the mountain. It's not long before two of the Entrepreneurs overtake Will. The next scene shows Will and Piers Conrad on a high rock ledge overlooking a vomit-inducing drop. The drone falls from the sky and zooms in on them.

'I don't know what they're talking about, but it doesn't look very friendly,' Julie comments.

'No. Will looks furious. Obviously, Piers has got under his skin. Good grief! For a moment there, I thought Will was going to punch him! Fiona exclaims.

'That's not like Will,' Gillian murmurs. Her comment again riles Fiona for some reason, as she narrows her eyes and stares at Gillian. Jackie notices and softly shakes her head at Fiona, a clear indication for her to drop it. Gillian is oblivious as her attention is focused on the TV screen.

⤳⟫⟫ ⟪⟪↜

The women crack open their third bottle of champagne.

'What are we celebrating?' Jackie begins. 'The fact they've made complete fools of themselves or the fact they're on their way home?' The footage shows Will slowly rise onto the plateau of the volcano and pull a bottle of water from his bag.

'I guess the latter,' Fiona says with a downcast face.

'At least Will gave it a shot. I'm not sure why Flaky wasn't with him? It's most unlike him to throw the towel in,' Gillian says wistfully. Fiona rolls her eyes at Jackie.

'It is embarrassing though,' Julie says. 'They'd garnered so much good press over the last few weeks. They're national heroes and they've just blown all their goodwill in one day.' The drone zooms in on Will as he rubs at the lid of the treasure chest. It cuts away to the Weathergirls as they snake their way down the mountain marginally ahead of the Entrepreneurs in distance, but well ahead in time.

The living room erupts into shrieks of laughter as Will pulls Dorothy from the bag, attaches the key, and releases the bird.

'Oh, my God! Is he allowed to do that?' Fiona screeches.

'I'm not sure. Felix said all they had to do was to retrieve the key to stop the timer.' The footage becomes confusing as various drones follow different competitors around.

'There's Robbo!' Julie cries as Robbo sticks the key in the clock and turns it. The viewers don't see how much time has elapsed.

'Does it mean he's won?' Gillian asks.

'I'm not sure. A minute ago, they showed Piers as though he were in the lead, now they've just shown Chloe,' Fiona adds as she scratches her cheek.

'They're keeping us on tenterhooks. No doubt all will be revealed after the next ad break,' Jackie replies.

'They'll cram more than one break in before they announce the winner, I can guarantee,' Julie adds.

With the aid of clever editing, the big reveal of the Rock Stars victory comes at the halfway point of the show. The four women jump to their feet and hug each other cheering wildly.

'It means they're in the elimination shoot out! That's why the show's an extra hour long,' exclaims Fiona.

'I told you,' Gillian says triumphantly. 'It was obviously Will's brainwave that saved the day.' Fiona storms from the room and heads to the kitchen. She reaches up to the top shelf and pulls a bottle of gin down as Jackie enters behind her.

'Calm down sister!'

'Easy for you to say,' Fiona replies as she twists the top off the gin. Jackie pulls a tumbler from the cupboard and places it on the counter.

'Hey, it's nothing new. We all know that Gillian has had a thing for Will for years. It's a schoolgirl crush... that's all.' Fiona half fills the glass with gin. 'Tonic in the fridge?'

'Don't bother.' Fiona smashes the gin down in one, grimaces then emits a deep sigh. 'That's better.' Jackie frowns at her best friend. 'What?' Fiona snaps.

'Nothing.'

'Well, it's not your husband who she fawns and gushes over, is it? And as for being a schoolgirl crush... she's thirty-bloody-six! And slim and attractive,' she adds as an afterthought.

'You're slim and attractive.'

'I can handle it when we're all together; her making eyes at him and agreeing with everything he says, laughing at his lame jokes, but when he's not here... well. She thinks she knows him better than I do. I'm his wife. He's my husband. That's what makes my blood boil.'

'Fiona, he's your man. Will is a lot of things; moody, pig-headed, and set in his ways. But he's not a cheat. Believe me... I can tell. I have an acquaintance who has the hots for Geordie, and yes, it does rile. But I know Geordie would never go with another woman. Chill girl, I'm speaking sense.' Fiona drops another smidgen of gin into her glass.

'Yes. You're right. I just want him home... that's all.' Jackie throws her arm around her friend's shoulder.

'Hey, if they failed this current challenge then they will be on their way home—maybe tomorrow. If by some unforeseen miracle they win the challenge and go into the final, then they'll be home in the next seventy-two hours. We'll soon have our men back.'

'It's pathetic, isn't it?'

'What is?'

'Here we are, four clued up, on the ball businesswomen, managing a home, kids and the never-ending work and yet...'

'And yet?'

'We miss our men so much.'

'It's called love. You've found your soul mate. We're all like doves; we mate for life. For better or for worse.' Fiona wipes the wetness from the side of her eyes and sniffs.

'Yes, you're right. I feel better now. Thanks, Jackie.'

'No problem. Now, finish your gin and let's see what those dinglebats get up to next. My God, we're never going to die bored with those four around!'

Chapter 27

The Finale

My eyelids flicker. Murky light filters through the canopy as the wind cajoles and harasses limbs and branches into a chaotic dance. The ocean is thunderous, indignant. Another day unfolds. But it's not just any old day. It's the day of the final challenge, followed by a huge party, a recovery day, then we begin our journey home. I'm cold and hungry. I glance at the fire. Smoke and red dots swirl from it in an excited stampede but there's no fire as such. I lift myself from the hammock for the last time. I think I've developed scoliosis. The others are still asleep. I prod the embers into life then guzzle down two cups of water. What I'd give for a mug of strong black tea.

I lift the cover from our hidey-hole and pull the last remaining plastic bag up. It's light. I inspect the contents. A half-empty bag of brown rice, one can of baked beans and another near empty bag of split peas. It's going to be a continental style breakfast, again. Dorothy flutters down from her overnight perch and lands on Flaky's hammock, cooing gently.

'Morning, Dorothy,' he murmurs sleepily. Geordie rolls out of his hammock, stretches while groaning, and emits a thunderous fart.

'And there's my early morning wake-up call,' Robbo says, yawning. 'That's one thing I won't miss when we leave this place.'

'Oh, shut up. It's a perfectly natural bodily function.'

'Not the frequency and decibels that you drop them. I'd get booked in to see a proctologist when you get home if I were you.'

'What's for brekky?' Geordie asks.

'Rice and peas or baked beans. Or coconut,' I reply.

His face contorts. 'If I never see a coconut again, it will be too soon. Does anybody want the beans?'

'If they were piping hot on a bed of heavily buttered toast, then yes. But as they're not, I'll stick with the rice and peas,' Robbo says.

'Flaky?' Geordie prompts.

'No. I'll go with the rice.'

'Bill?'

'No, you have them.' He grabs the can of beans, peels the lid back and pours the contents straight into his mouth, dribbling sauce into his beard as he does so.

'My God,' Flaky exclaims. 'It's like watching the devolution of mankind in fast forward. Another month on this island and you'd be swinging from the trees.' It's true. Geordie has an uncanny appearance to the archetypal caveman but without the manners. Flaky strokes Dorothy in a motherly sort of way. 'It's a bittersweet day,' he moans, mournfully.

'There's no bitter about it. This is the sweetest day of my life,' Geordie says.

'Aren't you going to miss anything from this experience?'

'No. It's been hellish. I hope there's an earthquake and Crusoe Island is swallowed up by the sea... after we've left, of course.'

'I'm going to miss Dorothy. She's been a constant source of comfort to me throughout.'

'She could have been an instant source of protein if you hadn't been so bloody sentimental.'

'Don't you listen to the big bad ogre, Dorothy. He doesn't mean it,' Flaky says in a baby voice.

'Don't I?'

'Do you think she'll miss me?'

'I doubt it. No one else ever docs.' Robbo rises from his hammock and rolls his head from side to side emitting a few cracks.

'I've told you; take her with you,' he says.

'Don't talk bloody stupid! A tropical dove wouldn't survive a British winter.'

'She'd be beaten to death by the sparrows within a day,' Geordie says.

'No, I'm afraid today is our final goodbye. She belongs here. This is her home.'

'There is another solution,' Geordie offers.

'What?'

'You stay here. To be quite frank with you, I think you lost your bloody marbles a while back. I'm not sure how you're going to fit back into a civilised society.'

>>>> <<<<

Jerry is giving an extended speech to his crew and the competitors. I wish he'd get a bloody hurry on as the weather is turning nastier by the minute. It's cold and windy with the occasional flurry of showers.

'This guy could talk under wet cement,' Geordie whispers out of the side of his mouth. A raucous round of applause erupts as Jerry ends his thank you speech and honourable mentions. I'm not sure whether the applause is for his monologue or the fact the windbag has finished.

'Wait! Wait!' Jerry cries.

'Christ, he's off again,' Geordie moans. 'They should use him in a battery advert. We shoved four AAA batteries up Jerry's arse, and he talked non-stop for over a year.'

'Shut up,' Flaky scolds. 'I'm trying to listen!'

'Pardon me for existing,' Geordie says suitably chastised.

Jerry continues. 'Before we set up for our final challenge of the show, I've had a recent update on cyclone 04F.'

'Catchy name,' Robbo mumbles.

'It's been upgraded to a category 5 severe tropical cyclone. And worse news; it's changed course and is heading our way. We are slap bang in its path. Once we have the final wrap, we need to gather everything which isn't nailed down and relocate them to the shipping containers. It also means... and I'm deeply sorry to say this, but the party scheduled for tonight has been cancelled.' There's a chorus of wails and groans from the assembled throng.

'Piss the shitting bed!' Robbo declares, as though he's just had his appendix removed with a rusty hacksaw. 'I was looking forward to the party!'

'As for our remaining competitors, the Rock Stars, and the Weathergirls, you have two options; you can stay here on the island until the storm has passed or we can arrange for a chopper to get you off today once the final challenge has been completed. The storm is expected to last four days. The choice is yours, but you need to let me know what your decision is ASAP, before the challenge begins.'

I glance at my comrades in bushy beards. 'I say, let's go. I can't manage another four days. What do you guys think?'

'Aye. I just want to get home now,' Geordie retorts. It's a unanimous decision with only Robbo looking a mite disappointed.

I inform Jerry of our verdict as the production crew swing into action for the final time. I notice a couple of the cameramen donning wetsuits which fills me with dread; another water-based contest.

⸝⸝⸝⸝ ⸜⸜⸜⸜

The challenge seems like an anti-climax to me. After all the complex games we've competed in, this one is rather mundane... but what do I know.

We're positioned atop a pontoon six feet above furious waves. Another pontoon is next to us about fifteen metres away. Linking both platforms is a very narrow boardwalk, maybe six to eight inches in width. The wind is gathering pace as the temperature rapidly drops. No one is happy.

'Hang on, run the rules by me one more time. I'm confused,' Robbo says, face creased as he rubs at his shaggy locks.

'It's perfectly simple,' Flaky explains. 'One of us picks up the red baton and walks to the mid-point of the plank. The others follow behind. The last one onto the plank has to navigate past the other three and take the baton from the first player. When we all arrive safely on the other side, we place the baton in a holder and pick up the green baton and repeat the process... in the opposite direction. When we get back to the starting point—i.e. where we are standing now, we place the green baton in the holder and hit the flare, signifying we've completed the challenge. The first team to accomplish the task is the winner.'

'Fuck me rigid! I thought you said it was simple. I'm more confused than before,' Robbo says, alarmed at Flaky's description.

'Robbo, think of it like a game of leapfrog and the last person to go collects the baton from the first person and places it in the holder. Then it's repeated.'

'Oh, I see. Why didn't he just say that?'

'Because Flaky is one of those people who likes to use a hundred words when three will do,' Geordie says adding his tuppence worth. Flaky becomes distracted as he stares over at the Weathergirls on their pontoon.

'We're fucked!' The three of us stare at him in surprise. I think it's maybe the third time I've heard him drop the "F" bomb in twenty-odd years.

'What's the matter?' Geordie asks, concerned by Flaky's profanity.

'Look at them,' Flaky says. 'There's not one of them over five-foot-eight; none over sixty kilos.'

'Your point being?' Geordie replies. The three of us gaze at Geordie as our hopes of winning float off into the dark sky.

'The point being, they don't have an oversized knuckle-dragger in their team!'

'And they all do Pilates and yoga,' I add just to hammer the final nail into our coffin.

'Yes... nimble is the word,' Flaky says.

'And nubile,' Robbo adds.

Geordie glances at the women then back at our faces. 'Oh, I see! You think I'm too big and uncoordinated for this challenge... is that it?'

'Yes,' three voices cry in unison.

'I'll show you lot. We won't fail because of me! When I was at school, I was the district boxing, javelin and hammer throwing champion.'

'Shame it's not a boxing, javelin and hammer throwing challenge, then,' Robbo says, rather presciently.

'I think the chances of us winning the one-million pounds for my halfway-house has evaporated,' Flaky moans sadly. I cast my gaze around as Felix waffles on in the background in front of three cameras, building the finale up to a crescendo for the viewers back home.

'Hmm... not necessarily. The wind is gathering pace,' I say as Geordie emits another gigantic fart. Three of us take a step back.

'You're not wrong there,' Robbo says screwing his nose up.

'Sorry,' Geordie says. 'It's those bloody baked beans I had for breakfast.'

'What's the plan of attack, Will?' Flaky asks.

I think for a moment whilst trying not to gag. 'Okay, the last one on the plank has to be the most agile. That rules out Geordie and Robbo,' I begin. 'Flaky... you go last. You've the best chance.' We've not been paying attention. The starter gun sounds and the Weathergirls rush onto their platform.

'Shit the bed!' Robbo cries. 'What's the order again?'

'Geordie, you go now and don't forget the bloody baton! Then Robbo, me and Flaky will be right behind you.'

It's a complete shemozzle of the highest order. Geordie grabs the baton and heads to the mid-point marked on the plank by a white stripe. Robbo follows but loses his footing and drops into the sea. It takes him a good thirty seconds to swim back to the platform and precariously navigate his way onto the boardwalk.

I take my time and inch along, sideways, until I'm two feet away from Robbo. Flaky nervously shuffles along until he's at my side. I look over my shoulder at the Weathergirls. Chloe, who must have been last in the queue has already navigated past two of her colleagues. We are miles behind. I grab Flaky's hand as he pushes up against me. There are a few wobbles, but he passes safely. He takes a little longer to get past Robbo but manages it. Geordie is a different matter. We lose even more time as the girls start their return leg to victory. Eventually, Flaky edges past Geordie, grabs the baton and with a hop, skip and a jump lands safely on the platform. The rest of us eke cautiously along until we too are safe. The air temperature is dropping, and the sea is frothing as an angry vortex whips it into a frenzy. The girls are at the halfway mark of their return leg.

'Flaky was right,' Robbo says puffing from his exertions, 'we're fucked.'

'We cannae throw the towel in. You never know what unexpected events may occur,' Geordie says, rather optimistically. 'Flaky, can you not ask Jesus for a helping hand?'

'I'm afraid it doesn't work like that.'

'Thought as much. Well, our only chance is the intervention of fate.'

'What are you hoping for; a lightning bolt, an asteroid hit?' Robbo says. 'I thought you said this would be like leapfrog? It's more like blind man's bluff.' I glance at the ever-darkening clouds rolling in on the horizon as Robbo's words ricochet around my head.

'Wait! I have a plan!' I declare.

'Oh, no,' Flaky whispers. 'What?'

'We let Geordie go last.'

Flaky's face screws up as though he's just been handed an unexpected tax bill. 'Give me strength! It means the lumbering moron has got to navigate past the three of us. That's a plan for failure.'

'Oi, watch your mouth, Peewee, otherwise you'll be taking a dip!' Geordie snarls.

'No, listen. If us three edge out to the middle and squat it will give us more balance. Geordie can step over us instead of having to wriggle past us.' There's silence for a moment. I'm waiting for epic congratulations but all I get is an "Aye. It's worth a try," from Geordie. A scream and a wail diverts our attention as a Weathergirl tumbles into the sea.

'That's our divine intervention, right on cue,' Geordie says with a cackle.

Robbo picks up the green baton and crabs to the mid-point. Flaky and I inch along behind him. When we reach our positions, we crouch down.

'Rest your forearms on your thighs and grab your knees,' Flaky yells. 'It will give you more stability.' I throw a glance at our competitors. Lucy was the one who fell in, and she's already climbed back up the ladder and is stepping out onto the plank where her teammates await. Geordie throws one leg over Flaky, followed by the other, bypassing him safely.

'Good plan, Bill. This is a breeze. Why didn't you think of it at the start?' I keep my mouth shut even though I've an overwhelming desire to jab him in the throat with a very sharp object. He straddles me with ease as I hunker down even further. We are well ahead of the Weathergirls. This is ours to lose. Geordie casts his left leg over Robbo, who is a little wobbly. As Geordie's left leg lands safely on the platform he turns sideways and grins at Flaky.

'Here's looking at a million quid coming your way, kiddo!' I flinch as the sound of brazen thunder assaults my ears, and yet, there's no accompanying flash of lightning. It's followed a few seconds later by Robbo's protestations.

'You dirty, Scottish git!' He doesn't get a chance to elaborate as he emits a yelp then somersaults into the foaming sea below.

⤞⤞⤞ ⤝⤝⤝

It's a rush job as the weather deteriorates at an alarming rate. I'm about to be interviewed by Felix. There are hundreds of people running around in a mad panic collecting, dismantling, and retrieving various objects. I'm in a small marquee with a camera crew and Felix.

'So close and yet so far!' he declares. 'We've watched you. The viewers at home have watched you. There have been so many times when we thought you were going to be eliminated. Yet, you survived. It's a testament to your team building, to your brotherhood, you got this far. Unfortunately, today you fell at the final hurdle. Tell me where it went wrong?' I feel slightly dizzy after so many cliches in one opening statement. However, I have to put my best and bravest face on. I always thought of myself as a musician, but apparently not; I'm a media figure and need to come out with some bullshit which can traverse through the ether and around the world in seconds.

'Hi, Felix, hello viewers and fans!' I say waving and grinning at the camera 'The facts are plain and simple. We were beaten by a better team. The Weathergirls were top of the leaderboard from day one and never relinquished their position. When it came to the final challenge, they won, we lost... end of story.' It's not the answer Felix wanted. He'd prefer something more dramatic. He asks me a follow-on question.

'Yes, I accept that. But I'm asking what went wrong?'

'I'm not sure what you mean, Felix?'

'You were in the lead. The challenge was yours for the taking. One of the Weathergirls had taken a bath and had to start again. Geordie had circumnavigated two of you when disaster struck. What caused Robbo to fall?'

'Ah, I see. Let's just say a violent gust of wind took him by surprise. It upset his sense of balance and has left him with a permanent bald spot on the back of his head. But let's not detract from the facts; the worthy winners were the Weathergirls, and any other result would have been an injustice.' Felix pulls his most commiserative feign and drops his voice by an octave. I sense some charity news is about to begin.

'That's very noble of you. But it means the charity of your choice, the outreach centre for young offenders, will not be receiving a cheque for one million pounds.' He's about to wrap up but I'm determined to have the last word, even if it does get cut in the edits.

'Not true. Me and the boys had a quick confab a moment ago and we've agreed, when we get back home, we're going to donate one million pounds from the band's bank account to Flaky's charity. The money will be transferred within one week. I hope the Weathergirls nominated charity receive their money in a similar timeframe. And lastly, to the Weathergirls I say this; you were deserved winners. Maybe the next incarnation of "Celebrity—I Will Survive" will feature as many women as men and possibly a few more ethnically diverse individuals.'

'Well done, Billy Boy! I couldnae have put it better myself.'

'Yep, nice one, Will. A nice undercurrent of agitation,' Robbo adds. I spot Chloe not far away as she beckons me over.

'Cheers, boys. I'll see you back at camp.' I wander over to Chloe.

'Hard luck,' she says, apologetically. 'Your closing statement was very magnanimous.'

'I meant every word.'

'I know you did. Please tell me you're all staying until the cyclone passes?'

I shake my head. 'No. The chopper will be here in less than an hour. It will give us just enough time to pack our belongings. One night in Dubai then a charter plane home. I take it you're stopping?'

'We're meteorologists, of course we're stopping. It's not every day you get to be caught in the eye of a force 5 cyclone.'

'Yes, I suppose you're right. I guess this is goodbye then.'

Her lips and eyelids droop. 'Yes. I guess it is... although it doesn't have to be. I'd like to see you again once we're back home.'

I take a deep sigh. 'Chloe, I'm a married man with a young child. I...'

She cuts me off. 'Hey, I'm not asking you to divorce your wife, leave your child and run off with me! All I'm saying is I enjoy your company. A slight affair is all I'm suggesting.'

'A slight affair?'

'Yes, occasional, if and when it suits. With my job, I'm always visiting various parts of the country. I'm sure you're in a similar position. If we both happen to be in the same city on the same night, then what's wrong with meeting up and catching a film or having a meal together. It can be rather lonely on the road.'

'Yeah, I guess. Just company... right?'

She leans in and kisses me on the lips. 'Yes. Just company. Why let sex get in the way of a good relationship.' She grabs my hand and slips something into it. 'It's my number. Straight away you're handed your mobile phone back, put my details in and text me.' She turns and walks back to her friends.

I wave to them as they all call out offering their condolences on our team's loss.

Chapter 28

Truth Be Told

Flaky and Robbo hoist their backpacks on as I bundle my belongings into mine. Dorothy sits forlornly on the rope of Flaky's hammock, surveying the scene. I'm beginning to think Flaky is right about the damned bird; it has a sixth sense. It seems to know what's happening. Its constant cooing has ceased. I think it's depressed.

'Goodbye Dorothy,' Flaky says with tears streaming down his cheeks. He gives the bird one last loving caress. Robbo drapes his arm over Flaky's shoulder.

'Come on, soft lad. Let's head off. Goodbyes are never easy.' They turn and walk solemnly towards the beach track and disappear from view. Geordie is shaking his head from side to side.

'It's been an emotional few weeks for him,' he says.

'He'll be fine once he's back home in the bosom of his family.' I zip up my bag and sling it across my shoulder. 'We better put this fire out.'

'Aye. I'll do the honours.' He wanders over to the water buckets as I peer into the smouldering embers.

'This fire was the centre point of everything. The only constant.'

'No wonder the ancients were in awe of it. Without fire, there is no life.' I pull Chloe's telephone number from my pocket and drop it onto the hot coals. The edges blacken before it ignites and curls up into nothing but flimsy ash.

'Sometimes fires need to be snuffed out before they get going,' I mumble.

'What do you mean?'

'Nothing.'

'Stand back!' He launches the water over the fire which erupts with hissing fury, sizzling and spitting its contempt. Another bucket is delivered and the fire dies. 'Okay, Billy Boy, I think it's a wrap, as they say in the movies. Come on, old pal, let's go.' Dorothy lets out two gentle coos before fluttering up to her perch.

'Au revoir, Dorothy! I'm going to miss you,' I whisper.

'You daft bastard. You're as bad as Flaky.' We leave the camp and walk on for a few strides before Geordie grabs me by the arm.

'What's wrong?'

'I think I left my colouring book behind. Stay here, I won't be a minute,' he says as he sprints back to camp. I'm intrigued and stalk him. I stand behind a bush and observe proceedings. Colouring book my blue-arse! Geordie pulls a packet of seeds from his pocket and scatters them on the ground.

'Come on, Dorothy, din-din time,' he gently encourages. The bird flies down onto his shoulder where he gives it a few loving strokes before it hops to the ground and pecks at the seeds. 'Take care little one,' he murmurs sadly as he turns to leave.

⟩⟩⟩⟩ ⟨⟨⟨⟨

We clamber aboard the chartered Cessna plane and relax into ridiculously comfortable seats.

'This is the way to travel,' Geordie says with a big cheesy grin.

'It's the least they could do considering what we've been through,' I reply.

'Such a cheerful soul, aren't you?'

I fasten my seat belt, pull out the newspaper and turn to the crossword page. 'I'll be cheerful just as soon as I walk through my front door.'

'Hey, Will what's the first thing you're going to do when you get back home?' Robbo asks.

I ponder for a moment. 'Pull my phone out and ring Fiona.'

'No, I mean when you get back to your house?'

'Oh, erm, put the kettle on and make myself a refreshing cup of Yorkshire Tea.'

'He's always liked to live dangerously,' Geordies says with a chuckle.

I ignore him. 'I'll cuddle Mary in my arms for about an hour and kiss those little red cheeks non-stop.'

'Do you want to know what I'm going to do?' Geordie asks.

'I think I can guess,' I reply.

'First, I'll have a bit of rough and tumble with my lads. Then I'll sling Jackie over my shoulder and carry her upstairs to the bedroom, lock the door and not come out for a good two hours.' A worried frown spreads across his face. 'That's if the mother-in-law is at home to look after the boys.'

'You really are a charmer, aren't you?' Flaky declares. 'And what if your wife isn't in the mood or happens to be on her menstrual cycle?'

'I don't care if she's on her fucking unicycle! I intend to have my wicked way. Anyway, I can assure you, she'll be hanging out for it more than me. It's not natural for a man to go so long without sex. Nearly thirty days and nights. I haven't gone this long without sex since I was fifteen,' Geordie says.

Flaky is shocked. 'You mean you lost your virginity when you were fifteen?'

Geordie turns to him. 'No. I lost my virginity when I was fourteen.'

'Who with?'

'Bendy Wendy, a Gypsy contortionist in a travelling circus,' he replies wistfully as he stares out of the window.

'And how old was she?'

Geordie appears distracted. 'What? Oh, I don't know. Mid-twenties, I guess.'

'That's child abuse!' Flaky exclaims.

Geordie grins. 'Rest assured, the only abuse was Gypsy abuse.'

'Did she know your age?'

'No. She probably thought I was old enough.'

'Why?'

'The beard.'

'Was the beard on you or Bendy Wendy?' Robbo asks with a chuckle.

'Very amusing. She was a bonny lass, despite her lazy eye and withered arm. Do you know, she could get both legs behind her head and walk on her hands.'

'Good life skills,' I mutter.

'I often wonder what she's up to now,' he adds with a wisp of melancholy.

'Maybe she changed career. She might be a neurosurgeon these days,' Robbo says.

'I didn't lose my virginity until I was twenty-three,' Flaky murmurs.

'I'm surprised you lost it at all,' Geordie adds. 'Who was your first?'

'Gillian, of course.' We all stare at him, surprised. Geordie appears mortally offended at the statement.

'You mean to tell me you've only ever had sex with one woman?'

'Yes. Is that so unusual?'

'It's not unusual, it's downright outlandish. We spent five years touring the world when we first got signed and you're telling me you didn't fill your boots?'

Flaky shrugs. 'The opportunity never came along.' The rest of us huff our disgust.

'Do you remember those days, Robbo?' Geordie asks with a cheeky grin.

'Oh, aye. I spent more time in the clap clinic than I did on stage. Good times.' Flaky makes himself comfortable in his seat and peers across at Robbo who is tucking into a bag of peanuts. 'And what's the first thing you'll do when you get home, Robbo?'

'Probably the same.'

'My God! You lot are sexually depraved.'

'No, I meant the same as Will. I just want to spend the next few weeks with Julie and Sally, smoke a few joints and chill. And you?'

'Strange as it may seem but I'm hoping the weather is atrocious then Gillian, Katrina and I can get rugged up and go for a long walk in the countryside. Autumn is a beautiful month. Leaves on the ground, the earthy aroma, the stark contrasts.'

Geordie mimics putting two fingers down his throat to make himself vomit.

Once the plane has reached altitude, the steward arrives with refreshments, and we crack open our first beer in weeks. It has an immediate effect on me as I experience a rush of euphoria and optimism. I stare at the first cryptic clue.

"Babe takes tea at the baseball game. It's no lie!"

I press a button and the chair reclines as my eyes become heavy.

~»»» «««~

A bump, accompanied by the squeal of rubber on concrete, jolts me from my sleep. I gaze out of the window at the mundane greyness of everything. Home sweet home. Robbo and Geordie are still in the land of nod but Flaky rouses. I release my seatbelt, stand and stretch.

'Have we landed?' Flaky says as he yawns.

'I hope so, otherwise, we're flying way too close to the ground for my liking.'

'You're keen. There'll be at least another fifteen minutes wait before we can get off the plane.'

'I need the loo. I'm bursting,' I say as I hurry down the aisle. I bolt the toilet door behind me, pull out my mobile, and tap her image. 'Hi, it's me. Just landed. Yes, yes... I've missed you as well. Yes... I love you, too. Listen, I'll give you a call once I'm alone in the taxi heading home. We need to talk... about you know who.'

Thank You

I hope you enjoyed this latest instalment in the Shooting Star series. It is available as an ebook, paperback and hardback. The perfect **birthday or Christmas gift.**

If you are new to the series, then why not go back to the very beginning and read Book 1 "Arc Of A Shooting Star".

The boys will be returning in time for the festive season **(Nov 2021)** in a new full-length novel that sees them spending the Christmas holidays at a castle in Scotland. What could possibly go wrong? If you would like a reminder of when the book is out, then read on below.

OUT NOVEMBER 2021

Let's Keep In Touch

If you wish to keep up to date with my book news, there are a few simple ways to be notified. You can subscribe to my entertaining (subjective) monthly "**Discombobulated**" newsletter. This not only keeps you abreast of new releases, but occasionally I have a free book to giveaway or promotional discounts. The newsletter is designed to entertain, with short, pithy takes on the world and life... mostly my life. There's no hard sell and I won't be inundating you with spammy "buy, buy, buy" nonsense – which I personally detest. You can sign up by following the link below, which will take you to my website.

I would like to subscribe to your newsletter.

Alternatively, you can go to the following sites and click on the "**Follow**" button.

Amazon

BookBub

Facebook

For paperback readers, the links above won't work no matter how many times you tap your finger on the paper. Below is a manual link to type into your browser.

https://www.subscribepage.com/author_simon_northouse_home

If you enjoyed this book, then all **reviews** are greatly appreciated. To contact me, my email address is:

simon@simonnorthouse.com

I enjoy a chat, and will always reply.

Also By Simon Northouse

The Shooting Star Series

Arc Of A Shooting Star (Novel)

The Resurrection Tour Diaries (Short Story)

Catch A Shooting Star (Novel)

Fall Of A Shooting Star (Novel)

What's It All About... Geordie? (Novel)

Nuts At Christmas (Novella)

Eggs Unscrambled (Novel)

I Will Survive (Novel)

Bells At New Year (Novel) – November 2021

The Soul Love Series

Soul Love (Prequel Novella)

Love Is The Goal (Novel)

Love On A Roll (Novel)

Love Of The Coal (Novel) - January 2022

The Discombobulated Newsletter Series

Keep On Keeping On (Novella)

Keep Karma and Carry On (Novella)

The Lockdown Diary Blues (Novella)

Keep On Keeping On Again! (Novella) - August 2021

The School Days Series

The School Report - Before We Were Tsars (Novella)

The School Report - The Final Term (Novella)